FORBIDDEN
HIGHLANDER

FORBIDDEN
HIGHLANDER

DONNA GRANT

St. Martin's Paperbacks

This is a work of fiction. All of the characters, organizations, and events portrayed in this novel are either products of the author's imagination or are used fictitiously.

FORBIDDEN HIGHLANDER

For information address St. Martin's Press, 175 Fifth Avenue, New York, NY 10010.

ISBN: 978-0-312-38123-3

Printed in the United States of America

St. Martin's Paberbacks edition / June 2010

St. Martin's Paperbacks are published by St. Martin's Press, 175 Fifth Avenue, New York, NY 10010.

10 9 8 7 6 5 4 3 2 1

For Lisa Renee Jones—
Your advice, encouragement, and friendship
are priceless. I'm lucky to call you friend, and I
know my world is a better place with you in it.

Love,

DG

ACKNOWLEDGMENTS

This series wouldn't be here without thanks to many people.

Thank you to my family for being so supportive! To my husband for coming up with great ideas for fight scenes, and my children for being so proud of my books. To my parents for always being there when I needed them.

To my exceptional editor, Monique Patterson. Thank you for all the support, encouragement, and marvelous editorial input and vision. You rock! To the best assistant out there—Holly, you're amazing. Thank you to the art department for putting the torc around the model's neck. Thanks also to everyone at St. Martin's working behind the scenes to get this book on the shelves.

To my extraordinary agent, Irene Goodman, for having such passion and belief in me.

To the other great Dangerous Authors for being so supportive. I'm lucky to be involved with such a wonderful group of authors.

ONE

Summer 1603
Edinburgh Castle

Fallon stood in the corridor outside the great hall, his fists clenched at his sides as he struggled to keep his breathing steady. The sounds within were deafening. He'd been in Edinburgh Castle for only a few hours, but the need to run, hard and fast, to the shelter of his castle on the west coast of Scotland consumed him.

Calm. Stay calm.

An image of his brothers flashed in his mind, and he was reminded of why he had left the safe haven of his home for a nest of vipers.

I'm here for Lucan and his mate, Cara. I'm here for Quinn. I'm here for our future.

Fallon licked his lips and forced himself to open the doors and enter the great hall. As soon as he was through the doors, he moved to the shadows to watch and observe. His gaze took in the long hall, the hammer beam ceiling, and the candelabras that stood around the room offering light in addition to the sun that poured through the windows on either side.

Edinburgh Castle was massive in size, and the great

hall was no different. Unlike Fallon's hall, Edinburgh Castle's bespoke opulence that could only come from the king himself. Everything was polished to a sparkle.

Fallon's chest tightened at the number of bodies in the hall. He was used to having his own space and, sometimes even, the entire castle to himself. He didn't like the crowd or how close they moved around him, brushing against him as if it were all right to do so.

It amazed him that they had no idea what he was, what was inside him that could unleash at any moment and rip them to shreds. To them, he was just a man. But he knew the death and destruction the primeval god inside him was capable of.

His heart pounded violently in his chest. If he didn't concentrate, he would run from the hall and make his stay at the castle that much longer. With that frightening thought in mind, he forced his lungs open and leaned against the stone wall to let his gaze move around the room.

Edinburgh Castle was a fortress, a magnificent work of art. The castle, on its rocky outcrop, dominated the city. Long ago, a Celtic tribe had built a fort atop the hill for they had known the advantage of the rock. The future kings of Scotland had also seen the benefit.

"You look ill at ease, friend."

Fallon tensed and glanced at the scrawny, pale man who sidled up next to him. He was tall, but his face was long, his nose hawkish, and his lips so thin they were almost nonexistent.

When Fallon didn't respond, the man shifted his feet. "I'm Baron Iver MacNeil."

"Baron," Fallon said with a small incline of his head.

He didn't have time for pompous idiots, especially the skinny lump beside him.

A smile pulled at Fallon's lips at the thought that he could break the baron in half with a touch from his pinkie. It was no wonder Fallon didn't see many brawny Highlanders at the castle. They preferred to stay on their land and rule their clan. It was the oafs, the ones more interested in furthering their own ambitions, that preferred to stay as close to the king as they could.

It sickened Fallon to a degree that he wanted to lash out at everyone. Rage filled his vision. He felt his skin prickle, the telltale sign that he was about to lose control and let the beast out.

"Are you here to see the king?" Iver asked, unaware of the turmoil inside Fallon.

Fallon swallowed and fought to keep from rolling his eyes. By sheer will alone, he pulled his anger under control. "Aye. I've a need that I'd see settled posthaste."

"You know the king isn't in residence," Iver said with a smirk. "He rarely visits Scotland anymore."

This was not what Fallon wanted to hear. "He's not here?"

"Not at the moment, though I did hear a rumor that he was on his way."

Shite. "Thank you for the information."

Iver cackled, the sound harsh and loud to Fallon's enhanced hearing. "I'm as close to the king as any. If you'd like, I can help you. Who are you, friend?"

"I doubt you can aid me. And my name is Fallon Mac-Leod."

Just as he expected, Iver's eyes widened. "Mac-Leod?"

"Aye, you heard correctly."

Iver's licked his lips nervously. "The MacLeod lands are long gone. They were divided by other clans centuries ago."

As if Fallon didn't know that already. "I know."

"What does your laird want? Does he think King James will be able to gain him back his lands?"

Fallon turned his head to look the weasel beside him in the eye. He didn't trust Iver and knew the insignificant man couldn't help him in the least. Yet, Fallon got perverse pleasure in seeing him squirm. "*I* am laird, and though my family may have lost our lands, the castle still stands. It's mine."

"Ah, I see," Iver said with an anxious laugh. He licked his lips again and glanced around him. "I truly may be able to help you with your request."

Fallon decided he would hold his tongue just in case Iver could indeed help. Fallon crossed his arms over his chest and thought of his brothers, of his home, of the peace he wanted more than anything.

He had left his younger brother Lucan and Lucan's new bride, Cara, at MacLeod Castle—a castle he was in Edinburgh to ensure reverted back to the MacLeods. The only one not at their family castle was Quinn, the youngest of them.

A fresh wave of pain washed over Fallon as he thought of his baby brother. Though it was only a little over a month since their lives had changed so drastically, it felt more like a lifetime.

Fallon still remembered finding the parchment stuck between two crumbling stones in the gatehouse wall.

He had known without reading it who it was from. Deirdre.

Bile rose in his throat every time he thought of the depraved bitch. Deirdre was a *drough*, a sect of Druids who took a blood ritual and gave themselves to evil and black magic. It was black magic that had released the god inside Fallon and his brothers, a god that gave them immortality and powers to wreak havoc on unsuspecting mortals.

At least that's what Deirdre, the most powerful *drough*, wanted in her quest for dominance. Fallon and his brothers had been the first to have their god unbound three hundred years before. He still recalled the excruciating pain when his skin had sizzled and his bones popped in and out of their joints as if the god stretched inside him.

He was a Warrior, descended from the first Warriors who accepted the primeval gods into themselves to drive Rome from Britain. The Druids, once a mighty people, had divided into two groups. The *droughs*, who preferred black magic, and the *mies*, Druids who used their magic only for good.

It was the threat of Rome and their dominance that had pulled the two sects of Druids together. They had combined their magic to create a spell that would call forth ancient gods imprisoned in Hell and long forgotten.

Their plan worked. The warriors whom the gods chose were the greatest in their tribes, and with the combined power from the gods, the men turned into Warriors. An unstoppable force that saved Britain.

For a time.

After the Romans left, the Druids were unable to coax the gods from the men as they had expected. The only recourse left to the Druids was to bind the gods. Once again, the *droughs* and *mies* combined their magic.

No one, least of all the Druids, expected the gods to move through the bloodline from father to son through the generations, residing in the strongest of the lineage each time until they could be called forth again.

The MacLeods had been such a family.

How Fallon loathed what he was. It was Deirdre who had found them, Deirdre who had destroyed his entire clan, and Deirdre who had ruined his life.

He still wasn't sure how he, Lucan, and Quinn had escaped Deirdre and her mountain all those centuries ago, but once they had, they had kept themselves hidden. For over three hundred years they lived like ghosts in the crumbling ruin of their home, hiding from the world, hiding from themselves, but battling Deirdre in her quest for supremacy.

Then Cara had come into their lives. None of them could have foreseen what would happen to the MacLeod brothers when Lucan walked into the castle with Cara's unconscious body in his arms.

A small smile pulled at Fallon's lips as he thought of how protective Lucan was of his woman. Lucan, who had been the rock for him and Quinn during those awful years, deserved the love and happiness he had found.

They had discovered almost too late that Deirdre was after Cara for her Druid blood. A great battle had ensued, but not once had the brothers thought to send Cara away to save themselves. Lucan wouldn't have allowed it anyway.

That night, that battle, changed Fallon almost as much as when his god had been released. He was no longer the man who had kept a bottle of wine in his hands at all times to dull the god's voice within him.

He had ignored his god, denied what he was, so that when it came time to save Cara, he hadn't been sure if he could. Yet, his god had answered his call and turned him into the Warrior, the monster, he had feared for so long.

In doing so, he had been able to help save Cara. The MacLeods had thwarted Deirdre yet again. Or so they had thought.

Until Fallon had found the parchment.

He'd memorized the words. They haunted his sleep and his waking hours, just as Quinn's face did.

Something pricked his palms. He glanced down to see his black claws had extended and were digging into the flesh of his hands. He glanced at Iver, but the fool was too preoccupied staring at a servant's ample breasts to notice and talking nonstop about his fortune and title. Fallon took a deep breath to manage his temper and didn't let it out again until the god receded.

It was always so whenever he thought about how Deirdre had captured Quinn. She held him in her fortress, Cairn Toul Mountain, awaiting Fallon and Lucan. The bitch knew they wouldn't allow her to hold their brother. But she wanted them to come.

And they would.

Fallon couldn't wait to get his hands around her slim neck. He would squeeze until he heard her bones break, until her eyes bulged, and the life left her body. Only then would he be satisfied. He would live the rest of his life as the monster he was in peace. Just knowing the evil that grew over the land would be gone was all he needed.

"You look like you could rip someone's head off," Iver said with an uneasy chuckle.

"Relax. It's not you. Yet."

Iver let out a sigh and moved a step toward Fallon. "Depending on what you were willing to give in return, I may be able to get some of your land restored to you. If, of course, you have proof you are a MacLeod. Truth be told, I had assumed there were none left."

"I gather you've heard the legend of my clan." Though Fallon hated to bring up, what had happened to his clan, the fear and curiosity, might work to his advantage.

Iver's beady black eyes became intense as his interest grew. "Oh, aye, MacLeod. Everyone has heard the tale. Is it true? Was your clan murdered?"

"Aye. Every man, woman, and child was killed."

When Iver's smile widened in glee, Fallon had to stop himself from punching him in the nose.

"What happened?" Iver asked. "The account is that none survived."

"Three survived. Three brothers, to be exact. Fallon, Lucan, and Quinn."

"Fallon," Iver whispered. "You were named after your ancestor."

Fallon didn't correct him. Let the fool think he was a descendant. Iver wouldn't believe the truth anyway. "I am rightful laird of the clan MacLeod."

"Aye, you are. You deserve your lands." Iver rubbed his hands together, anticipation making his black eyes glow. "I will send a missive to the king immediately."

But Fallon wasn't fooled. "Thank you, but I'd rather see the king myself. Are you sure you heard he was on his way to Edinburgh?"

"Aye," Iver said. "That's why so many more have come to Edinburgh Castle. It has been many years since the king has come to Scotland."

Fallon quirked a brow. There was much he wanted to say regarding that fact, but decided it wouldn't be wise to badmouth a king when he was about to ask that same king for his castle to be returned.

"I appreciate the news," Fallon said, and moved away before Iver could speak again.

As he walked to a new corner and settled himself to see if he could hear more about the king's arrival, the crowd around him thinned and he caught a flash of color. He turned his head and found himself staring across the hall into a face of unbelievable grace and beauty. A face he knew he would never forget, even if he lived for eternity.

She was so stunning that he had pushed away from the wall and started toward her before he realized what he was about. The need to get closer, to take in her loveliness, goaded him onward, much as his god pushed at his rage.

Fallon kept his feet rooted in place by force of will alone, but he couldn't tear his gaze from her mesmerizing oval face. She held herself with elegance and dignity, a noblewoman by birth.

Someone bumped into her from behind, and there was a subtle shift of awareness about her that only a Warrior would understand, only a Warrior would note.

He was intrigued more by the moment. Though

Highland women were known to be strong and coura-
geous, they weren't Warriors.

Just as quickly as she had taken a stance, she relaxed, the perfection back in place.

Fallon let his gaze wander to his heart's content. It
had been so long since he'd laid eyes on something
so . . . stunning. Her lips were wide and full, her smile
easy and contagious as she spoke to others around her.

She had impossibly high cheekbones and a small
nose that had the slightest lift at the end of it.

His enhanced hearing picked up a conversation that
made him pause.

"She's incredible, isn't she?" a male whispered. "Lady
Larena Monroe is her name. There isn't a man in the
castle that doesna want her in his bed, and there isn't a
man that wouldna kill for her if she but said the word."

Fallon knew they had to be speaking of the woman
his gaze was locked on. He wanted to hear more, but
he wanted to be closer to her as well.

Unable to stop himself, he weaved through the mob
around the perimeter of the great hall. He edged closer
to Larena Monroe, admiring the cut of her burgundy
gown and the way it clung to the swells of her breasts
before hugging her trim waist. She held her hands together at her waist, her long, slim fingers intertwined
as she listened to an older woman with a bulbous nose.

Fallon peered through the space of two men and
watched Lady Larena. Her skin was the color of cream,
and she had eye-catching blond hair that was piled art-
fully atop her head. She had wide, expressive eyes that
captured whoever she looked at, and a mouth he couldn't
stop fantasizing about kissing.

He was enraptured, awestruck by one woman.

Fallon's blood quickened, his heart raced, and God help him, his balls tightened. Lust roared within him, demanding he taste the unblemished skin that beckoned him so sweetly.

Then Larena turned her head and looked straight at him with eyes a dark, smoky blue that seemed to see him for what he really was. Fallon sucked in air to his lungs and held himself still. She tipped her head in acknowledgment, her golden halo of hair a beacon in the hall.

As soon as she turned her gaze away, he stepped back through the crowd and into the shadows of a corner. He recognized the yearning that flared inside him. He recognized it . . . and feared it.

He was here to make sure his castle stayed his, not slake his need between a woman's thighs. Despite how comely the woman was.

The MacLeods might have lost their lands with the massacre and Quinn's subsequent disappearance, but Fallon would fight with everything he had to secure the castle as theirs for eternity. No longer would he and his brothers hide away like ghosts. It was time to take a stand, and if others discovered what they were and tried to harm them, then they risked their own lives.

Fallon ran a hand over his jaw as he hungered for a taste of wine, anything to help dull the ache of desire in his loins. If James VI were in residence here instead of England, Fallon might be able to return to the castle soon. As it was, Scotland's king preferred to live in England and rule both countries from there.

The rumor that James was on his way to Scotland

was just that, a rumor, but Fallon needed to discover if it was true or not.

There wasn't time to travel to London and seek an audience, despite his power to travel many leagues in the blink of an eye. Fallon could only use his power to "jump" to places he had been before. Since he had never been to London, he could end up in a field or with half his body in a wall.

Fallon would give himself the rest of the day to learn if the king was indeed coming to Edinburgh. If so, then he would stay. If not, Fallon would return to MacLeod Castle and talk with Lucan about whether they could take the time for Fallon to travel to London.

Despite the king's absence, Edinburgh Castle still teemed with nobility and people seeking to exchange favors with powerful lords. Maybe Iver had been correct and people were converging on the castle because the king was coming.

Fallon remembered vividly the day his father had brought him to Edinburgh. It had been just a year prior to the massacre, and his father had wanted to introduce him to the king and the nobility as the future laird of the MacLeods.

Da had told him often that it was in his best interest to know everyone, especially if they influenced the king in any way. It didn't mean Fallon had to support them, but a laird needed to know the ins and outs of nobility and royalty to keep the clan safe.

His father had been correct. It was too bad no one had known about the beautiful, evil *drough* who would destroy everything just a year later.

Disgusted with himself, his lust, and the hand fate had dealt him, Fallon turned on his heel and left the hall. He couldn't stand the crush of people or the stench of sweat that hung in the air. He missed the view from the towers of his castle where he could watch the waves crash into the cliffs and listen to the birds squawking and flying with the air currents.

He made it back to his chamber, a cold sweat running down his face as he leaned against the closed door inside his room. His hands shook, but in the solitude of his chamber, he didn't hide them.

His gaze landed on the bottle of wine he kept near him always, to remind him of what he had ignored, of what he had almost lost, and the war he had before him.

Lucan had shouldered the brunt of the responsibility while Fallon had sunk into the oblivion of the wine day in and day out. It was Lucan who had dealt with Quinn's rages, it was Lucan who had mended and cleaned the castle to make it habitable. As eldest, Fallon should have been the one who had seen to all those things.

Fallon had neglected his brothers. Quinn, who had lost his wife and son in the slaughter of their clan, hadn't been able to control his anger, which fueled the god inside him. It was rare that some part of the Warrior didn't show on Quinn. He couldn't manage his wrath, and so couldn't command the god at will.

Instead of helping his brothers, Fallon had ignored them, intent on his own pain, his own fury.

Fallon stumbled to the table and gripped the wine in his unsteady hand. His father would be ashamed of him. He hadn't been the leader his father had told him he was, had trained him to be. Fallon had been a coward afraid of facing the truth of his future and learning how to control the god as Lucan had.

Except now he had a chance to redeem himself.

After several moments as Fallon battled with himself, he released the wine and pushed from the table. His castle was being renovated and pieced back together. It might never shine with its former glory, but it would be a home again. A future awaited him there.

It wasn't just the brothers anymore either. There was Cara, and the other four Warriors who had come to their aid when Deirdre attacked. And they had a second Druid, Sonya, who had been told by the trees to help Cara learn her powers.

MacLeod Castle would be open to any Druid or Warrior who wanted to fight Deirdre and the evil she wielded. If it was the last thing he did, Fallon would see it done.

TWO

Larena Monroe's heart jumped in her throat when she heard the name MacLeod whispered in the great hall. As soon as it was spoken it spread like wildfire throughout the room. Everyone wanted to know who the MacLeod in attendance was—she most especially.

"Excuse me, Lady Drummond," she said as she turned to the woman behind her. "I thought I heard you say 'MacLeod.' Surely I was mistaken."

The name MacLeod was synonymous with death, heartache, and the unexplained. The myths of the MacLeod brothers hadn't died in the three hundred years since the clan had been destroyed. It was a story told over and over again, but not one usually heard in the middle of the day in Edinburgh Castle. It was usually saved for stormy nights.

"Ah, dear Larena," Lady Drummond said. Her droopy hazel eyes held a note of mischief. "You heard right. There is a man at the castle, a man who claims to be *the* MacLeod."

Larena fisted her hand in her skirt while excitement ran rampant through her. For so long she had searched for the MacLeods. Could fortune have smiled on her, and had one come to her? After all these years. She had to find him, had to speak to him.

She mentally shook her head. It was most likely some confusion in the name. The MacLeods were hunted, not by any Highlanders or even the crown, but by something much, much worse. They were hunted by the epitome of evil, Deirdre.

Larena started when she realized Lady Drummond had spoken to her. "My apologies. My mind was wandering."

Lady Drummond leaned close, her great jowls swinging. "I asked if you saw him? The MacLeod? I caught a glimpse of him, my dear." She fanned herself with her wrinkled hand. "If I were younger . . . He's devilishly handsome."

"Is he?" Larena wished she had seen him.

Lady Drummond laughed and sidled closer to Larena. "He wears a torc like the Celts of old. A true Highlander," she whispered, her high voice tinged with a note of awe.

Larena's heart missed a beat as she realized the man Lady Drummond spoke of and the one that had heated her body were one and the same. She had seen him, the MacLeod. It had been just a moment, but she had locked gazes with the most amazing, most unusual dark green eyes she had ever seen. They had been turbulent, like a stormswept sea, and intense.

She'd had to look away or make a fool of herself. When she had glanced back, he was gone. In all her years, there had not been one man who had ever had that kind of effect on her. It frightened her at the same time it captivated her.

After a thank-you to Lady Drummond, Larena excused herself and moved around the hall intent on finding this curious Highlander with the beautiful eyes and the gold torc.

He'd been dressed in a kilt with a plaid she didn't quite recognize, but he didn't wear it with the ease of a man who had been born to it. Yet, he *was* a Highlander. One look in his eyes and she had seen the wildness, the untamed spirit that was the Highlands.

When Larena couldn't find the man claiming to be the MacLeod, she headed to the garden for a breath of fresh air. She had been living in the castle for too many months in her bid to learn how far Deirdre's magic had stretched.

Larena was putting her own life in jeopardy by being at the castle, but what she hid from the world was worth it.

She wasn't at the castle just for Deirdre though. She knew enough about the infamous MacLeods to know she needed to discover anything she could of them.

How she yearned to see the mountains of the Highlands and feel the snow on her face. But she couldn't leave. Not yet. There was still information to be gathered.

Larena walked past a bush of vibrant yellow roses and sat on a stone bench that offered some seclusion. The fragrance of the flowers swirled around her, taking away the reek of stale breath and sweaty bodies.

With her hands planted behind her, Larena leaned back and tilted her face to the sky where the rays of the sun filtered through the heavy clouds. It would rain soon, and she would have to stay indoors.

Her mind wandered until she recalled the news that

had reached her two weeks past about the MacLeod brothers. She trusted Camdyn MacKenna because he was a Warrior, and he had no reason to lie.

There were few people she relied upon. She had learned the hard way that trust was something someone earned. Camdyn had earned her trust, or at least part of it. There were things that no one could know about her. The ramifications were too dangerous for everyone involved.

Among all the people of her acquaintance there was only one she truly trusted, her cousin Malcolm. Malcolm shouldn't know her secrets either, but he had learned one of hers when he was just a young lad of seven summers.

She knew she needed to try and convince Malcolm to return to his clan, the clan that had banished her. Every time she brought it up, he would argue that as powerful as she was, she needed someone to help her.

And since she was a woman, apparently that was the truth.

The crunch of a shoe on the grass brought Larena's head around. She smiled when she saw Malcolm's steady bright blue gaze on her. He was tall and carried himself like the lord he was. As the first son to the Monroe, he had the upbringing and the blood of a noble.

It was his face, though, that made women swoon. His features were perfectly proportioned, with a square jaw and long, regal nose. His mouth was wide and his lips full. And he could charm the gown off a nun.

"I thought I would find you here." His deep voice

was low, smooth, as he sat beside her. "I gather you've heard?"

"About the man claiming to be a MacLeod?"

He nodded and swept his fingers through his blond waves that constantly fell into his eyes. "I tried to meet him, but I've been unable to find him."

"I saw him speak to Iver MacNeil."

Malcolm groaned as his lips flattened. "That imbecile? I avoid Iver at all costs, but for you, my dear, I will see what I can discover."

She smiled when he lifted her hand to his lips and kissed it. The warmth in his eyes wasn't that of a lover, but that of a man who was more of a brother. "You are too good to me."

"Nay. If I was, we would be long gone from this vile pit. I know you wish to leave."

She placed her other hand over the one that still gripped hers. "I have a destiny, Malcolm. I will see it through."

"If it is one of the MacLeods, what will you do?"

"I will talk to him."

"And if he doesna believe you?"

She glanced away, hating the fear that swam in her stomach. "Then I will show him."

"You're taking a terrible risk, Larena. This could be a ruse from Deirdre."

"She doesn't know of me. I've fooled her so far. I will continue to do so until the time comes to bring her down."

Malcolm lowered their hands to the bench. "I'd rather be with you when you talk to MacLeod."

"Nay. I must do it alone. There are things that need

to be said. If he is a Warrior, he won't trust anyone to speak as freely as I need him to."

Malcolm leaned close and kissed her cheek. "Just be careful."

"Don't worry. Soon, I will be gone and you will be free to marry that pretty auburn-haired girl I've seen you smiling at."

Malcolm threw back his head and laughed, his blue eyes crinkling at the corners. "You've been so intent on other things I didna think you had noticed."

"I noticed. I also observed how she watches you when you aren't looking. She's quite taken with you." She let her smile drop. "I want you to marry, but marry a woman who will make you happy. You deserve at least that, Malcolm. Find a good woman who will give you many children."

His laugher gone, he rose with a sigh and paced in front of her. Larena looked at the Monroe kilt with its bold red and green plaid. She had always loved the tartan, even though it had been many, many years since she'd had it stripped from her.

"I will do as you say," Malcolm said as he stopped in front of her and went down on his haunches. He took her hands in his and turned her to face him. "But only if you give me a promise in return."

Larena was afraid what the promise would be, but they had been friends for too long for her to think of denying him. "What would you ask of me?"

"Doona leave without telling me good-bye."

She blinked back tears that suddenly sprang to her eyes and cupped the side of his face with her hand. "I would take you with me if I could. You are the finest man I've ever known. I cannot thank you enough for all you've done for me."

He waved away her words and straightened, his eyes downcast. "Enough. You'll cry, and you know how I hate tears."

"I don't cry." Though she found her eyes burned when she thought of leaving Malcolm. He was the only family, the only friend, she had in the world. She wanted away from Edinburgh and the crowds to the quiet of the Highlands, but she didn't look forward to being alone. Again.

"Come," he said, and offered her his arm. His smile was a little forced, but still true. "Let's take a stroll through these magnificent gardens."

Larena took his arm, grateful for the change in subject. She didn't like to think of what the future held. There was too much uncertainty, too much death that awaited her. And she hated to see him worry, for there was nothing he could do.

"Remember when I spoke with Camdyn a few days ago?"

"I do," Malcolm said with a nod. "What of it?"

"He spoke of the MacLeod brothers, that they had been found. After all this time. And now one is apparently here. Which one is it, do you suppose? Fallon? Lucan? Quinn?"

Malcolm smiled. "I couldna begin to guess."

"I pray what Camdyn told me is the truth. My kind has too much to lose to put our faith in men who aren't the real MacLeods."

"I agree. Yet, didn't you tell me that Camdyn spoke of Deirdre being in a violent rage a month ago?"

"Aye. You think there is a connection to MacLeod's being here?"

Malcolm shrugged a shoulder and maneuvered her to the side to allow a couple to pass by them. "Could be, Larena. You yourself said that Camdyn was surprised that so many Warriors had been leaving their hiding places. Where are they going, by the way?"

"Camdyn didn't know. The MacLeods are the oldest Warriors and would be our best advantage for defeating Deirdre once and for all. The MacLeods escaped Deirdre and evaded her for over three hundred years. None have managed to do as they have."

"You have told me that Camdyn rarely comes out of hiding for anything. The fact that he came to find you to tell you of the MacLeods says a lot."

She nodded, recalling the Warrior. Camdyn MacKenna loathed crowded places almost as much as he hated Deirdre. "Anything that prodded him out of hiding is important. Apparently, the markings he found were vital enough that he waited around the castle in hopes of seeing me."

"What did the markings say?"

"That a Warrior Camdyn called friend left his forest." Larena, like all Warriors, could read the ancient Celtic language they used to speak with each other by markings on trees. She wished she could have seen the markings herself.

"Do you recall the name of this Warrior?"

Her brow furrowed as she thought for a moment.

"Shaw? Aye, that's the name. Galen Shaw. I've heard Camdyn speak of Galen before. He's well respected."

"But where are they going? Did Camdyn say?"

She shook her head. "Nay. Just that they were traveling north. I'm sure there are other markings to help point the way, but that was the only one Camdyn had seen."

"Did he go to find Galen?"

"He did."

Malcolm stopped her near a tall hedge. "Would you know the markings if you saw them?"

"It's been a while since I've read them, but I could decipher them."

"Then we should go look."

She smiled at his exuberance. Always Malcolm was eager to help, eager to place his life in danger if it would hurry Deirdre's death. But Larena wouldn't allow him to jeopardize his existence. Malcolm had already defied his father's wishes to remain with the clan in northeast Scotland to be with her.

"I wouldn't know where to begin to look," she said. "Camdyn didn't tell me what forest, so it is a moot point."

"And you wouldna let me come with you anyway."

"Nay. You're too important to the family."

"To hell with them," he ground out, his jaw clenched.

Larena tightened her grip on his arm. "Cousin . . ."

"Don't," he warned. "Just don't, Larena."

But she had to remind him. He was endangering his future to make up for what his grandfather and great-grandfather had done to her. As soon as he'd learned she intended to go to Edinburgh Castle, Malcolm had decided to go with her. For protection, he'd said. She smiled every time she thought of that. If anything, she would be the one protecting him.

Larena glanced at the ground. "For whatever reason, I am what I am. Your great-grandfather and your grandfather made the decision to banish me from the Monroe clan. I don't want the same for you. Already the clan distances themselves from you because of your involvement with me."

"My father wouldn't dare exile me, and I doona care what the rest of the clan does. As for my grandfather and great-grandfather, they were just resentful that the god chose you and not my grandfather."

She winced, recalling the day the god had chosen her instead of Naill. Everything she had ever known and loved had changed in a blink, never to be the same.

"Maybe. As far as I know, there are no female Warriors."

"Besides you," Malcolm whispered.

She licked her lips and tried to find the words to help him understand. "It cost me my family and my clan, Malcolm. I don't know how the other Warriors will treat me once they find out I am one of them."

"You didn't lose everything. You had Robena."

Larena smiled at the mention of the old Druid who had unbound her god. "Robena was the only one not surprised to learn I was the Warrior and not your grandfather. She whisked me away from the clan and started my instruction immediately."

"I used to watch you train."

"I remember." Larena smiled as she recalled the times she had let him think she didn't know he watched.

"You must have been only six or seven summers the first time I spotted you."

Malcolm shrugged. "It was fascinating watching you transform. I envy you that. And your immortality."

"Don't," she cautioned. She was eighty years his senior, but in the eyes of mortals, it was Malcolm who could tell her what to do. "It may look exciting, but my very life hangs in the balance."

"Your secrets are safe with me. You should know that."

And she did. Malcolm had been her only connection to her clan after she had left and Robena died. Though banished from the Monroe clan, Larena had always lived close enough to visit her father from time to time.

Through the years Malcolm had always stayed her friend, giving her news and anything else she needed. It had been his idea to come to Edinburgh and act as her brother. Malcolm had sacrificed much in order to help her, and she feared she would never be able to repay him.

"Does Camdyn know that which you guard?" Malcolm asked.

Larena shook her head. "Nay. It's enough that he knows I'm a Warrior."

"Be careful, Larena. You may be a Warrior, but Deirdre will find out about you sooner or later."

"I know." She glanced away as icy fingers of foreboding raked down her back.

Malcolm touched her hand to gain her attention. "What will you do when she comes after you? For you know she will stop at nothing to acquire what you protect."

"This I know as well. I've been prepared for it."

"She has black magic. There is nothing that can prepare you for that."

It was true, but she wouldn't let him know how much she feared Deirdre's discovery. For a hundred years she had lived her life as her own. Once Deirdre began hunting her, things would change. And not for the better.

If Deirdre learned of what she was, Larena would forever be running. She didn't fear being captured by Deirdre. She feared what would happen when Deirdre learned Larena guarded the Scroll.

The Scroll was a list of all the surnames of every Celtic man who had been inhabited by a god to drive out the Romans. It was a list that Deirdre would want at all costs since she could then easily find the men whose bloodline housed a god.

Larena would never forgive herself if the Scroll fell into Deirdre's hands. It was one of the reasons she kept the secret to herself. The only reason Malcolm knew was because he was family and had been told by his father.

"It's why you want to talk to the MacLeod, isn't it?" Malcolm guessed, breaking into her thoughts. "You think he and his brothers can protect you."

"If anyone can help keep me from Deirdre, it's the MacLeod and his brothers."

"And if he says nay?"

She blew out a breath, not even wanting to think of the possibility. "Then I will face Deirdre on my own."

Malcolm's arm muscles clenched beneath her hand

before he turned and led her back to the castle. "I pray you're right about MacLeod."

"So do I," she murmured.

Her life was nothing, but the Scroll she guarded was too precious to fall into evil hands.

THREE

Fallon watched Larena Monroe from his window. He had been surprised to see her walk into the gardens alone. For a moment she had dropped the smile and let herself relax. In that instant, he had seen the despair and anxiousness in the small frown that marred her smooth forehead.

As soon as the man had joined her, she quickly brought the smile back, however. It was an easy smile, not the obligatory one he saw in the great hall. Whoever this man was, she obviously cared for him. And that annoyed Fallon more than he cared to admit.

Larena and the man had sat for several moments talking before they stood and walked through the garden. Fallon knew he shouldn't spy on her, but he couldn't help himself. Everything Larena did fascinated him. From the tilt of her head to the lift of her hand, her every movement was graceful and elegant. The golden curls that framed her face tantalized him with a view of her slender neck.

In the quiet of his chamber, he was able to observe her at his leisure, and he found he quite enjoyed what he saw. The more he looked, the more he wanted to look. It was no wonder every man in the castle wanted her. It wasn't just her beauty, it was the strength and resolve inside her that drew men's gazes like a moth to flame.

The way the man held her, as if she were his, caused Fallon's fists to clench. Was he observing a clandestine meeting? He hadn't bothered to ask anyone if she was married. As much as Fallon told himself it didn't matter, the simple truth was it did. Because he wanted her for himself.

"It cannot be," he told himself.

Yet, as daft as it was, he did want her.

Fallon turned and walked to his bed. He fell face-first on it and took a deep breath before rolling to his back. His gaze moved to the burgundy velvet canopy that reminded him of Larena Monroe and the gown she wore.

He wished he knew what was going on at his castle. Had Deirdre sent additional Warriors to attack? Were the repairs going according to plan? Had more of Galen's Warrior friends found their way to the castle? Had Cara and Sonya found the spell that would bind their gods?

Too many questions and no answers. But those questions weren't what kept him awake at night. Nay, it was his worry of Quinn in Deirdre's dungeon. He had no idea what Deirdre was doing to his youngest brother, and that scared him as nothing else could.

"I'm coming, Quinn. Hold on, brother. Hold on," he whispered into the chamber.

He had wanted to go after Quinn immediately, but cooler heads had prevailed. They needed leverage against Deirdre. Besides Lucan's wife, Cara, there was only one thing Deirdre wanted more—the Scroll.

The Scroll was a list of all the names of men who had housed the gods when the Celts fought the Romans. Deirdre had her own ways of discovering these men who could have the god inside them, but the Scroll would give her all the surnames instantly. It would help her to triple her Warriors in a matter of weeks instead of years. And with those Warriors, Deirdre would have control over Scotland—and the world—all too soon.

Fallon wanted to discern whatever he could about the Scroll, but so far he had found nothing that led him to believe the Scroll was even real. So much got added to stories in the retelling that the legend of the Scroll could have been included at any time.

He sat up when there was a soft knock on his door. Fallon rose and let his claws lengthen. He didn't trust anyone, and he would be damned before he was caught unawares by Deirdre.

"Who is it?" he called.

"A servant, sir, sent by Baron MacNeil. He has sent you a message," said the feminine voice.

Fallon walked to the door and opened it a crack to find a young girl with auburn hair standing before him. She held out the missive, her hand shaking and her eyes downcast.

He retracted his claws and reached for the parchment. "Thank you."

She dipped into a hurried curtsy and started to turn away.

"Wait," Fallon said. He opened the note and read it. Fallon clenched his jaw when he learned Iver had sent a missive to the king even after Fallon had told him not to.

"Aye, milord?" Her gaze briefly met his.

Fallon folded the parchment. He would deal with Iver later. He leaned his shoulder against the doorway and pushed the door open wider. "Tell me what you know of Lady Larena Monroe."

The young girl fiddled with her skirts. "She is very beautiful and kind to everyone."

Fallon lifted a coin and held it before her. "Is it true all the men want her?"

"Aye, milord. She is sought after by many. Her brother is very protective."

Damn. He handed her the coin and lifted another. "A brother, aye? Who is he?"

"Lord Malcolm Monroe. He's a handsome devil. He's as sought after as his sister."

Fallon narrowed his gaze as his mind raced. "Is that so? Which man is seeking Lady Larena's favor now?"

"Milord?" the servant asked, her brow furrowed.

He sighed and held up another coin. "What man is in her bed?"

The girl's eyes grew large. "I wouldn't know, milord. For all the gossip, there is no man I've heard claim that he's had her."

"Interesting." Fallon pulled out some more coins and handed them to the servant. "Thank you for the information."

Once the door shut, he leaned back against it. He had learned more than he expected. There might not be men boasting of having Larena, but he imagined many had shared her bed. She was, after all, a very beautiful, very alluring woman.

And they were in the king's castle where favors were

traded for anything. It only made sense that Larena
and her brother had come to the castle to gain something, as everyone did. Why the men kept quiet about
their affairs with Larena was intriguing. Did they do it
out of respect? Or did they fear her brother?

It had been a long time since Fallon interacted with
people, but he found it more than odd that there wasn't
at least one man willing to claim he'd had Larena.

Fallon tossed aside the missive and left his chamber.
He wouldn't get anything accomplished staying in his
room, and he needed MacLeod Castle turned over to
him.

Three hours later and Fallon was no closer to finding someone who could help him learn if the king
really was coming to Scotland or not. Everyone had a
different opinion.

He had thought he could come to Edinburgh and see
the king. It never occurred to him the king of Scotland
would prefer to rule in England. Of course, it still bog-
gled his mind that the king ruled both England and
Scotland.

How times had changed his Scotland. And not for
the better.

Just another example of why he and his brothers
shouldn't have remained holed up in the castle for three
hundred years. There was so much to get caught up on.

His stomach growled with hunger, but the thought of
sitting in the great hall with all those people made him
break out in a cold sweat. His steps slowed as he reached
the double doors that led into the hall.

More than likely he had learned all he could in Edinburgh. It was the thought of returning to Lucan without anything that made Fallon pause. His brothers were counting on him. He had promised Lucan he would get their castle back. How could Fallon fail once again?

"Damn," he murmured.

Fallon ran a hand down his face and sighed. He would seek out Thomas MacDonald during the evening meal. MacDonald's name had been mentioned as someone who knew what the king planned. Maybe Fallon could find out once and for all what the king planned to do. The thought of staying in the castle another hour made him ill, but he would do it for his brothers.

He wished it was Lucan here instead of himself. Lucan knew how to charm people to do whatever he wanted. But Lucan had done too much during the last three hundred years while Fallon had stayed drunk. This was the least he could do for his brothers, and he *would* see it done. One way or another.

The soft scent of lilies drifted on the air, halting his thoughts. Fallon turned to find none other than Larena Monroe standing behind him. For a moment she looked unsure of herself. Then, she smiled, and he noted the hands clasped in front of her shook a little. Was she nervous? The woman everyone wanted?

Fascinating.

She had changed from her burgundy gown to one of the deepest blue that brought out the color of her eyes. And he couldn't look away.

Her hair was different as well, softer, with more curls framing her face. One hung alongside her cheek to land near her mouth. He wanted to reach over and tug on one of the strands to see if it was as soft as it looked.

"This may seem unforgivably ill-mannered," she said, "but I was hoping you could tell me if you are the MacLeod everyone is speaking about?"

Her voice was as smooth as honey and as rich as the finest wine. Her smoky blue eyes searched his, as if she sought more answers than the one question could provide. He could easily drown in her almond-shaped eyes and lose himself in her scent.

His body reacted with alarming speed at the sight of her. Heat and blood centered between his legs as his rod thickened, and the lust he had pushed aside earlier returned with a vengeance.

"Aye," Fallon answered after a moment, when he knew his voice would work. "I am Fallon MacLeod."

She let out a breath as her eyes briefly closed. "Fallon. An unusual name."

"I suppose so."

"I am—"

"Lady Larena Monroe," he finished for her. He had to force his gaze from her lips, lips that he ached to kiss, to taste. "It seems as though your name is just as well known as mine, though for a different reason, my lady."

Her brows furrowed for the space of a heartbeat. "It is the castle of the king, sir. Gossip abounds. You shouldn't believe anything you hear."

There was truth to her words. Still, too many whispered their lust for her. Could it be true none of them had sampled her?

"I was hoping I might have a moment of your time?" she asked.

Fallon was intrigued. Too damned intrigued. What could she want with him? He was no palace dandy, and as much as he found himself attracted to her, he didn't have time for any kind of affair, however short-lived it might be. He had to stay focused on his task.

"I'm sorry, my lady, but I doona have the time."

Her smile faltered. "I assure you, sir, it is important."

Fallon frowned. "Then tell me now."

She glanced around them, noting the people in the corridor before she stepped closer to him. "What I have to say is not for others' ears. I would prefer a moment alone. Please."

Fallon was tempted to take her up on her offer, just to see what she had to say. "I'm sorry, my lady, but I must decline. My business is short, and I wish to return home as quickly as I can."

He turned on his heel and walked into the great hall before she could say more. It had been the right thing to do to walk away from her, although the scent of lilies followed him, reminding him of the exquisite woman that had wanted him, even if it was just to talk.

It wasn't talking Fallon wanted to do though. He sank onto the end of the first bench he came across and fisted a hand beneath the table. He had been more than rude to Larena, but he hadn't trusted himself with her.

Just one look at her and he was ready to fall to his knees and beg her to let him touch her, kiss her. The desire consumed him, making it difficult to breathe or think of anything other than her. Larena Monroe.

Fallon needed to keep his sights on why he had come to Edinburgh despite the tightening of his balls and the racing of his heart at the nearness of a woman. There would be time enough later to slake his lust.

But never with one so lovely.

As true as it was, Fallon inhaled deeply and turned to the man beside him. "Can you point out Thomas MacDonald for me?"

Larena stared at the closed doors, her blood pounding in her ears. She couldn't believe Fallon had refused her. Though she didn't think her face any prettier than others', she had learned not long after reaching Edinburgh that a simple smile could make men do just about anything.

Fallon MacLeod, however, was proving to be different. And she liked that. He guarded himself well. It could be because he was a Warrior, or his name could be mere coincidence and the legend of his clan caused him to be cautious.

She understood cautious all too well, but she would wager the Scroll that Fallon was a Warrior. Once Malcolm spoke with Iver MacNeil they would know what Fallon wanted in Edinburgh. There wasn't much a person couldn't procure in Edinburgh Castle, and she would make sure she was the one who would give Fallon what he wanted.

Then, he would listen to her.

She lifted her chin and walked into the great hall.

Fallon nodded to the man across from him. After learning that Thomas MacDonald was expected in Edinburgh that evening, Fallon had sat through the meal only half listening to the conversations. All it did was make him miss his brothers and his castle more.

He would talk to MacDonald as soon as he could, then he would leave Edinburgh and use his power to arrive back at his castle. Just being there would help to calm the itch in his blood, although not for long. With Quinn held by Deirdre, Fallon would have that same prickle.

Fallon reached for his goblet, wishing it were wine instead of water. Just as he brought the cup to his lips his eyes clashed with smoky blue ones. For a moment Fallon was held by Larena's gaze. Finally, he tore his eyes away.

She sat at a table to his right and was surrounded by men, each hanging on every word she spoke. But her eyes were riveted on him. Fallon got perverse joy out of the dark looks the other men threw his way.

Despite his wish to quit the hall, he couldn't stop watching her. Every time she took a bite of food or drank from her goblet his eyes found her mouth, a mouth he wanted to taste desperately.

Fallon cursed and rose to his feet. He had to leave or risk going to Larena and kissing her in front of everyone. He might have stayed away from people for three hundred years, but even he knew that would be frowned upon.

No sooner had he started toward the doors than he saw her exit in front of him. Too curious for his own good and powerless to control his desire, Fallon followed her. As he let the great hall doors close behind him he saw her walk down the long corridor. Alone.

Unable to help himself, he pursued her. Her strides were long and purposeful as she moved through the castle. Fallon kept to the shadows, not wanting her to see him. He wanted to learn more about her. He tried to tell himself it was in order to discover why she wanted to speak with him, but Fallon knew it for the lie that it was.

He simply wanted to know more.

And so he hid in the shadows and listened as a man blocked her path. The man was dressed not in a kilt, but some revolting extravagance of velvet and stockings with padded breeches that stopped at his knees. In short, he looked ridiculous.

The man had a lecherous smile aimed at Larena, his intentions clear. Larena dodged his hands and raised a brow when he tried to kiss her.

"I cannot tell you how many times I've watched men try to get the better of her."

Fallon turned to find the man who had been in the garden with Larena. He cursed himself for being so engrossed in a woman that he hadn't heard someone approach.

The man gave him a friendly smile. "I'm Malcolm Monroe."

"The lady's brother. Shouldn't you help her?"

Malcolm folded his arms over his chest. "She can handle herself or I would ensure the man might never have children."

Fallon watched the tall, blond Highlander. There was something very amiable about him. Maybe it was his blue eyes that seemed so honest and open, much like Quinn's had been when he'd been a lad. Time and Deirdre had changed that.

"There is much you do not know, Fallon MacLeod."

Fallon raised a brow at Malcolm. "You know me?"

"You're new to Edinburgh Castle. Everyone knows you."

"And why I'm here?"

Malcolm shrugged indifferently. "Gossip does travel swiftly."

"So what is it I don't know?" Fallon asked. He turned to face Malcolm fully. His first instinct about the man was that he liked him, but appearances could be deceiving.

Larena's brother was just an inch or so shorter than Fallon, but his wide shoulders and thick chest told Fallon he wasn't a dandy, but a Highlander who was used to hard work.

The smile dropped from Malcolm's face. "Larena isn't the woman people think she is. The castle gossips. Men hunger for things they cannot have. Women, in their vindictiveness, spread rumors that aren't true."

"That is true enough."

"Larena needs to talk to you. She doesna seek men out, MacLeod, they come to her. If she tells you she has something to discuss with you, then I would listen to what she has to say."

"Do you know what she wants to talk to me about?"

Malcolm shrugged again. "It isn't for me to say. All I ask is that you doona judge her. We all wear guises in some fashion." He bowed and started to turn when he paused. "I've heard that Iver sent a missive to the king.

If you've pinned your hopes on Iver's helping you, you chose the wrong noble. King James tends to ignore Iver, as most of us do. I do know someone, however, that the king will listen to."

Fallon wasn't fooled for a moment. "I told Iver not to send the missive, but apparently the idiot doesna listen well. Tell me why the king would listen to you?"

"A fair question," Malcolm said with a smile. "My family, the Monroes, are in good standing with the king. I've traveled to London twice to see him. He will listen to me."

Fallon still didn't like the idea of being beholden to anyone, but he didn't want to fail his brothers again. He had been charged with getting the castle back in the hands of the MacLeods. He could either accept Malcolm's help or travel to London himself and take that much longer to rescue Quinn.

There wasn't really a choice. Still, it was difficult for Fallon. "And what do you want in exchange?"

"I would tell you I'm doing it because I want to, but you wouldn't believe me. So I ask that you listen to Larena. That's all you have to do. Just listen to her."

Fallon watched him walk away. People weren't kind for no reason at the castle of the king. They were all out for themselves. They would do you a favor if you could do one in return. Was it worth it to listen to Larena?

When he turned back, Larena was also gone. Fallon ran a hand down his face. He was so tired. And damned thirsty for wine. He held his hand in front of his face and cursed when he saw it shake.

He spun on his heel and stalked to his chamber. He was fidgety, anxious. He wanted to sit atop his castle and let his god loose. He wanted to look out over his sea and watch the waves roll in the dark water. He wanted the comfort of his hall and the calm of home. He wanted his brothers.

Fallon eased his door shut behind him. No candles flickered in greeting. He preferred it this way. It reminded him of what he had left behind on the coast.

He barred the door and froze as he realized someone was in the chamber with him. He reached out, his hand wrapping around a thin wrist.

Fallon pulled the intruder out of the shadows and into the light of the moon from his window. He lengthened one of his claws and put it in his assailant's side as he pinned a wrist to the door. His eyes widened when he saw he had none other than Larena Monroe in his grasp.

The scent of lilies washed over him. He realized too late he had her against the door, his body pressed against hers. His gaze was riveted to her breasts that rose and fell rapidly, matching the beat of the pulse at her throat.

His anger vanished, replaced with something more primal, more urgent. His blood roared in his ears as desire surged through him. He could feel every inch of her soft body, and God help him, he wanted more. He fought for control, fought to release her and step back.

Then he heard something through the door. A sound distant and fleeting, but with his enhanced hearing he was able to catch it. He leaned his face toward the wood of the door and found his head next to Larena's.

The sound was forgotten as the feel of her silky cheek rubbed against his. He turned his head and breathed in the scent of her hair. A silken strand touched his face, and before he knew what he was doing, he bent and licked her neck. His lips slid over her jaw and he heard the whoosh of air that passed through her mouth.

His balls tightened as blood rushed to his cock. He had to get away from her, to forget about sampling her lips and tasting her creamy skin. To forget the feel of her curves against his body and the way she fit against him perfectly. To forget the taste of her on his tongue and the scent of her that filled his nose.

But Fallon made a fatal mistake. He looked into her eyes.

FOUR

Quinn tugged at the chains holding his wrists and ankles in the darkness of his prison. How long had he been in the mountain? A day? A month? *A year?*

With every moment he was Deirdre's captive he could feel himself slipping under the god's control. His god, Apodatoo, the god of revenge, wanted complete power.

There had been a few weeks before Deirdre captured him when Quinn had been tempted to give the god that command. He had resisted. But then again, he'd had his brothers to help him, even though they hadn't known what was going through his mind.

His brothers.

God, how he missed them. He missed Lucan's easy smile that relaxed him, and Fallon's intense gaze that gave him strength.

Lucan and Fallon had always been there for him, even when he hadn't wanted them. Now, Quinn would chew off his own arm just to be with them again. To sit in their ruin of a castle and share a meal together.

Quinn had wanted to run away. It was what had gotten him caught, but looking back now, he realized that he hadn't run from his brothers. He had been running from himself.

What a fool he'd been. What a fool he still was. Apodatoo had grown stronger every time Quinn couldn't manage his rage. It wouldn't be long before the god had him in his command. And that's when the true hell would begin. For with the god's control, then Deirdre would dominate him.

Quinn had no doubt his brothers would come for him, but he prayed it was before Apodatoo and Deirdre took control. If he fell, he knew in his heart, his brothers would follow. And Quinn couldn't let that happen.

Lucan had just found Cara, and though she was mortal, they had a love that Quinn could only dream about. Then there was Fallon. He had stepped back from his drinking, and he had let his god out to save Cara.

The only one that hadn't changed was him. Not that Quinn deserved a second chance at anything. He hadn't been there to save his son and wife, and he had let his brothers down too many times.

Then fight your god!

It was much easier said than done. Yet, Quinn knew his very life rested on this.

The chains that held him were strengthened with magic, which prevented him from pulling loose, unlike the first time Deirdre chained him. Since he couldn't get free, the only thing he could do was battle his god.

Quinn took a deep breath and fought to manage the anger that ripped through him. With each beat of his heart he concentrated on pushing his god down. After agonizing moments, he felt the god retreat. For the time being.

He blinked in the darkness. Deirdre hadn't even left a candle for him, but then again he could see well enough in the dark not to need one. He didn't need light to know his skin was no longer black, his claws and fangs had retreated, and his eyes were once more normal.

He had won against Apodatoo this time, but each time would be more difficult. And in his human form, it left him vulnerable to the attacks he knew were imminent.

Larena held her breath, waiting for Fallon to lean in and place his lips over hers. Her body shivered in anticipation as she gazed into his dark green eyes. She saw loneliness, but she also saw hunger in his depths.

And to her surprise, she felt her own hunger rise up within her. She desperately wanted Fallon to kiss her, wanted to know what his lips felt like.

Already her blood had heated and her heart raced with the feel of Fallon's body against hers.

She forgot about hiding from Deirdre, she forgot about the Scroll she kept secreted away. All that mattered was the man who held her between his rock-hard body and the door.

Just as she thought she would get her kiss, he spun her away from him and jerked open the door.

Larena blinked at the empty space that Fallon had just occupied. She couldn't believe he had left. She had felt so sure the passion was mutual between them.

Then the screams registered in her ears. She rushed to the doorway and leaned out. Something had panicked the entire castle.

She lifted her skirts in her hand and ran toward the shrieks. Halfway to the great hall she heard it—the unmistakable screech of a wyrran.

"Nay," she whispered, and ran faster.

Why was a wyrran at the castle? Had Deirdre learned of her? Or was it here because of Fallon? None of it mattered at the moment. The only thing that did matter was killing the ugly creature.

When she reached the corridor that led to the great hall she had to push and shove her way through the crowd running from the hall. She heard someone shout her name and looked over to see Malcolm. His blue eyes held a wealth of worry, telling her without words that her worst fear had come to pass. Deirdre had found her.

Using the strength she usually hid, Larena shoved aside the people blocking her path and pushed into the great hall that was now devoid of people. She skidded to a halt when she found Fallon already there and facing off against the yellow-skinned wyrran as it clung to the upper wall near the ceiling.

She watched Fallon's claws lengthen, their obsidian color shining in the candlelight. She waited for the rest of him to change. She wanted to know what he looked like as a Warrior, to see all of him as dark as his claws.

Instead, the wyrran raised its gaze to her and let out another ear-piercing screech. It leaped at her, but just when Larena was about to let her goddess out, Fallon caught hold of the creature's leg.

"Get out!" he bellowed.

She gave a quick nod and hurried from the hall. But Fallon had another thing coming if he thought she wasn't going to fight.

Fallon couldn't believe there was a wyrran at the king's castle. But more worrying than that was the fact Larena had followed him. Most women would have run upon hearing the screams. But not her.

He didn't know whether he liked her courage, or wanted to shake her for putting her life in danger.

He thought he'd do both.

First, though, he needed to kill the wyrran, and he couldn't take the chance of changing into his Warrior. The residents of the castle had already seen too much with the wyrran's appearance. There would be no explaining away his black skin, fangs, and claws.

Fallon unsheathed the dagger he kept in his boot and tracked the small creature, praying that during the few moments Larena had been in the hall she hadn't seen his claws.

The wyrran were diminutive, but the long claws on their hands and feet could tear a person in half. He hated looking at them with their thin, yellow skin. Their faces were hideous with a mouthful of sharp teeth that their lips could hardly fit over. And their large, round yellow eyes made his skin crawl.

"Did you come for me?" he taunted the creature.

The wyrran opened its mouth and issued a long shriek.

Fallon grimaced as his ears rang from the sound. "I really hate you little shites," he murmured. "Come on and fight me!"

The wyrran jumped from the wall to the ground. The slight bastards could crawl on anything, in any direction. For the first time since he had let his god out to help save Cara, Fallon wanted to transform. He wanted to toss aside his dagger and use his claws to rip the wyrran in half.

The wyrran's lips peeled back in what was supposed to be a smile, as if it knew what Fallon wanted.

"Can you read minds now?" Fallon asked as he jumped toward the wyrran. His dagger landed in the creature's arm. Fallon ripped the blade down, scouring open the thin skin.

The wyrran's claws raked down Fallon's chest as it struggled to get free. Fallon ignored the pain and tried to hold on, but the wyrran's diminutive, lean frame was hard to hold on to. Somehow, it jerked free of Fallon and the dagger and leaped to the wall.

It gave another screech before it bounded out of the great hall and into the castle through the door Larena had left open. Fallon's only thought was of Larena. She would be defenseless against the wyrran.

Fallon rushed from the hall and into the empty corridor. When he was sure the wyrran and Larena weren't there, he continued through the castle. The few people he saw quickly ran into chambers and slammed the doors. But he didn't find the wyrran.

With a curse Fallon slid to a halt and returned to the great hall. The wyrran was fast, but he couldn't outrun a Warrior.

FIVE

Larena knew the wyrran would leave the hall. So she sat and waited. She wished she could watch Fallon battle the ugly creature, but she couldn't chance it. The wyrran had to die.

How many of the vile creatures had she fought and killed over the decades? Too many. And what exactly was it doing in Edinburgh Castle?

That confused her even more. She could only guess it was here because of Fallon, but if she didn't consider the possibility the wyrran was there because of her, then she would be foolish.

Between the shrieks of rage from the wyrran, she imagined Fallon was doing a good job of wounding the beast. Larena smiled. Had Fallon changed into a Warrior? She didn't hear a roar, but how she wanted to see him in his Warrior form.

There were too many people in the castle for Fallon to chance it, and it wouldn't be long before someone got up enough courage to come and check the hall.

Her musings came to an end when the wyrran burst from the great hall into the corridor before leaping out a window down from her. It was a good thing she had already tossed her gown out the window and transformed because a moment later Fallon came out and looked right at her. But he couldn't see her. No one could.

She waited until he left then she followed the wyrran out the window and down the rocky facing of the castle. The wyrran was fast, but not as fast as it should have been if it had known what tracked it.

Deirdre had made the creatures crafty, but not nearly fast enough to outrun a Warrior.

Larena jumped in front of the creature and made herself visible once they were on the ground. The wyrran bared its mouthful of teeth and hissed. Larena just smiled and readied for the kill.

The wyrran lifted its hands and showed her its long, sharp claws. She wasn't impressed. Larena bent her legs and waited for the creature to attack. She used to fear using the power coursing through her, but now she relished it. Her goddess had never let her down before.

And it had been quite a few months since Larena had loosened the goddess inside her. Her goddess smiled within her, as eager as Larena for a fight.

The wyrran rocked back and forth on its feet as if trying to decide how to attack. Suddenly, it jumped on her and used its lethal claws to rake down her arms.

Larena grimaced in pain and plunged her claws into its chest. The wyrran's eyes bulged when she wrapped her fingers around its heart.

"You don't belong here," she told it just before she ripped out the heart.

Larena tossed aside the small organ as the wyrran fell dead upon the ground, its lifeless eyes staring at the stars. As much as she wanted to leave the creature, she couldn't chance anyone coming upon it.

So she grabbed the wyrran by one of its ankles and dragged it into the forest where she hid it. Larena would return later and set it on fire along with the heart. She was covered in blood and shivered in the cool evening air, alone.

She was so tired of being alone. Malcolm was a wonderful confidant, and a true friend, but he could not fully comprehend what it was like to have a goddess inside him. Malcolm couldn't understand the raw power that surged in her when the goddess was turned free. And Larena feared if he did learn just how much power she had, he would never come near her again.

Larena had already lost her family and her clan when the goddess chose her over a male. She couldn't stand to lose Malcolm as well.

Yet, she knew the time was coming when she would have to leave him for good. He would never face his own future as long as she was near. Malcolm felt responsible for what his family—her family—had done to her, and he was determined to make up for her banishment.

She took a deep breath and turned back to the castle. As usual, when she returned to her chamber Malcolm would be there with water for her to wash and a gown. He never asked questions, not even when he saw her wounds.

Even though he knew she was immortal, it had taken him actually seeing her body heal for him to realize that she couldn't be killed unless someone took her head.

It made her throat ache to have to tell Malcolm farewell. Malcolm was one of the few people she trusted.

He had been there for her when others hadn't. But she knew that if Fallon was really the MacLeod she had been searching for, she would have to learn to trust him, because the MacLeods were the only ones who could keep her hidden from Deirdre.

Larena sighed and brushed the hair from her face that had fallen when she tracked the wyrran. She would have to tell Fallon she was a Warrior, but the one thing he and the others could never learn about was the Scroll she guarded.

She had taken a vow upon having the goddess released. That vow meant everything to her, especially when she had seen the pride in her father's eyes. She had been so scared of what the future held for her, but her father had believed she was the perfect person to guard the Scroll. She prayed he was right.

If for some reason Fallon MacLeod wouldn't aid her, she was still going to have to leave Malcolm behind. Even then Larena was taking a huge chance. He knew too much. If Deirdre ever discovered how much Malcolm knew of the Warriors, Deirdre would come after Malcolm with a vengeance.

Larena knew she had been selfish sharing her burden with Malcolm, but she had needed a friend. He had never failed her. That would change, however, if Deirdre ever captured him. Malcolm would try to hold out, but in the end he would tell Deirdre everything.

When that happened, there would be no place Larena could hide where Deirdre couldn't find her.

What a mess Larena had dug for herself. She should have been stronger, she should never have told Malcolm more than he already knew or guessed. And most of all, she should never have involved him in her schemes to find the MacLeods.

She touched the spot on her neck that Fallon had licked. She shivered as she thought about how it had felt to have his hot, wet tongue touch her. Larena closed her eyes as she recalled every inch of his body against hers, how his warm breath fanned her cheek, and how his long dark hair had tickled her face.

Her nipples puckered, sending spirals of desire shooting between her legs as she recalled the feel of Fallon's hard body pressing against hers, flattening her breasts. No longer did the cool night air bother her as her body heated and throbbed with a need she couldn't ignore.

Larena opened her eyes and took in a steadying breath. She needed to get control of herself. Fallon couldn't know how his nearness unnerved her. It would give him an advantage she couldn't allow.

After seeing his claws tonight she knew he was the MacLeod of legend. It was time she spoke to him. If Fallon couldn't help her, then she needed to hide. Whether the wyrran was here for her or Fallon, it had come to the castle.

And that wasn't a good sign.

Larena turned herself invisible before she made her way back to the castle and her chamber. Just as she expected, Malcolm stood waiting for her. She grabbed a blanket from the bed to shield herself before she made herself known.

Malcolm blew out a breath when he caught sight of her. "I was worried."

She forced a smile so he wouldn't know the turmoil inside her. "I can take care of myself."

"No wyrran have come to the castle before, Larena."

She moved to the tub, not caring that the water wasn't hot. She waited until Malcolm turned his back to her before she climbed in. "I don't know why the wyrran was here. Was it for me? Or was it for Fallon?"

"It could have been for either of you."

Her stomach pitched wildly at his words. "I know. I must speak to Fallon tonight. No longer can I wait. I must know if he can help me or not."

Malcolm sighed but kept his back to her as he took a chair near the hearth and sat. "I saw Fallon searching the castle for the wyrran. He's cautious, Larena, which could be a benefit if he helps conceal you."

"He's been hiding for three hundred years, of course he's cautious. I'm curious to know why he's here though. Did you learn anything?"

"Aye. He wants his castle given back to the MacLeods. He had come to seek an audience with the king."

She nodded to herself as she continued to wash the blood from her body. "The wyrran is dead so we needn't worry about that for the moment. I'm going to need to go back and set it afire. It was surprised to see me, so I think it was here for Fallon, though why it showed itself in the great hall I don't understand."

"I'll take care of the wyrran. Where is it?"

"You shouldn't take that chance."

Malcolm mumbled something beneath his breath. "Larena, though you are a Warrior, a man can get away with things at this castle that a woman canna. Now, tell me where the damned beast is."

Sometimes she hated that she was a woman. "It's in the forest near an oak with a double trunk. I hid it well."

"I'll see to it tonight. I doona suppose you were able to talk to Fallon before the wyrran appeared?"

"Nay, I didn't." She recalled Fallon's warm breath that fanned her skin, the feel of his tongue as it branded her neck, and the smell of orangewood as she learned the feel of his muscular body. "We were interrupted."

Malcolm turned his head to the side so she could see his profile. "You're going to him now."

It wasn't a question. "I am. I cannot wait to speak with him any longer."

Malcolm rose to his feet and walked to the door. "I'll be in my chamber after I get rid of the wyrran if you need anything."

"Thank you, dearest friend."

He paused with his hand on the latch. "Thank me when MacLeod takes you to his castle."

Larena waited until the door closed behind Malcolm before she let out a breath. She picked up the soap again and scrubbed her body a second time. She couldn't stand the wyrran's blood on her.

Fallon slumped down on his bed. He had half expected to come into his chamber and find Larena inside once again. To his disappointment, there had been no one.

He didn't like that frustration, or the nervousness that hadn't left him since he had seen her in the great hall. It would have been nice to find the wyrran to take out some of his anger on the creature instead of coming back to his chamber and to his memories of Larena in his arms.

He could still feel her. That small contact of her face against his had embedded her in his body. He had held her against him, felt her supple body and womanly curves. He wanted to bury his face in her hair and inhale the scent that was hers alone.

And God help him, he wanted to lick every inch of her.

Fallon rose and removed his boots, tartan, and shirt. It wasn't that he didn't like wearing the kilt, it was just so different from what he had worn for the last three hundred plus years. He could get used to it though. He especially liked wearing the colors of the MacLeod for all to see.

With a sigh he slid beneath the covers. Sleep wouldn't come, not with a wyrran on the loose and knowing he had to find Thomas MacDonald in the morning before he left for MacLeod Castle. He closed his eyes, but all he could think about was Larena. He could still taste her on his tongue from that brief lick against her neck. She was the sweetest taste of sin.

By the saints, how he wanted to savor more of her! Too bad he would never get the chance.

Larena climbed in through Fallon's window. She was careful not to make any noise that would wake him, not that he would see her if he did. Once she was inside, she moved to the corner near the hearth and reached for her robe that lay on top of the chest.

It was one of the things she hated about using her power of invisibility. She might become invisible, but whatever clothes she had on didn't. The only thing that she was able to wear and not be seen was the ring on her middle right finger because it held magic. That ring never came off. For any reason.

Her goddess receded as she threaded her arms through the sleeves of her robe. She had brought it with her and left it when Fallon had found her in his chamber. She hadn't expected to talk to him then. Nay, her plan had been just what she was doing. There was only one way to talk to a man like Fallon, and that was to get his attention.

Arriving naked would do that, but she wasn't ready to show him everything. At least not yet. She would use her body if she had to. She didn't like that idea, but too much was at stake. First, she would try and talk to him.

To her horror her body heated just knowing she might get to kiss Fallon.

She walked in the moonbeams that shone through his windows. The chamber wasn't as large as hers, but it was still nice. The burgundy velvet bed hangings were the best that coin could buy. The candles were scented, and there was plenty of wood stacked near the hearth in case he wanted a fire.

Larena put a finger on an unopened bottle of wine. It sat in the middle of the small table, almost like a gift. Except she had the feeling Fallon had put it there himself. So, not a gift, but a punishment then?

She thought back to dinner. He hadn't taken any wine or mead. He had only drunk water. Odd for a man such as he.

Her head turned to the bed. She had kept herself from looking at him, but no longer. Her feet started to move and took her to the bed. He slept with his face toward the windows, the light of the moon illuminating his chiseled features and silent strength.

He was spectacular. He had an angular face with

hollows beneath his cheekbones that made him appear hardened and menacing. His chin was square, his jawline hard and unforgiving. Just like a Highlander.

His nose was long and straight and thin. When her gaze landed on his lips, she sighed, recalling how they'd grazed her cheek.

His eyes, though closed now, were the most beautiful green she had ever seen. Dark brows slashed over his eyes. There was a small scar near his left eye that must have occurred before his god was unbound.

She wanted to touch that scar and ask him how it had come about, and how he had managed not to lose his eye and sight in the process.

The paleness of the linens was a stark contrast to his skin, bronzed from the sun. In the moonlight his hair looked almost black, though she knew it was dark brown with hints of gold running through it as though he had spent much time out of doors.

Her gaze traveled to his bare chest that rose and fell slowly. His abdomen rippled with honed muscles and power. The same was true of his arms and shoulders, and even his hands that lay slack by his sides.

Larena leaned in close to get a good look at the thick gold torc around his neck. Two boars' heads with their mouths open and teeth visible stared at her.

She straightened, unable to believe her luck in finding one of *the* MacLeods. She had kept her distance from everyone for so long, that the need to know everything about Fallon MacLeod startled her. The mistakes of her past wouldn't let her forget, yet she couldn't take her gaze from Fallon.

She let her fingers comb through a lock of his dark

hair. It reached past his shoulders and was thick and cool to the touch. She wanted to run her hands through it again and again. She wanted to hold him and lull him to sleep with the gentle scrape of her nails on his scalp.

Larena pulled her hand away, afraid she would touch more of him if she didn't. She hadn't felt anything like this for a man before, and to be frank, it frightened her.

Her gaze moved to his lips once again. Ah, such a beautiful mouth. Wide, firm lips that weren't too thin or too full. Lips that were made for teasing and kissing.

She trembled at the thought of his mouth on hers. Her hand reached up to touch the cheek where his beard had brushed against her. Even in the dim light she could see the thick whiskers growing out on his jaw. It made him look wicked and dangerous. Forbidden.

He shifted in his sleep, his mouth parting. He looked so different as he slept. Gone were the worries that bracketed his mouth and eyes. Gone was the furrow on his forehead. He looked young and almost mischievous now.

Larena smiled, trying to picture the lad he had been. She imagined he'd caused his mother to fret. As the eldest, he'd had to be strong for his brothers. Just the type of laird a clan like the MacLeods had needed. It was a tragedy Deirdre had wiped them out.

Thinking of Deirdre made Larena remember why she was in Fallon's chambers. She turned away and went to stand next to the window. She needed to forget the temptation Fallon's body posed.

Why? Why not use him? You felt his attraction to you.
It was true, she did know he was attracted to her.

But could she chance being intimate with a man again? Did she dare after what had happened the last time?

Fallon is a Warrior. He doesn't want to use you.

Larena considered her conscious. What would it hurt if she gave in to the desire Fallon brought out in her? She would be in control. And just one time, she would know what it felt like to be held by a man like Fallon MacLeod.

SIX

Fallon wasn't sure what woke him. He'd been deep in a dream of a time before the massacre of his clan. He had brought his mother flowers, as an apology for stealing the bread from the kitchen again.

His mother had always said he knew just how to find forgiveness with any woman. He had laughed, thankful she couldn't stay angry at him long.

Just as the dream had taken the sinister road toward the death of the clan, he could have sworn he smelled lilies.

Larena.

Instantly, the dream changed. He held Larena in his arms up against the door. Her beautiful smoky blue eyes were heavy lidded as she looked at him with lips swollen from his kisses. He took her mouth for another kiss, a moan escaping him when she rubbed her hips against his arousal.

By the saints, he wanted her with a desperation that bordered on insanity. He would do anything, say anything, just to claim her as his own.

Then, with a smile she had moved out of his arms and beckoned him with her fingers to follow. Her scent, that amazing lily scent, went with her.

Fallon woke with a longing that made his chest ache. He kept his eyes closed, trying to go back to the dream and follow Larena. He might not be able to have her, but he could in his dreams. In his dreams, they could have everything.

A sound like a soft sigh reached him. Fallon cracked open an eye to find a woman standing by his window, the moonlight spilling around her and making her golden locks shine as they hung down her back.

Larena.

He couldn't move, couldn't breathe. He wasn't sure if she was real or if he was dreaming, but it didn't matter. She was in his chamber.

He watched, mesmerized, as she ran her fingers through her damp hair. Her stunning yellow tresses fell in soft waves over her shoulders and down to her breasts. She took a small strand and began to braid it absentmindedly.

It was then Fallon realized she was deep in thought, her gaze looking out over the land. He let his eyes roam over her, surprised to find her in a thin robe of pink. He could see every curve, every swell of her body through the sheer material.

He'd already been aroused by his dream, but now he was rock hard.

Suddenly her hands paused and her gaze swung to him. His mouth went dry, and he was most thankful that he hadn't kicked the covers off as he normally did.

She couldn't be in his chamber. He didn't have time to dally with a woman, any woman, but especially one that had invaded his dreams. He had a mission to complete, and he would see it done before anything else.

"What are you doing here?" he asked once he realized she wasn't going to speak.

She licked her lips, drawing his gaze to her plump mouth. "I told you I needed to speak with you."

"So you did. This makes twice now you've come into my chamber. What you have to say must be very important."

"It is."

There was a soft waver in her voice. Was she frightened of him? Somehow that didn't give him the joy it should have. She had shown him such strength in the little time he had observed her. He couldn't imagine her frightened of anyone.

He sat up and swung his legs over the side of the bed, careful to keep the blankets over his throbbing rod. "Go on, my lady. Say what it is that is so important that you've stolen into my bedchamber in the middle of the night."

She opened her mouth, then closed it and faced the window. "It was so much easier in my mind."

Before he realized what he was doing he rose from the bed and walked to her, uncaring that he was nude. He had gone daft, but no matter what he told himself, he couldn't stop from going to her. She turned to face him, her large eyes wide and searching. But searching for what?

"You shouldna be in here," he said. It was taking every ounce of his control not to pull her against him and take her mouth in a kiss with enough fire to engulf them both.

She swallowed and let her hands drop to her sides. "I had to."

"Leave."

"I cannot."

He grabbed her by her upper arms and gave her a little shake. "Leave," he ground out between clenched teeth. Touching her had been a mistake, but he had to make her understand he couldn't control the hunger that coursed through him.

"I can't," she repeated.

He inhaled the fragrance of lilies and nearly groaned. His cock throbbed between them, aching to feel her wet heat. "Larena, you have to leave. Now."

She looked into his eyes and lifted her face to his. "Nay."

He knew he was lost then. He couldn't make her leave, and to make matters worse, he was damned glad she hadn't. "Then you damn us both."

Larena knew he was going to kiss her. She'd seen it in his eyes when he'd risen from the bed. She expected a rough kiss born of anger and lust. She never expected the soft touch of his lips and the desire that swarmed her when his tongue swept into her mouth.

She was flooded with the taste of him, and, oh God, how good he tasted. His hands left her arms to move to her neck where he cupped each side of her face. He tilted her head to the side and deepened the kiss.

Larena couldn't stop the moan that tore from her. The kiss was intoxicating, lulling her like the sweetest wine. And it made her want more. So much more.

The kiss went on forever as heat built in her body and her heart pounded in her chest. Fallon moved an arm to her lower back where he pressed her against him, his arousal pushing into her stomach and making it difficult for her to continue standing. She wound her arms around his neck, loving the feel of his back muscles moving beneath her hands.

His potency stunned her, his tenderness surprised her. She had felt desire for Fallon the first time she had seen him, but now, with every touch and kiss, she was falling farther and farther under the spell of passion he wove around her.

Her mind shouted warning bells, but her body was too far gone. There was no way she could walk away from him now. She was stronger than she had been the first time, and she would make sure no one took advantage of her again. Even if that man could weave such a spell of pleasure around her as Fallon did.

"My God, Larena," he murmured between kisses.

She couldn't agree more, but now was not the time for talking. Now was the time for touching and feeling, of loving.

His hands were everywhere, caressing every part of her body, and still it wasn't enough. She trembled when his hands parted her robe and skimmed over her breasts to her waist. His mouth slanted over hers again, their tongues mating in a frenzy of undeniable lust. She lost all sense of time and place. All that mattered was Fallon and what he was doing to her body.

She gasped at the contact of his skin on hers. She hadn't realized he had removed her robe. Yet, she sighed at the feel of his heated body against hers. He was so hard, so *hot*! Her nipples pebbled at the contact of his chest against her breasts.

Heat flooded her and pooled between her legs, making her ache and throb. She wanted to touch Fallon as he touched her, but every time she tried, he stopped her.

"Not this time," Fallon said before he kissed her again.

Larena gave up. For now. She was determined to have Fallon again that night, so she would have a chance to know his body. For now, it was enough that he wanted her.

A laugh escaped her when he tossed her back onto the bed and quickly crawled over her. She gazed into his turbulent green eyes. She saw desire as well as worry in his beautiful depths.

"I should have known I couldn't ignore the hunger you brought out in me," he said.

Larena reached up and touched his face. "You take my breath away," she confessed. She knew better than to tell a man such things, but it was out of her mouth before she could stop it. She knew it was the truth and it terrified her, but there was something about Fallon that tugged at her soul.

He bent and placed kisses down her neck and across her chest then to the valley between her breasts. His big, muscular body settled between her thighs, his arousal bumping against her aching sex.

She trembled with the need to have him inside her. It had been decades since she had last lain with a man. That one time had been a mistake, one that had cost her dearly. She had guarded herself since then. But somehow, that wasn't possible with Fallon.

His large, callused hand cupped a breast as he ran his thumb over her nipple. She moaned and arched her back, wanting more, needing more. The pleasure that simple action brought her was unbelievable.

Her breasts swelled and her nipples hardened with the pleasure that pooled within her. While he rolled one hard nub between his fingers, he covered the other with his mouth and sucked.

Larena cried out and buried her hands in his hair. Desire and pleasure swirled around her, making her forget to breathe as she thought only of the man in her arms.

Passion thrummed within her, making her ache and tremble. Fallon's mouth and tongue drove her wild as he alternated between sucking and licking one nipple while his fingers pinched and rolled the other.

The torture was exquisite, the pleasure endless. Larena moaned when he pulled her nipple deep into his mouth and suckled. The drag from his lips brought a flood of desire. She was close to peaking just from him touching her breasts. It seemed impossible, but the more Fallon touched her, the more she gave her body to him.

She ground her hips against him, seeking some relief from the maddening desire that pumped faster and wound tighter inside her. He shifted to the side and moved his hand from her breast down her body to the curls that hid her sex.

Larena moaned as his fingers parted her. He leisurely skimmed his deft fingers over her sensitive, throbbing folds. Each touch of his fingers only heightened her awareness of him and increased the ache within her. Then, *finally,* he pushed a finger inside her and delved into her heat.

Her fingers clutched the blankets as she moaned and begged for more. She should be mortified at herself, but with Fallon touching her, nothing else mattered.

In and out his skillful fingers moved within her, bringing her closer and closer to her orgasm. When he skimmed his fingers over her clitoris, she screamed his name, her body jerking with the pleasure.

When he pushed his fingers back inside her, there were two this time. He pumped into her slowly then faster and faster until she trembled with the need for her release.

"Saints help me," Fallon said with a groan. "It's been too long, Larena. I cannot wait."

She didn't want to wait. Not another moment. "Then don't."

He moved over her and guided the head of his cock against her slick folds. She cried out when the tip of him rubbed against the most sensitive part of her, sending waves of need rolling through her.

And then he pushed inside her.

Larena gripped his back as he filled her, stretched her. She brought her legs up to his waist and he went deeper, seating himself completely.

For a moment they both lay still, their harsh breaths filling the room. Fallon looked down at her and one corner of his mouth lifted in a smile.

"I've missed this," he said.

Larena shifted her hips and grinned when Fallon hissed in a breath. "Don't stop. Please. Not now."

"Never," he vowed.

He pulled out of her only to thrust hard and deep. Larena moaned and gave herself up to the delicious sensations racking her body. She wrapped her legs around his waist, locking her ankles together. He whispered her name as his hips began to pump faster.

Larena couldn't believe the feel of Fallon inside her. It was beautiful and felt so good that she never wanted it to end. The climax came quickly, blinding her in its intensity as it consumed her. Larena succumbed to her body's need, a need that had long been denied. As she came down from her peak, she opened her eyes to find Fallon staring at her.

"My God," he whispered.

With her body still convulsing from such a powerful orgasm, she raised her hips to meet his. Fallon threw back his head as he plunged inside her, his body tense and shaking. Larena held him as he climaxed. When the last of his tremors left him, he lay atop her.

Larena wrapped her arms around him, stroking him, caressing him. She could feel him still deep inside her. She wished they could stay as they were forever, but it was a fanciful dream.

Eventually, he pulled out of her and rolled to his side. Larena was loath to break contact with him, so she faced him. Their gazes clashed and held. His hand came up and he ran the back of his knuckles along her cheek.

"Why?" he asked.

How could she explain it? "You said you felt the lust. I knew from the first moment I saw you that you were special."

"Special?" He frowned. "Nay."

"Aye," she said, and smoothed her fingers over his brow to remove the frown. "I know I shouldn't have come to your chamber, but what I have to say has to be done in private."

He took her hand in his. "Tell me."

Now that she had his attention, she was scared. How would he react? Would he welcome her? Would he believe her? Would he scorn her?

She didn't think she could take his disdain.

"Larena," he urged gently. "Tell me."

She rolled to her back and looked at the deep burgundy of the bed hangings above her. "It's difficult to know where to begin."

"I'm not going anywhere. Why not start at the beginning?"

The beginning. It was so long ago, with memories she would rather forget. But Fallon was right. She needed to start at the creation of it all.

"My clan, the Monroes, aren't the largest clan, but they are powerful. We can trace our roots back to the time of the Celts, and even then our clan was strong. We've endured."

Larena couldn't contain the anxiety within her and rose from the bed to walk to the window. This was the difficult part, and she needed some space from him to be able to get it all out.

"I know what you are, Fallon, what's inside you. My family had passed down stories from generation to generation about the ancient Celts and the Romans. Stories that spoke of why Rome left our shores."

She paused and waited to see if Fallon would say anything. Only silence greeted her. She continued to gaze out the window at the trees swaying in the wind.

"Added to those stories were new ones. Ones about the MacLeods and an evil Druid named Deirdre."

She heard the bed squeak and knew he had sat up. "The laird, my uncle, knew our time was running out. Soon Deirdre would find her way to our clan and take the strongest male to turn him into her Warrior."

"God's blood," Fallon murmured behind her.

"We had an advantage though." Larena made herself face him. "We had a Druid in our clan. She and her family had watched over us, keeping the stories alive. She knew the spell to unbind the god."

Fallon's brow furrowed and his eyes narrowed.

"The family gathered in the great hall. My uncle and his son Naill, who everyone thought was going to be the future Warrior, stood in the middle of the hall. The Druid Robena began the spell. Only it wasn't Naill whom the god chose."

"Who?" Fallon asked.

She swallowed her dread. "I was next to my father when the pain started. I tried to hold back my cries, but soon it became too much. I fell to my knees, my skin on fire, my bones breaking. I must have blacked out, because when I came to, Robena stood over me with a smile on her wrinkled face.

"My father helped me stand as Robena announced the god had chosen. It was me, not Naill. My uncle and cousin were so furious they banished me from the clan. With time only for a hug from my father, Robena and I fled to the forest."

Fallon stared at her in shock. "The god chose you?"

"It's a goddess actually."

She had expected many things, but not stunned disbelief. He wouldn't believe her until she showed him. "My goddess is Lelomai, the goddess of defense."

She held out her arms and let herself transform. First her claws, long and sharp, next her fangs, and then, her body. She stood before Fallon, hoping, praying, he would be the salvation she sought.

SEVEN

Fallon could only stare awestruck at Larena. He'd never seen anything so beautiful before in his life. She was a stunning woman, but when she transformed she was . . . breathtaking.

He rose and walked toward her. She glowed with all the colors of the rainbow, muted though they were. He touched a lock of her hair, amazed to find the iridescent color was also there. Of all the Warriors he had seen, none had had hair that changed color.

His gaze took in her shapely form that glimmered, sparkled. He lifted her hand in his and looked at her long claws of the same color as her skin. They were narrower than his, but just as deadly. A glance at her parted lips showed him her fangs.

She was definitely a Warrior. A female Warrior. Who would have guessed one existed?

"You're beautiful," he murmured.

Her troubled iridescent gaze met his as she removed her hand from his. "I'm the only female Warrior that I know of, Fallon. Deirdre knows nothing of me. Yet. But it is only a matter of time."

He understood then why she had sought him out. "You want my protection."

"I do."

How could he possibly turn his back on her? He was here to help his brothers, but finding Larena would also help their cause in fighting Deirdre. Another Warrior only improved their odds. "You have it. How long have you been a Warrior?"

"A hundred years."

She'd been alone for so long. He ached for her. "And why did you come to the king's castle?"

"Malcolm agreed to help me try to uncover anything we could regarding Deirdre."

"Where have you been before this?"

She shrugged and looked away. "Though I was banished from my clan, I stayed near because of my father. It was in the forest that Robena helped to train me with the things I would need to know to be a Warrior."

"Why come to Edinburgh now?"

Her gaze met his and he saw defiance and determination in the depths. "It is my duty to stay out of Deirdre's grasp. I was learning nothing of Deirdre or other Warriors in the forest."

"Maybe, but you were hidden."

"Not exactly. I've been battling wyrran since my goddess was unleashed. Since most Warriors are loners and hidden, I figured I would have a good chance learning how far Deirdre's reach had gotten while in the king's castle."

"You think Deirdre has control of the king?"

"Nay," she said with a shake of her head. "At least not yet. But it was while I've been here that I discovered the MacLeods had been found."

"And why you sought me out," he finished.

"I may have been alone, but I can defend myself."

He glanced at her claws and smiled. "I imagine you can."

"Just because I'm a woman doesn't mean I cannot take care of myself. I've killed a man before. I gave him my body because I was naïve and believed he cared for me. He betrayed me and murdered my father."

"By all that's holy," Fallon murmured, unable to believe someone would do such a thing.

"I was so angry. Once the fury took hold, I wasn't myself. The next thing I knew, I was looking down at his dead body."

Fallon nodded. "You were betrayed, Larena, by someone you trusted. Your goddess defended herself, and in the process killed the man. Don't let your father's murderer and your betrayer haunt you anymore."

She gave him a shy smile in answer. The more he learned of Larena, the more he was impressed by her bravery and courage. "What other powers do you have?"

Right before his eyes she disappeared. Fallon turned one way and then the other. "Larena? Where did you go?"

"I'm standing in the same place," she said.

He heard her voice, but he couldn't see her. The power she held was vast and could greatly aid in their coming battle. "Amazing."

She materialized before him and her goddess faded away, leaving the beauty that he had lain with just moments ago. "As I said, I can protect myself, and I can help you."

"I would have taken you back to the castle anyway. You are a female Warrior, Larena. Deirdre would stop at nothing to have you."

"I've been careful, but I fear she will find me soon."

"Then we'll make sure that doesn't happen."

He saw the relief in her eyes and gathered her in his arms. For the first time in a very long time he felt needed, as if he could make a difference. He wouldn't make the same mistakes he'd made with his brothers. He would protect Larena—with his life if necessary. He might have disappointed his brothers all these centuries, but he would not fail Larena.

"Thank you," she said, her voice trembling.

"You're not alone any longer, Larena. You have me. Once we get to my castle, you'll meet my brothers and the other Warriors and Druids who are there. You will be protected."

She nodded. "I thought you would be repulsed."

"Repulsed?" He pulled her out of his arms and tilted her face up to his, the urge to kiss her strong. "You didn't get to choose the goddess. The goddess chose you. You bear the same trials that the rest of us do, regardless of whether you are a man or a woman."

There was something in her eyes. She had more to tell him, a secret she didn't think she could trust him enough with. He understood that. He wouldn't trust him either, but he would earn her confidence. It wouldn't make up for all the wrongs he had done his brothers, but it would help. He would be the man his father had wanted him to be.

"Does Malcolm know?" he asked.

"Aye. He knows everything. I tried to keep it from him, and I fear now that Deirdre will learn he has helped me."

Fallon inwardly cursed. "Malcolm has put himself

in a dangerous position. Deirdre will go after him if she learns of him."

"I know," Larena said. "I've used the same argument before, but Malcolm said he wanted to make up for what our family did to me. He's next in line to be laird, and I don't want anything to happen to him. He shouldn't even be here with me."

"Then he needs to return to your clan. Immediately."

She nodded. "I agree. Once I assure him you'll protect me, I'll send him home."

Fallon had an uneasy feeling. How had Larena stayed hidden from Deirdre all this time? "The wyrran?"

"I killed it," she admitted. "I waited until it left the great hall."

"Did anyone see you kill it?"

"Nay. I then took the body into the woods. Malcolm is there burning it now."

He ran a hand down his face. "And you came back to the castle the same way you left?"

"Aye. Unseen."

It was a large castle, full of nosy people. Could they have been lucky enough for Larena to have escaped detection? "I wonder if the wyrran was here for me or you."

"I think you," she said. "After all, Deirdre doesn't know about me. I've been here for over a year, Fallon, and not once has a wyrran appeared in the castle. Not until you came."

"Good. I also think we should leave first thing tomorrow."

"All right," she said, and walked to the bed. She sank down on it, unmindful of her nakedness and the effect she had on him. "I'll tell Malcolm as soon as I see him."

Fallon felt his cock stir. He wasn't surprised he wanted her again. Being with Larena had been . . . amazing. It might have been three hundred years since he had lain with a woman, but he knew no one had touched him the way she had.

She smiled and dropped her eyes to the floor. "I've looked for the MacLeods for so long. It seems strange to have found you now."

He moved to stand in front of her and cupped her face in his hands. He lost himself in the beauty of her smoky blue eyes. He could only imagine what it had been like to be forced from her clan. It brought to mind how many times he had failed his own family.

"I give you my word, Larena. I'll not abandon you."

Unable to help himself, he bent and placed his lips over hers. She wrapped her arms around him and sank into the kiss. The spark of desire flamed once more. Fallon could no more stop the lust from swarming his veins than he could stop his body from breathing.

He gently pushed Larena back onto the bed and covered her body with his. Her soft curves, all womanly and seductive, made his head spin. How he had gone so long without the touch of a woman surprised him. He had missed the warmth of a female's hand, the soft sighs, and gentle caresses.

Just knowing that she was a Warrior, that she knew what he was and what was inside him, unleashed something primitive. He wanted to claim Larena for his own. The thought of another man, another Warrior, touching her made him see red.

Fallon skimmed his hand down her side to the indent of her waist and over her gently flared hips to the curls nestled between her legs. He was wild for her already. He wanted to sink into her heat and thrust inside her again and again and again.

He groaned when he felt how wet she was. "You're ready for me."

She nodded, her eyes glazed with desire. "I don't know what you do to my body, Fallon, but don't stop. Please, don't stop."

He wouldn't. Not now, not ever. God, what was wrong with him that he had no control over his body when he was around her? He saw Larena, or smelled her, and he had to have her.

Fallon lifted her leg and thrust inside her. She cried out, her nails raking down his back. Her passion only spurred him on. He pulled out until only the tip of him remained, then he plunged inside her until he touched her womb.

She cried out his name, her body bucking beneath his. He felt his climax roaring closer, but he didn't want to go without her. Fallon moved his hand between them and found her clitoris. He stroked the little nub in soft circles until it was swollen and Larena writhed with mindless desire.

He loved how she responded to his touch. At one time he had thought he'd forgotten how to pleasure a woman, but it all came back with one touch to Larena's luscious body.

"Fallon," she cried, her hips rising to meet his.

He knew she was close to peaking. He closed his mouth around one of her nipples and sucked it deep in his mouth. Her body jerked beneath his as her orgasm claimed her.

Fallon lifted his head and watched the look of utter abandon on her face. It was beautiful. He forgot everything when he felt her clenching around his cock. No longer could he hold off his own climax. He thrust his hips once, twice, and then it took him. He closed his eyes, his body throbbing as his seed spilled inside her.

Sweat covered their bodies, and his arms were shaking from holding himself above her. He opened his eyes to find her watching him.

"What have you done to me, Fallon MacLeod?" she whispered.

He had no idea, but he wanted to continue doing it.

EIGHT

With her body sated, Larena began to drift off to sleep. He moved the covers over them so they wouldn't get chilled and kissed the top of her head.

Fallon mumbled something, but she couldn't decipher it. She wanted to ask him what he'd said, but the delicious way his fingers skimmed over her arm and back made her think of the pleasure they had just experienced. She wanted months, nay years, with him.

"You are a good man, Fallon MacLeod." She tilted her head to look at him. She didn't know of any other Warrior who would go against Deirdre in such a manner.

His brow furrowed and his gaze became distant, as if her words had brought forth a long-buried memory. "Nay, Larena, I'm not. Not yet. My brothers are good men, and I am trying to be."

"Tell me of your brothers. Before your god was unbound. What was your life like?"

A faint smile touched his lips. "We had a good life. Our parents' marriage had been arranged, but they had fallen in love. That love was evident in everything they did. My father was stern, but he was clever and well loved by his clan as well as respected by other clans.

My mother had the gentlest touch. Her voice could calm anyone, and she had a look that she would give us lads that would make us tell her anything she wanted to know."

Larena chuckled. She easily envisioned his family and what his life had been. "Your parents sound wonderful."

"They were the best. I saw the way some of my friend's parents were, so I knew what my parents had was special."

"My parents didn't love each other, not like that. However, they did care for each other."

"You were luckier than some."

"Aye."

"Did you have any siblings?"

She sighed. "It was just me. I always wanted a sister."

"I couldn't imagine life without my brothers. We did everything together. Rarely were we apart. I remember when Quinn married. It seemed strange that he wouldna be running around with me and Lucan anymore."

"What are your brothers like?"

"Strong. Intelligent. Cunning. Honorable. They are the best men I know. Lucan was always the one that grounded Quinn and me. Lucan got our mother's calming influence, and he used it judiciously. Whereas I had a habit of thinking things through for too long, Quinn was rash and always jumped into things without thinking about the consequences. Yet, for all the times Quinn found himself in trouble, he's always been clever enough to get out of it."

"I think I'm going to like your brothers," she said with a smile. Her eyes drifted closed while Fallon's fingers lazily skimmed her back once again.

"You will. They will like you as well."

"And after Deirdre worked her magic and unbound your god. What happened?"

He let out a long breath. "It was hell. While we lived in the mountains we ate whatever we could find when we could find it. We were quickly turning into wild animals, and though I ken I needed to be the leader my father trained me to be, I couldn't get a handle on the god inside me."

"Don't be too hard on yourself, Fallon. In order to help your brothers, you had to help yourself first."

Fallon grunted. He had helped himself all right. He had tried to block the memories of those years after Deirdre, but he liked talking to Larena. And for some reason, he wanted her to know him—the real him, not the man she thought he was.

Because you're afraid you'll fail her as you did Lucan and Quinn.

That was the truth of it. As painful as it was to acknowledge.

"I'm not sure where Lucan found the wine," Fallon said slowly. "He had gone looking for food, and when he returned to our cave he carried a jug of wine. I started drinking. It didna take much for me to realize the more I drank, the less I heard and felt my god."

"So you kept drinking," she said in a small voice.

He paused. Should he tell her? She would think of him differently once she knew, he realized. It could also destroy everything that was building between them, but maybe that was for the best. Destroy all hope now before he lost her later. Besides, she would find out once they reached his castle. It was better if she knew just what kind of man he was now.

Better for both of them.

"Aye," he answered. "I kept drinking. When Lucan wouldn't bring me the wine, I went out and found it myself."

"Oh, Fallon," she murmured.

He gripped her arm, afraid that she would move away from him, and he couldn't finish the telling if he had to look in her eyes. "Instead of being the leader I was supposed to be, I let Lucan shoulder the responsibility. I knew he needed me to help him control Quinn, but I drowned in my wine anyway.

"Every morning I woke to see Quinn's rage evident on the walls of the cave where he had clawed at them. The loss of his wife and child rode him hard. In all this time he's never really gotten over it. I should have been there for him. For both my brothers."

"What would you have done?" Larena asked. "People deal with grief differently."

"I turned away from both of my brothers. Lucan begged me to stop the drinking. He tried to hide the wine, but it only resulted in a vicious fight between us. I thank God we couldna kill each other, because I fear I might have. Just to have my wine."

Her fingers trembled on his chest and he felt her eyelashes against him as she blinked. He wondered what she was thinking, but he didn't dare ask. Her impression that he was a good man was now shattered, and though he hated it, it was for the best. He wasn't the man he should have been, and he didn't want to fail her as he had his brothers.

"I doona know when Lucan realized he couldn't stop me. I just know that he always made sure I had wine. When he asked us to return to the castle, I wanted to refuse. Being near the place that now held nothing but death and destruction was not how I wanted to spend my days. But after all Lucan had done for me I couldn't say no to him, even though I wanted to be anywhere but between those stone walls."

"He thought it would do you good."

Fallon shrugged. "I suppose. It did benefit Quinn in a way, and it gave Lucan purpose. He helped Quinn and me as best he could, and there is nothing I can do to ever repay Lucan. For close to three hundred years I buried my god with wine. For three hundred years I left my two brothers alone. When wyrran would come near the castle, I would fight them, but with my swords only."

"You didn't release your god?"

"Nay. I didna dare. Not even when Lucan brought Cara into the castle and Deirdre's Warriors attacked the first time. Because I didn't change, the Warrior nearly got away with Cara. I'll never forget the look of dread in Lucan's eyes when he saw that a Warrior had Cara."

"What happened?"

"The three of us have always been good fighters. No one ever bested any of us, and when we fought each other, it always ended in a draw. We were great when we fought alone, but unstoppable when we fought together. I guess that's why Apodatoo, the god of revenge, chose to be inside all three of us."

She nodded, her hair tickling his nose. "I wondered about that."

"We had the Warrior cornered, and we attacked. Lucan got Cara away, and Quinn and I killed the Warrior. But we knew Deirdre would attack again. I wanted to be able to help my brothers, but that would mean letting loose my god."

"You couldn't do it, could you?"

Shame washed through him. "I had spent too long ignoring what was inside me, including the powers that came with it. I feared I would hinder Lucan more than help him. I knew I could stand my ground with my swords, so that's what I planned."

He thought back to that battle and how Cara had tried to hold her own against the wyrran. Lucan had stayed near her, always near her, but the unthinkable had happened. A Warrior caught her and left before Lucan could follow.

"There were so many wyrran. I've never seen so many. You killed one and five more took its place. They swarmed the castle along with four Warriors. What Deirdre didn't realize is that we had four more Warriors on our side."

Larena smiled against his skin. "The odds were in your favor."

"Or so we thought. But somehow a Warrior captured Cara. I was the only one who saw, and I knew I had to be able to help her. If Quinn had nearly gone daft with the loss of his wife and child, I knew Lucan would never recover. Cara *is* his life. So, I followed the Warrior and Cara, intent on keeping them at the castle until Lucan could find us.

"Most of the castle is still in ruins, and the Warrior went to a tower that backed to the sea. He made Cara hold on to his back as he descended the tower. One wrong move and Cara would plummet to her death."

Larena leaned up on her elbow and looked at Fallon. "By the saints. Deirdre wanted Cara badly, then?"

"Aye. Cara's mother was a *drough*, and Cara carried her mother's blood."

"Ah. The Demon's Kiss. Robena told me all about it."

"Exactly. That blood, along with Cara's, would give Deirdre more power. We couldn't allow that."

Larena nodded and bit her lip. "How did you stop the Warrior?"

"A few weeks before, I had quit drinking as much as I normally did. By the time of that battle, I was consuming the wine only rarely. I was coherent enough to realize Lucan would lose Cara that night. Cara and Lucan had a love like that of my parents, and after everything I had put Lucan through, I couldn't let him lose the only thing he had ever fought for. So, I unleashed my god."

"You saved Cara?"

Fallon shook his head and looked away. "I slowed the Warrior. That allowed enough time for Lucan, Quinn, and the others to arrive. In the end, we did get Cara away."

Soft fingers caressed his cheek, her nail scratching over his stubble. "You didn't fail your brothers or Cara, Fallon."

"After that night, I vowed to never touch the wine again."

"Is that why there is a bottle in your chamber?"

"Aye, to remind me of what I almost lost. If Cara had died, I would have lost Lucan. Quinn was almost beyond us already, but without Lucan there would be nothing holding us together."

Her hands never stopped touching him. He fisted one hand to stop it from shaking. Talking about the things that had haunted him for so long felt good, but he was ashamed of the man he had become.

She traced his eyebrow and the curve of his lips. "And now? How are your brothers?"

"The morning after the battle I found a piece of parchment rolled between two stones of our castle wall. I had gone looking for Quinn, but as soon as I saw the parchment, I knew."

"Deirdre."

He nodded. "She had trapped Quinn. She wants all three of us, and she knew all she had to do was get one of us and the other two would come to her."

Larena shifted and sat up, tucking her legs beneath her. "Did you get Quinn free?"

"Not yet."

"Then what are you doing here trying to get your castle back?"

Fallon finally looked at her. "It's my contribution while the others learn what they can of the Scroll."

"The Scroll?"

He didn't miss how her voice had risen and her body had stilled. She knew something, but what exactly? "Do you know of it?"

"The list of names of each family that bore a Warrior?"

"Aye."

"I've heard of it." But she looked away as she said it. *She's lying.* Fallon couldn't blame her. She didn't know him. Everything depended on the Scroll to release Quinn.

"What do you want the Scroll for?" Larena asked.

"To get Quinn out of Deirdre's mountain, if it's real. As far as I know, it could just be part of a tale."

Larena's smoky blue eyes swung to his, anger simmering in their depths. "You want to give Deirdre the names to turn other Warriors to save your brother?"

Fallon didn't tell her the rest of the plan. There was no need, not with how heated she had become. She either wouldn't believe him or wouldn't understand. "Wouldn't you do the same for Malcolm or your father?"

The tension eased out of her. "I would do whatever it took to get them away from such evil."

"Then you understand why this is so important?"

"I do," she whispered. "Deirdre could have a trap for you and Lucan though."

Fallon pulled her back down to his chest and let his fingers run through her long golden locks. "Maybe. Maybe not. I doona plan on ever being her prisoner again. But knowing my youngest brother has been in her mountain for over a month makes my stomach turn."

"I can only imagine."

Fallon said no more. Too much had probably already been said. At least Larena was still in his arms. She hadn't run from him, nor had she looked at him with pity. There hadn't been accusations. Only understanding in her beautiful eyes.

Hope blossomed in his chest for the first time in three hundred years.

NINE

Larena had never shared so much with someone before. The fact that Fallon was being so open with her helped her to trust him more. Still, there was much she wanted to know about him.

"The stories about what Deirdre did to your clan are told all over the Highlands."

"I know," he said in a flat voice.

"Will you tell me what happened that day?"

He paused for a moment, as if weighing her words. "Sometimes I can still smell the blood and death of that day. All the happy memories I had of my clan, my family, and my home were gone in a blink. I was the next laird, yet I was powerless to do anything to help my people."

"You couldn't have done anything against Deirdre."

"I know," he admitted. "But at the time I had no idea it was a Druid who had done this to me, to my brothers. Our lives were over in an instant. And then she brought us to hell."

She caressed his chest, wishing she could take away some of his heartache. "I know the pain of having my god unbound, and though I didn't know it was going to be me, I knew what was happening. You didn't know anything, did you?"

"Nay. Deirdre chained us as soon as we entered her mountain. Lucan jerked at his chains so hard that they cut into his skin. There was so much blood, and nothing I said to him could still him. And then there was Quinn. He couldn't stop yelling at her. I doona know if he knew what he was saying, the ache of losing his wife and son had nearly killed him. It all seemed so surreal at the time. I was the eldest, I needed to show my brothers that I could stay calm in the face of such a crises."

She swallowed past the lump forming in her throat. "Fallon."

"But the moment she started chanting, all my good intentions flew out the door. I was ripped apart by the pain, blinded by the fury at what was happening. I knew something had come to pass, and it wasn't for the better. I wanted to kill her, to seek vengeance for what she had done to my people. I ripped at the chains, expecting to get nowhere like Lucan, and then they broke. My brothers followed suit. As much as I wanted to kill Deirdre, and I would have had the chance, too, I knew we had to leave. She was stunned that we were able to break away, but I took my brothers out of the mountain. And we ran and ran and ran."

"I can't believe you got away."

"We caught her by surprise. She wasna expecting us to run. The wyrran that came after us we killed. We hid for many years in the mountains, moving constantly. Then, we returned to our castle."

He paused and she could feel his pain as if it were her own. She ran her hand over his chest wishing she could heal the wounds deep inside him.

"Our lands were gone, our castle falling down, but

we stayed. We hid in the darkness, keeping away from everyone and everything."

For long moments they sat in silence. Larena didn't know what to say in response to Fallon's admission. His tale was similar to what she had heard as a child, but she had never known what had happened to him at Deirdre's hands.

And somehow, hearing it from him made it so much worse. How anyone so evil and vile as Deirdre could come into such power seemed unbelievable.

"You're going to fight her, aren't you?"

"Aye," he said, and smoothed his fingers through her hair. "Our castle will house anyone who seeks to hide from her or fight against her."

"I want to fight with you."

He smiled against her forehead. "I'm glad."

"It's almost dawn. We've been talking all night."

Fallon chuckled. "I doona think I've ever spent so much time talking to a woman before. And here I could have been making love to you again."

Larena rolled on top of his chest to look into his dark green eyes. "Hm. I quite enjoyed our talk."

"Apparently, though I did all of it."

"I've told you all there is to know about my life."

He gripped her buttocks and rocked her against his arousal. "We've time for another round."

She wanted nothing more, but she also wanted to leave Edinburgh as soon as she could. Ever since she had seen the wyrran she'd had an uneasy feeling.

"Do we have time?" she asked.

Fallon glanced out the window. "Shite. When can you be ready?"

"Give me at least until dawn."

"Why not just leave Malcolm a missive?"

She wrinkled her nose. "After all he's done for me, that isn't fair. I'll hurry to get ready, and if he hasn't come to my chamber by then I'll go find him."

"All right. Meet me in the gardens. There is a bench surrounded by yellow roses."

"I know the one," she said, and reluctantly rolled from him and the bed. She stood next to him and bent to give him another kiss. "I'll see you soon."

He sat up as she moved to the window. "Doona be late," he called just as she turned invisible.

"I won't," she promised.

Larena couldn't stop smiling. Ever since she had returned from Fallon's chamber, she had been walking in a daze. Fallon had not only returned her desire, but he was going to take her to his castle. And protect her.

She knew she should be more cautious. After all, the first time she had given herself to a man, it had ended with her father's murder.

But Fallon is different.

Was he? She trusted him with her life, she was trusting a man she barely knew. Then there was her biggest secret—the Scroll. Fallon wanted the Scroll to give to Deirdre. It was something she couldn't allow.

But she had looked into Fallon's eyes. Her instincts told her Fallon hadn't lied when he vowed to protect her, but Larena knew she would also have to guard herself. Already she was thinking of being in his arms again. Nothing good could come of her unquenchable desire for Fallon.

For so long she had been on her own, hiding and running. It was going to be nice to have a place where she knew she was safe, where everyone knew her secret and didn't care. She was going to miss Malcolm, but she knew this day had been coming for a while. Malcolm deserved a life, and she was going to ensure he had one.

She rose from her bath and dried off. She was sore from Fallon's lovemaking, but it was a delectable soreness, one she wanted to experience again and again.

She had learned her lesson though. She didn't trust anyone but Malcolm and other Warriors. The man who had claimed her body first had wooed her with pretty words and promises. She had seen too late what he was about, and even with her powers she'd been unable to save her father.

Even now, so many decades later, she could remember finding her lover standing over her father's body, the dagger still buried in her father's chest. Blind rage had consumed her, and when she had returned to herself, her lover was dead. By her hand.

It was the first time she had taken a human life, and though he had murdered her father, she still felt the weight of that life taken every day.

It was a bitter lesson, but one she had needed to help sustain her through her long, lonely years.

Larena dressed in a gown of the softest cream. The wired collar with decorative lace edging was all the rage, but she hated it. Just as she hated the cartwheel hoops she wore under her gown. It was ridiculous for a woman to wear such trappings. She couldn't move freely to engage in battle if a wyrran came upon her, and it took her too much time to get out of the gown.

She adjusted the wide, lace-edged cuffs of her sleeve and longed to don the simple gowns she had worn while she lived with her clan. She much preferred life in the Highlands with men in their kilts to the stuffy, overindulged buffoons that walked around with knitted stockings and padded breeches.

As her maid combed and pinned her hair, a knock sounded on her door. Her heart leaped, thinking it was Fallon, but she realized a moment later Fallon wouldn't come to see her.

"Enter," she called.

She smiled as she saw Malcolm through the mirror of her dressing table. "Any news?"

"I was about to ask you the same thing," he said as he leaned against the door. "Are you almost finished?"

"That will be all." Larena dismissed the maid.

Once they were alone, Malcolm walked to the chair. He sat and braced his elbows on his knees. "Tell me you have good news."

"The best." She couldn't stop the smile from spreading. "Fallon has agreed to take me to the castle. He wants to leave immediately."

Malcolm grinned. "I'm relieved to hear it. I think the sooner you're away from here the better."

He wasn't ready to say farewell, and she wasn't either, truth be told. But Malcolm had sacrificed too much. "You must promise that you will forget about me and get on with your life."

He chuckled. "Never. You've given me adventure the likes of which I'll never know again."

"You need to find a wife and sire plenty of children. You've a clan to lead, Malcolm, and I've no doubt you will be the best laird of the Monroes yet."

He rubbed his chin, his brow furrowed. "Are you sure about MacLeod?"

"You know my issues with trusting people better than most. Fallon has given his vow to help protect me. I believe him."

"That's all I ask."

She rose and held out her hand to him. "Thank you. For everything."

"I'm going to miss you."

She leaned up and kissed his cheek. "Aye. I feel the same."

TEN

Quinn's body ached. He'd been cut, bruised, and beaten, yet he hadn't given in to his god as Deirdre wanted. He smiled and then winced as his busted lip cracked open and began to bleed again.

Deirdre had actually come down to his cell. She had stood in the entrance and watched her Warriors beat him. After a while she had called a halt and told Quinn to turn, to let his god free.

He had looked at her through the one eye that wasn't swollen shut and laughed at her. The beating had started again, and this time the Warriors used their claws. They had repeated the process several times until Deirdre had left the prison.

He knew the instant she departed because the Warriors went at him as though they wanted to kill him. And they nearly had. He would heal, though it would take time.

His shoulders ached from hanging by the chains, but it was better than rolling around with the rats. He shuddered. God, he hated the rats. They were always there, their squeaking heard throughout the dungeons. Quinn had felt them run across his feet too many times.

With both eyes swollen shut now he couldn't see, but

he could hear the rat coming toward him. He knew by the sound of its tiny claws on the rocks that it was almost upon him.

Stop.

The rat paused, but kept coming.

Stop! Dammit, stop!

And to his confusion, the rat did.

Quinn felt something in his mind. He wasn't sure what it was, but he would try anything to keep the rats away from him.

Don't come near me. Keep the others away.

His heart leaped into his throat when the rat turned and scurried away. Quinn wasn't sure what had happened, and he was too tired to think about it. His head felt as if someone had tried to crack open his skull. All he wanted to do was sleep and dream of home, of his brothers.

He wanted to tell his brothers he had pushed aside the anger that hadn't left him in three hundred years. That fury had allowed his god to rule him, and when Quinn discovered that's what Deirdre wanted, he had fought his god with everything he had. He would die now before he let his god out.

Fallon paced his chamber as he watched the sun break the horizon, his mind occupied with thoughts of Larena. He hadn't wanted to let her go, but if they were to leave for his castle, she had to get things in order.

He still couldn't believe she was a Warrior. Never would he have guessed there would be a female Warrior. Though why he should be surprised, he wasn't sure. It was well known that some of the fiercest Celtic warriors had been women.

A chill wrapped around his heart as he thought of Deirdre discovering Larena. Fallon had experienced for himself the treachery of Deirdre, and he didn't want Larena coming anywhere near that evil bitch.

The need to get to MacLeod Castle was great. If he'd had his way, they would already be there, but Larena was insistent on talking to Malcolm first. He understood, Malcolm had done much for her, but Fallon couldn't help thinking the longer they stayed at the king's castle the longer Larena put herself in danger.

They were to meet in the garden in less than an hour. Larena had no idea they would be at MacLeod Castle in less time than it took to blink. He couldn't wait to return, though regrettably he would have no news of the Scroll that could help free Quinn from Deirdre.

Fallon blew out a breath. He hadn't been able to talk to the king. He would, however, ask Larena if she knew anything of the Scroll. There had to be some Warrior or Druid who knew if it was real or not.

Fallon found himself staring at a bush of dark red roses. His mother had loved roses. His father had brought a shrub back from a trip to Glasgow one year. Fallon smiled as he recalled how his mother had reverently planted the shrub, watching over it every day. Fallon had doubted it would survive in their rocky soil, but with her care, the plant had grown and bloomed with flowers of virginal white.

He should have taken care of the roses, but like everything else, he had let them wither and die.

The sound of a knock on his door brought Fallon out of his thoughts. He opened it to find Malcolm. Fallon looked at the young lord with new eyes. Malcolm had put his own life at risk helping Larena.

"I owe you a debt of thanks," Malcolm said. He pushed away a lock of blond hair that kept falling in his eyes.

Fallon nodded and invited Malcolm inside his chamber. "She told me what you've done for her. I doona know if you realize how much danger you're in."

Malcolm shrugged. "My family did wrong by her. I'm just trying to make it right."

"Is she ready?"

"I've come to tell you she's already in the garden. She's eager to leave Edinburgh."

"Thank God," Fallon said.

Malcolm barked with laughter. He lost his smile and stepped closer to Fallon and lowered his voice. "Larena has been alone for much of her life. She's used to fending for herself, and she doesn't trust easily. Give her time."

"I willna constrict her," Fallon promised. "I'm merely taking her somewhere she'll be safe from Deirdre. My castle is being repaired as we speak. There are four other Warriors at the castle as well as two Druids."

"Two?" Malcolm repeated, his eyes wide. "How did you find two?"

"One of them is my brother's wife. The second found us."

"Found you? How?"

"The trees told her," Fallon said with a smile.

Malcolm whistled low. "Amazing."

Fallon nodded. "It is. You know much about us, Monroe. If Deirdre ever gets her hands on you . . ."

"I would never endanger Larena. Never," he swore. His eyes were narrowed, his cheeks reddening in anger. "There is nothing Deirdre could do that would make me tell her anything."

Fallon was skeptical, but he gave a nod of his head to Malcolm. "I hope you are right."

"You have my word, MacLeod."

"It seems I do."

Malcolm bowed his head. "Take care of her."

"I will. And Malcolm, if you ever need anything, you are welcome at my castle anytime."

"Thank you."

Fallon watched him leave. Malcolm was a fine Highlander. His clan should be proud of him for putting his life on the line for Larena. Fallon made a silent vow that if Malcolm or the Monroe clan ever needed assistance, he would lend it in any way necessary.

Without a backward glance at his chamber, Fallon strode from the room. He was ready to leave Edinburgh as well. He couldn't wait to show Larena his power.

Fallon had found his power quite by accident. Lucan called it *leum,* the Gaelic word for "jumping." The term had taken hold and everyone at the castle now used it.

Fallon still couldn't believe he could do it. For hundreds of years he'd had a powerful tool to use, but he had drowned himself in wine instead of learning to control his power. He feared there would come a time when he needed to use it and he wouldn't know how.

He followed a path through the garden until he came

to a bench where Larena sat. It was secluded. Perfect for them to depart.

Fallon recalled the first time he had "jumped." It had been by accident. He had let loose his god so he could learn not to fear it so. He'd been in the great hall and wished he was down at the beach. The next thing he knew, he stood ankle deep in the sea.

After that, he spent his time learning how to call up the power at any instance. He hated that he had to let his god loose in order to use the power, but he was determined to learn to use it without the god. He was sure it was possible, and he was going to make it so.

"Will you tell me now why we had to meet in the garden?" Larena asked, a welcoming smile on her face.

It struck Fallon that he had someone else now depending on him. Was it a trait of his to fail everyone? He hoped to God it wasn't, because he couldn't stand to have Larena look at him in disappointment.

"We're leaving from here. By my power."

Her brows rose. "Indeed? I cannot wait to see this power. What is it?"

"My brother calls it *leum*."

"Jumping?" she asked with a frown.

He laughed and held out his hand. "Is there nothing you want to take with you?"

"Not a thing."

"Then let me show you what *leum* is."

Just as Fallon began to transform to use his power he heard a wyrran. He jerked and looked around for the creature.

"Another one?" Larena asked.

Fallon clenched his jaw. "You canna fight in your gown. Stay here. I'll find this one."

Larena didn't like being left behind, but she knew Fallon was right. She sank back onto the bench and listened for the wyrran.

Fallon had told her to stay here, but she would help if she could.

As she sat there she contemplated all she had learned of Fallon. Never had she felt so beautiful, so cherished as she did in his arms. Every touch of his hands made her feel as though she were the center of his world.

Not even his admission of having been a drunk had any effect on her wanting him. He was trying to change from what he had been, and who was she to judge him after everything he had been through. She had known by being around him that he no longer drank. The reasons he had started she could understand, and she was happy to hear he had stopped.

The love he had for his brothers was obvious. All anyone needed to do was listen to his voice as he spoke of them. His brothers were all that mattered to him.

Larena wondered if she would matter to someone like that one day. She knew that something linked her and Fallon, but would it last? That, she couldn't answer.

The one thing that bothered her was Fallon's talk of the Scroll. He had no idea how close he was to it, and she wondered if he would take her ring if he knew what was inside it. She didn't think so, but she knew he would ask her for it.

And could she blame him for that?

It wasn't that she didn't comprehend why he wanted it, but it was more than foolish to turn over such an important document to Deirdre. She didn't like the idea of anyone being in Deirdre's captivity, but nothing was worth the risk of Deirdre's getting the Scroll.

There had to be another way to free Quinn, and she would help them figure that out. The Scroll wasn't an option they could use, and she needed to guard her heart lest Fallon betray her for it.

Fallon already had her respect, and it wouldn't take much more for her to care deeply for him. Once that happened, she wouldn't be able to keep the Scroll from him.

She would have to keep her distance from him now. How was she going to endure seeing him day after day at his castle and not kiss him, not want his arms around her? It was going to be the most difficult thing she had ever done, but she didn't have a choice.

Larena was ready for a new adventure even though it meant leaving Malcolm and being near a man who had touched her more deeply than she thought was possible. The connection between her and Fallon frightened her because it had been instantaneous, its pull too alluring to resist.

And she couldn't afford another mistake like the one that had gotten her father killed.

ELEVEN

MacLeod Castle

Lucan stood beside his wife in the bailey as they surveyed the castle. Cara's chestnut hair hung in a thick braid over her shoulder and her mahogany eyes looked up at him with a wealth of love that he never tired of seeing.

"Fallon is going to be so happy," Cara said. "I can't wait for him to see how much progress has been made on the castle."

Lucan glanced at the new gate and then to one of the reconstructed towers. "Aye. I think he will be pleased. I hope he returns soon."

"He will," Cara declared. "He didn't want to go, so I cannot imagine him staying longer than necessary in Edinburgh."

Lucan smiled. He remembered when Fallon had volunteered to go. It was evident by his brother's curled lip that he would rather face an army of Deirdre's Warriors than go to the king's castle, but Fallon had said it was his duty.

It was easy to see Fallon had felt useless at the castle. While all of them worked to rebuild the once magnificent structure, little progress had been made on finding the Scroll, or even any information on it.

Lucan still found it hard to believe Fallon had stopped drinking. Lucan didn't know how long it would last, but he was happy to have his brother back again.

Now, they just had to rescue Quinn.

"We'll get him," Cara said.

He glanced down at his wife and kissed her forehead. Her powers as a Druid had grown since Sonya had arrived. "Reading my mind are you?"

"Nay, husband," she said with a mischievous smile. "I just know what you're thinking by the way your lips compress. Don't work too hard."

Lucan watched Cara return to the castle to work with Sonya on spells that might help them bind their gods. There was much he needed to do, but his mind was on his brothers. He worried about them constantly.

Quinn was strong, but was he tough enough to endure Deirdre? And Fallon. He hadn't been away from the castle in over two hundred years. He had just given up the wine, and he was still learning to control the god inside him.

Lucan prayed his brothers could withstand what destiny had put before them. They were stronger together since they shared the same god. He didn't like them being parted.

He breathed in the sea air. "Hurry, Fallon. Please hurry."

Larena leaned her hands back on the bench and looked up at the castle. Fallon had been gone longer than she expected. Was he having trouble finding the wyrran?

Just then she spotted one of the yellow creatures near her balcony and another at the castle's roof. She had no idea what they were about, but she couldn't sit here and wait for Fallon.

Larena jumped from her seat and hurried into the castle and up to her chamber. When she threw open the door, however, there was no wyrran to be seen. She listened to the sounds of the castle, waiting to hear the frightened shrieks as before, but none came.

Just where were the wyrran?

A sound on her balcony drew her gaze. When she saw the two Warriors, her heart froze in her chest.

She eyed the Warrior with skin so dark blue it looked almost black. He had wings that he folded against his back and that loomed over his head. He kept his gaze on her as he walked into her chamber as if he had every right to be there. Neither Warrior wore tunic or shoes, just loose breeches that hung low on their hips.

"Get out." She was proud that her voice sounded steady and commanding since she felt anything but. She didn't know why they were there, but she wouldn't unleash her goddess unless she had no other choice.

"That we cannot do," said the second Warrior, with pale green skin and short black hair. "We've come for you after all."

Larena knew the door to freedom was exactly fifteen steps from where she stood. She couldn't reach it before the Warriors got to her, so she didn't think twice about escaping.

She decided to play dumb instead. "Is this some new costume the king has ordered for a masked ball? You are very frightening to look upon. And my brother will not approve of another man in my chamber, much less two."

The dull green Warrior's lips peeled back over his fangs as he growled. "Do not play coy with me, Larena Monroe. You know what we are."

"All right." She dropped all pretenses. "Why are you here?"

"As I said, we're here for you. Deirdre is looking forward to meeting you."

"Deirdre has never known of me. Why am I now of such interest?"

The pale green Warrior tilted back his head and laughed while the blue Warrior cocked his head to the side, his shoulder-length blond hair falling against his face. His eyes were intense as they studied her. Larena didn't know which she feared more, the quiet one with wings, or the angry one.

It was the pale green Warrior who answered. "You're of interest as a female Warrior. You see, the wyrran you killed the other night wasn't the only one at the castle."

Larena's stomach dropped to her feet like lead. Sweat broke out over her skin, turning her palms clammy. If she had stayed with Fallon, she wouldn't be in this mess.

Sooner or later they would have cornered you.

"Why did Deirdre send wyrran here?" she asked.

"A seer told her Fallon had come," the winged one answered.

She took a deep breath to steady her nerves and lifted a brow. "I have no interest in going with either of you. Give Deirdre my thanks for the invitation, but I'm going to have to decline."

Larena could have sworn there was a hint of a smile

on the winged Warrior's face, but it was gone so quickly she couldn't be sure. As she expected, the pale green Warrior was the one who attacked.

She waited until he was almost upon her before she let her goddess out. She allowed herself a brief smile at the Warrior's startled expression before she launched herself at him.

Robena had done her job well. Larena knew how to protect herself but part of that defense had been hiding. Now that Deirdre knew of her, Larena would be battling Warrior after Warrior.

If you get free.

She wanted to scream for Fallon, but even if she did, he would never hear her. Malcolm was just in the next chamber, but she couldn't chance him coming in and getting injured, or worse—killed.

Larena let her claws sink into the back of the pale green Warrior and raked them down to his waist. The Warrior bellowed and swung a meaty fist at her, connecting with her cheek before she could turn herself invisible.

She staggered away, dark spots blinking before her eyes. Something tore at first one arm and then the other. She didn't need to look to know the Warrior had used his claws on her. Blood seeped from her wounds down to her own claws to drip onto the floor.

No matter how many times she tried to clear her vision, she couldn't. The hit had addled her brain. She wasn't thinking clearly, and if she couldn't get her head together, she wouldn't be able to get away.

Larena could sense the Warrior was close. She closed her eyes to stop the room from spinning and kicked out with her foot. There was a heavy thud and a grunt to let her know she had knocked the Warrior off his feet.

"Don't make this harder," someone said in her ear.

The dark blue Warrior. He had let the other battle her. Why? "I won't go."

"You have no choice," he said.

She shook her head and jerked out of his arms. She opened her eyes and saw that her chamber tilted from one side to the next. Her feet tripped over themselves as she tried to get to the balcony. She would jump if she had to, anything to get away.

Before she reached the terrace, the pale green Warrior bellowed and grabbed her ankle. Larena caught herself from falling just in time. She kicked with her foot and landed a hit on the Warrior's face. In an instant he was on his feet, his lips pulled back in another snarl to show his fangs.

"You will pay for that," he growled.

She saw his claws come at her, and though she tried to turn away, she wasn't quick enough. Larena bit back a scream as his claws plunged into her right side.

As a Warrior, she healed, but it always hurt to get injured. Her arms stung from the scratches, but it was nothing like the burning in her side. She clutched at her wound, feeling the blood flow thick and fast through her fingers.

"What have you done?" demanded the winged Warrior to the other.

The pale green Warrior shrugged and studied his left claws. "She shouldna have kicked me in the face."

"You wouldna dare." He spoke through clenched teeth, his fangs cutting his lips. "Deirdre will have your head."

The other laughed and walked to the balcony. Without a backward glance he jumped from the railing.

Larena stumbled as lights began blinking in her vision. She reached for the posts of the bed to steady herself. The bleeding should have slowed by now, and the pain should have receded. She glanced down at her side and saw the blood was gushing so rapidly that it coated her gown.

"I'm sorry."

She turned her head to the winged Warrior. "What did he do?"

"He dipped his one set of claws in *drough* blood. Your wounds willna heal, Larena. You need to find help, find Fallon. You must stop the bleeding before it's too late."

The longer she stood, the weaker she got. She let herself sink onto the bench before her bed. "Why are you helping me?"

"Deirdre wants you alive. I'd rather not have my hide ripped from my body because of an incompetent fool."

Before she could ask more, he was gone. She focused on keeping herself breathing. A couple of times she hollered for Malcolm, but the sound wasn't loud enough to carry into the next chamber.

She wasn't sure how much time had elapsed when the banging started on her door. She was slumped over the bench with blood everywhere. The ache from her wound had spread to her entire body, and each pump of her heart was like someone pouring fire in her veins.

The door swung open, and suddenly Malcolm was kneeling before her.

"My God, Larena. What happened? Why aren't you healing?"

She licked her lips. "N . . . no time. Fallon."

"I'll get him." Malcolm kissed her forehead and then raced from the chamber.

Larena tried to stay conscious so she could tell Fallon about her wound, but fate conspired against her. She blacked out on her next breath.

Fallon turned from killing a wyrran to finding three more waiting for him. As he began to chase after those, he spotted more climbing the outside of the castle.

"What is going on?" he grumbled to himself.

He easily caught two of the three wyrran he was chasing and bashed their heads together. With his strength, it killed them instantly. As much as he wanted to chase after the third, he had to get rid of the three he had already killed.

Fallon lifted the two wyrran at his feet and hurried back to the first he had killed. It was while he was returning from the forest that he saw Malcolm running toward him.

Malcolm gripped his arms, his blue eyes wide and darting around him. "Thank God I finally found you. I've been looking for you everywhere."

That's when Fallon noticed the stain on Malcolm's blue vest. "What happened?"

"It's Larena. You need to come with me right now. She's hurt, Fallon."

Fallon said no more as he followed Malcolm. They kept their pace more sedate than Fallon would have liked, but because Malcolm kept looking around him, Fallon understood something awful had happened.

As they climbed the stairs toward Larena's chambers

a servant went rushing by them, tears on her face. A moment later two ladies walked down the stairs, their hands covering their mouths as they whispered.

Fallon's chest tightened. Larena was a Warrior, which meant her body healed on its own and very quickly. There was nothing that could kill her except cutting off her head.

"Malcolm?"

"Not yet," the younger man said.

They reached the landing and turned the corner to walk down the corridor to Larena's chamber when Fallon saw the crowd. People, lords and ladies and servants alike, milled about the doorway to Larena's chamber.

"Let us through." Malcolm's voice boomed through the conversation.

The crowd parted. Fallon glanced at a few people as he followed Malcolm through the doorway. And then he stopped cold.

Larena was on the bench before her bed slumped over, with blood everywhere. A man knelt beside her and put his finger beneath her nose. Fallon couldn't breathe. His vision swam and the voices around him faded as if he were in a tunnel. It was a hand on his arm that brought him back to the present.

Malcolm's trembling fingers dug into his arm. "There was a man who attacked her," Malcolm told the physician who rose from beside Larena.

"Did you get a look at him, my lord?"

Malcolm swallowed and glanced at Larena. "He had black hair. He rushed past me when I entered. I didn't get a good look at his face."

"I'll report the death. My condolences, my lord. Lady Larena was well liked. Shall I take the body?"

"Nay," Malcolm said, a little too hastily.

Fallon hid his wince, but couldn't take his eyes off Larena. He stood to the side as people filed out of the chamber. Malcolm closed and bolted the door before he turned to Fallon.

"You must help her," Malcolm said.

Fallon put a hand on Malcolm as he started past him toward Larena. "What happened?"

"She was attacked. I don't know by what or who, but that is her blood all over her."

Fallon felt as if someone punched him in the gut. He rushed to Larena and lifted her head. He put his cheek by her nose and waited to see if she breathed. It was faint, so weak it was barely detectable.

"She's not dead, not yet at least," he told Malcolm. "Tell me everything."

Malcolm gripped the bedpost and cleared his throat. "I came in to find her just as she is. Blood gushed between her fingers as she held her hand over the wound. I asked her what happened and she told me there wasn't time. Then she said your name. I left immediately to find you."

"Did you tell anyone?" Fallon let one of his claws lengthen before he sliced open her gown. He tugged all her clothes off but her chemise. Everything was soaked in blood. He found her wound and ripped the chemise so he could see the injury better.

"Nay, no one," Malcolm answered. "A servant must have come in and found her."

Fallon saw the five slices in her side and cursed.

Malcolm moved closer to look. "What is it?"

"It wasn't a man, Malcolm. A Warrior was here. He's the one that attacked her."

"Oh, God." Malcolm staggered to the bed and sat. "How? Why?"

"I'm hoping Larena can tell us." Icy sweat covered Fallon's skin. He couldn't remember ever being so frightened in his life. He had foolishly thought he wouldn't have to worry about Larena dying, that he would be spared what Lucan went through every day. What an idiot he had been. She was in his arms dying even now.

He wanted to howl at the injustice, but more than that he wanted to find the Warrior who had dared to hurt her and tear him limb from limb. He reached for her skirts and tore off a long thick strip that he wrapped around her to help stop the flow of blood.

With Malcolm's help they removed the bell hoop from beneath her skirts so it would be easier for Fallon to carry her.

Fallon put his arm under Larena's shoulders and hugged her against him. "Larena? Can you hear me?"

Had he failed someone again so soon? He was trying to make himself into the man his father had wanted him to be, but everything he did backfired on him.

When Larena didn't respond, Fallon gave her a little shake. He couldn't stand not knowing what happened, or why the Warrior had attacked her and not him as well. Had the wyrran been a diversion so they could get to Larena? It made sense and angered him like nothing else could have.

"Has she ever been injured like this before?" he asked, and looked up to find Malcolm watching him with red-rimmed eyes.

"Aye," Malcolm answered after a moment. "She's always healed."

"They had to have done something. That's the only reason she would not have healed right away. I can't help her, not here, but the Druids at my castle can."

Malcolm stood. "Then take her. Now. I'll deal with things here."

"I need something to cover her with."

Malcolm rose and returned a moment later with a cloak in his hands. It took both of them to get it on her, and then Fallon lifted her in his arms. Her head fell to his shoulders and her eyelids fluttered.

"Larena," he said. "Can you hear me?"

"Fallon," she whispered.

"Aye, I'm here. What happened?"

"W . . . Warrior."

Fallon clenched his jaw. "Did he mean to kill you?"

She shook her head. "D . . . d . . ."

"Deirdre?" he supplied.

She opened her eyes and gave a single nod.

"God's teeth," Malcolm cursed. "How? How did she know?"

Fallon shook his head. "Deirdre is very powerful. There are many ways she could have learned of Larena."

"Get her out of here now," Malcolm said. "I'll check the corridor."

"No need." Fallon walked to the balcony. "I've another way."

Fallon had transported himself several times since

he first learned he could, but he had never tried it with another person. He looked down at the garden and found a secluded spot hidden by bushes. A heartbeat later he had released his god and they were standing in the garden. Larena was asleep once more, and he feared that this time she wouldn't wake.

Fallon couldn't take the time he needed to make little jumps. He had to arrive at the castle immediately. He hugged Larena to him and concentrated on his castle and the bailey. It was going to take everything he had, but he would get them there. There was no other choice.

All of his powers swirled around him, making the ground move beneath his feet. Larena's arm tumbled to her side and her head fell back, exposing her neck.

"Nay!" he bellowed.

TWELVE

Lucan heard the bellow from the great hall. He knew his brother's voice as well as his own. Lucan jerked to his feet from his seat at the table and rushed into the bailey to see Fallon kneeling with a woman in his arms.

"By the stars," Cara said as she joined Lucan at the door. "She's covered in blood!"

Lucan bounded down the stairs and ran to his brother. Fallon kept whispering something over and over into the woman's hair.

"Fallon," Lucan said slowly. He'd never seen his brother look so . . . lost. Lucan glanced up to find Galen and Ramsey beside him. Whatever was wrong with the woman, they had to get her out of Fallon's arms to aid her. "Fallon, look at me. Fallon!"

Finally, his brother glanced up, his dark green eyes clouded with grief. "I didn't save her, Lucan."

"Get out of the way," Sonya said as she shouldered her way through the men. She reached to touch the woman, but Fallon jerked her away. "Let me see if I can help her, Fallon. I will not harm her."

Fallon's face was grim as he let Sonya place her hands on the woman. "Her name is Larena Monroe.

She's a Warrior. Another attacked her, but I don't know why she isn't able to heal."

Lucan took a step back at Fallon's words. A female Warrior? His glaze slid to Galen in question. Galen shrugged in response. Lucan had thought only males were Warriors. But whoever this Larena was, his brother cared for her greatly. Because of that Lucan would make sure they did whatever it took to save her.

Sonya slid a small dagger from her boot and cut away more of the material covering Larena's wound. She leaned down and sniffed before she reeled back. "*Drough* blood."

"What?" Fallon asked before anyone else could.

Sonya sighed and touched Larena's forehead. "The Warrior must have dipped his claws in *drough* blood. *Drough* blood is poisonous to Warriors."

"Oh, God." Fallon's face had lost all color. "Is she . . . ?"

"Not yet," Sonya said. "But we must hurry. She's lost a lot of blood, and if we don't do something quick, she will be gone from us forever."

Fallon didn't loosen his hold on the woman as he climbed to his feet. Lucan started to help him, but Fallon shook his head. "Nay, brother. I'm taking her to my chamber. Send Sonya there."

And then Fallon was gone, using his power to jump to his chamber.

For a moment no one said anything. Lucan swallowed and turned toward the castle. The haunted look in his eldest brother's eyes was one he had never seen before, and it unsettled him.

"A female Warrior," Cara whispered.

Lucan looked at his wife. "I had no idea that was possible."

"Deirdre will want her," Galen said.

Ramsey snorted. "Deirdre will stop at nothing to have her. What I don't understand is why a Warrior would try to kill Larena. We all know Deirdre must have sent the Warrior for Larena, but not to harm her."

"True enough," Lucan said. "We may never have the answers unless Sonya can work a miracle and save the woman."

Cara leaned up to kiss his cheek. "I'm going to help. I have a feeling Sonya will need me. And Fallon will need you."

Lucan waited until Cara was inside the castle before he turned to the two Warriors, Galen and Ramsey. "Find the others. Let them know about Larena. They need to be aware that an attack could be coming soon."

"I'll see to it," Galen said, and walked off.

Ramsey folded his arms over his chest, his gray gaze sliding from the castle to the gatehouse.

"What is it?" Lucan asked.

"An uneasy feeling," was all Ramsey said. "Go to your brother, Lucan. I will patrol the area."

"Don't go alone." He waited until Ramsey lifted a hand in response before Lucan took the stairs three at a time and hurried into the castle.

His home had felt empty without his brothers, even with all the Warriors and another Druid around. It was good to have Fallon return. Then he recalled the look on Fallon's face when he'd come upon him in the bailey.

Fallon had looked the way Lucan imagined he would look if he were holding Cara's dead body in his arms. It sent chills down his spine. Fallon had just recovered from his thirst for wine. What would happen to him now if this female died?

Ramsey walked from the castle to the burned village, his eyes trained on the sky. He had hoped a message, or more importantly, a messenger, would have arrived by now.

He wanted to know Deirdre's next plan, and he couldn't do that without his spy inside her mountain.

With every day that passed, Ramsey worried about his friend being discovered. They had made a pact while chained together in Deirdre's mountain that one of them would leave while the other stayed to spy.

It had worked for over a hundred years now, but how much longer could they continue to deceive Deirdre before she discovered she had been duped?

Worse, Ramsey knew his friend would never survive once Deirdre learned of his deeds. And his friend was a good man.

Ramsey sighed. He should have been the one to stay behind. He had known it then, and he knew it now. It seemed that the instances he saw his friend grew more and more scarce, and there was always the doubt in his mind that his friend had switched sides and was now spying on them.

"Nay," Ramsey whispered to himself. He couldn't envision the man that had become more a brother than a friend doing that to him.

He waited for half an hour to see if his friend would appear before Ramsey turned on his heel and raced to the castle to check on Larena's progress.

Fallon laid Larena on his bed in the master chamber. Lucan had proclaimed it Fallon's the moment they had returned to the castle, but Fallon hadn't wanted it. The chamber reminded him too much of his parents. Lucan had insisted, however, saying Fallon was his laird after all.

Fallon tried to swallow as he looked at Larena's pale form on the large bed. Just a few hours earlier he had held her in his arms and revealed things he hadn't even told his brothers. He had made love to her sweet body, kissing and caressing her soft skin. He had heard her cries of ecstasy and filled her with his seed.

She can't be gone. Please, God, don't take her from me. Don't tell me I've failed again.

He glanced at her wound to find the blood had been reduced to just a trickle, but with all the blood that was on her clothes and in her chamber back in Edinburgh he was surprised she had any left.

The door opened and Sonya and Cara entered. Cara came to stand beside him as Sonya moved to the other side of the bed.

"Please. Help her," Fallon said. He was prepared to beg if necessary.

Sonya looked up at him and nodded. "I will do my best."

He prayed that would be enough.

Cara tried to get him to sit, but when he refused, she took his hand in both of hers. Fallon wanted to pull away, he should have pulled away, but he needed the strength Cara gave him.

He waited in the silence of the chamber as Sonya examined Larena's wounds. For the most part, Sonya kept her face passive, but Fallon caught her grimaces. His gut clenched each time. He could feel his world falling apart again, and this time, he knew, he wouldn't survive it.

With Larena he had tried to be the man he'd always wanted to be, had put the past behind him and looked to the future. Now, all of that was fading away, as it had the day his clan had been destroyed.

The need for a bottle of wine was so fierce he shook with it. But he wouldn't leave Larena.

Sonya placed her hands over the wounds and closed her eyes. A few moments later Cara joined her. Fallon shifted from one foot to the other as the two Druids poured their magic into Larena.

An eternity later Sonya opened her eyes to look at Fallon. Her face was lined with worry and stress from using so much of her magic. Sonya wiped her forehead with the back of her hand and blew out a breath. "She's lost too much blood to heal herself. All the magic in the world won't help her now."

"Then what will?" Fallon asked.

Sonya shrugged. "She needs blood."

Fallon stepped to the bed and jerked up the sleeve of his tunic. "Use mine."

"And mine if needed," Lucan said behind him.

Fallon looked over his shoulder to find Lucan standing in the doorway. His brother gave him a nod of encouragement. Fallon returned the nod, and then looked at Sonya. "What are you waiting for?"

"It could take a lot."

"I doona care," Fallon stated. "Just do it. Every moment we waste arguing is putting her closer to death. I cannot lose her, Sonya."

The Druid took a deep breath and reached for the blade in her boot when Lucan stepped forward.

"Let me," Lucan said as he extended a claw and held it over Fallon's arm.

Fallon met his brother's gaze a heartbeat before Lucan sliced open his arm. The slash was quick and went deep. Fallon clenched his teeth together and kept his gaze on Larena's face. The small amount of pain he suffered was worth it. The blood that seeped from his cut was dark and fell in a rush. Sonya moved his arm so the blood would flow over Larena's wounds.

It didn't take long for his wound to begin to heal. Lucan quickly scored his flesh again and again and again. Sonya held his arm steady so they didn't waste any of the blood.

The chamber began to swim and Fallon swayed on his feet. Lucan was there to steady him with an arm around his back.

"It's not going to be enough," Sonya said. "Lucan, we may need you."

"Nay," Fallon said. He tried to swallow, but his mouth was dry. "My blood. Only my blood."

"You're going to kill yourself," Lucan said in his ear. "Be reasonable, Fallon."

But Fallon shook his head. He didn't have his brother's strength, but he wanted Larena to have whatever potency was in his blood to make up for nearly getting her killed. "She's mine to protect, Lucan. She'll only have my blood."

Fallon's knees buckled before he finished speaking. Lucan held him as Cara rushed to get a chair. Once the chair was beneath him, Lucan let him slump in the seat. Fallon leaned on the bed and reached for Larena's hand with his good arm.

He glanced at Sonya to find that she held his other arm up for him. All he wanted to do was close his eyes and sleep, but that was a luxury for later.

"My cut is closing," he told Sonya.

She looked at Larena's wounds before she spoke. "Let's see if this will be enough before you slice yourself again."

Fallon was glad Lucan was there. He had missed his brother dearly while he had been gone, and there was so much he wanted to tell Lucan. Fallon hated that he hadn't accomplished his goals while in Edinburgh. Yet, he had found Larena.

Or rather, she had found him.

He tried to squeeze her hand, but his strength was rapidly departing. His gaze lifted to her face to find the color was returning, but slower than he wanted.

"Fallon."

He felt Lucan's hand on his shoulder. Always the rock, the steady one. It should have been Lucan who was firstborn. He would have known what decisions to make, and he wouldn't have neglected his brothers for a bottle of wine.

"You're about to pass out," Lucan said as he came to kneel in front of Fallon. "You arna going to do Larena any good if you're dead."

Fallon didn't disagree with him on that score. Though he wanted to be the one to save Larena, he knew it was selfish not to allow Lucan to help. "If she needs more . . . ?"

"I'll help any way I can," Lucan said before Fallon could finish. "You know that, brother. You shouldna even have to ask."

But Fallon did have to ask. He needed to prove to everyone, including himself, but most especially his brothers, that he was the man his father had taught him to be. A leader. A man who considered all possibilities and made the wisest decisions.

"Her wounds are closing," Sonya said into the quiet of the chamber.

Cara clasped her hands together. "Thank God."

Fallon cradled his cut arm against his chest once Sonya released him. All that was left of the last gash was puckered pink skin that would fade in the next few moments.

Sonya laid her hand on Larena's forehead before moving her fingers to Larena's neck. "She doesn't have a fever and her heart is beating faster. I think she's going to make it, Fallon."

"Thank you," he said to the Druid. "I don't know how to repay you."

Sonya smiled and tucked a strand of red hair behind her ear. "You've given me a home. This is the least I can do. Now, Cara and I used some magic to help speed up the healing. With the blood in her now, within a few hours she should be healed." She paused for a moment. "Is there anything I can do for you?"

He shook his head. Sonya couldn't heal the wound inside him, the cut that had nearly broken him in half at seeing Larena all but dead. Only time would help him. Time and Larena back in his arms.

"As you wish." She took a strip of cloth and dunked it in water. She wrung it out and began to clean the blood off Larena's arms and face.

Cara walked to the door. "I'll go see if I can find our new guest something to wear."

Fallon rubbed his hand over his face. Even though he knew Larena's wounds were healing, he couldn't let go of her hand. He would stay by her side until she woke, until he saw with his own eyes that she would live.

"By the stars!" Sonya hissed.

Fallon jerked his head to the Druid. "What is it?"

"Her ring." Sonya pointed to Larena's hand.

"What about it?" Lucan asked as he rose to his feet. "Is it worth something?"

Sonya's hand trembled as she ran a finger over the large milky-white oval stone. "You don't know what this is?" she asked Fallon.

Fallon shook his head. "I know she never takes it off. It goes everywhere with her."

"You sought information on the Scroll in Edinburgh. All the time she had it, Fallon. She must be its keeper."

Fallon looked from Sonya to the ring. He rose on shaky legs and peered into the ring. He saw something inside the stone, just as before.

His heart began to pound in his chest as he remembered telling Larena about wanting the Scroll to help get Quinn released. She had known all along where the

Scroll was and that it was real. Fallon had bared his soul to her, and she had hidden the very thing he needed for his brother.

"How?" he croaked out.

"Magic," Lucan said.

Sonya nodded. "No one would think to look for it there."

Fallon felt the betrayal all the way to his soul. The realization made his head swim. He needed to get out of the chamber and away from her. He tried to turn and ran into the chair. He would have fallen if not for Lucan's steady hands.

"What is it?" his brother asked.

Fallon couldn't tell him what a fool he'd been. "Get me out of here. Now."

Lucan half dragged, half carried him out of the chamber and into the corridor. "You need to rest."

"Aye." And he needed wine.

God, did he ever need the wine now. He had known there would be days when the need overtook him, but learning of what Larena had kept from him made that need overwhelming. He swallowed, his mouth drier than ever. The wine would fix that.

Aye. Find some wine. It will deaden everything just as before.

Fallon hated himself for his weakness. He was grateful he wasn't alone. If Lucan weren't with him and he could stand on his own two feet, he knew he'd search the castle for his wine.

"What happened in Edinburgh?" Lucan asked as he shouldered open a door to a chamber down the hall and walked inside.

Fallon collapsed on the bed and stared at the ceiling. "Too much. And not enough."

Despite her betrayal, he grudgingly realized Larena was only protecting the Scroll. He hadn't explained his plan in full, and in her place, he would have kept silent about the Scroll as well.

He'd been a fool, a complete and utter fool. Larena would never be his no matter how much he wanted it. And that was probably for the best.

THIRTEEN

Deirdre tapped her nails on the stone wall of her mountain. She had been waiting impatiently for James and Broc to bring her the female Warrior.

She smiled. A female. Who could have guessed the gods would have chosen a female? Deirdre certainly hadn't. She wondered if there were more female Warriors. She would send messages to her spies immediately and have them begin to look.

Deirdre glanced to her right to see one of a select few Druids she hadn't killed. Isla stood unmoving in the corner, so still she could have been mistaken for a statue.

The girl and her sister had been so innocent when Deirdre had captured them. Isla had eyes that could pierce right through you, and their color, so pale a blue they almost looked colorless, left men speechless.

She had used Isla countless times to break men. And kill others. While Isla's sister had come in handy as a seer. Deirdre considered sending Isla to Quinn, but thought better of it. Quinn was hers. She didn't want another female anywhere near him.

Just thinking of Quinn brought a rush of longing to her limbs and dampness between her legs. Ever since Deirdre had first seen Quinn she had coveted him. She had sensed the reckless power inside Quinn, seen the fury that consumed him. He was the perfect partner to rule beside her and fulfill the prophecy.

And she would convince him.

Deirdre leaned her face against the cool rocks and closed her eyes. *Talk to me*, she demanded of the stones.

"We are yours. Command us."

She relaxed shoulders she hadn't realized were tense. The stones had a way of soothing her as nothing else could. It was one of the reasons she didn't leave her mountain. Why should she when she had her kingdom all around her?

"The Warriors come. Empty-handed."

Deirdre whirled away from the stones and faced the doorway. This was twice her Warriors had returned without her prize. First, it was Cara, and now Larena Monroe.

James's tall, thick body filled the doorway. He paused and bowed his head before he moved into the light. The candles from the chandelier that hung from the ceiling shed its golden light on his pale green skin.

"Where is she?" Deirdre demanded.

"Ask James," Broc said as he entered the chamber.

Deirdre shifted her gaze to the blue-skinned Warrior. She longed to touch his wings as his cock filled her. Maybe tonight she would take him to her bed. "Tell me," she demanded of James.

"She fought back."

Deirdre raised a brow. "And you expected she wouldn't? I told you she was a female Warrior. Didn't she transform in front of you?"

James gave a nonchalant shrug. "She's quick."

Deirdre blew out a breath and turned to Broc. "Tell me what happened."

"James cut her with the claws he dipped in *drough* blood."

Rage consumed her. How could James have been so stupid? Deirdre raised her hand, her magic rushing through her, and James slammed against the stones with the force of her power. None of them knew just what kind of dark magic dwelled within her. Maybe it was time they learned.

"Bind him," she ordered the mountain.

James began to scream as the stones moved to lock around his arms, legs, and head. When he was secure Deirdre moved to stand in front of him. He dangled a few feet off the floor as he continued to try to jerk free of the rocks.

"The only way you'll get loose is if Larena lives. If she dies, James, the torture I have for you will last for centuries."

The Warrior swallowed and lowered his eyes to the floor. Deirdre turned away and tried to rein in her anger. The Warriors were hers because they couldn't control the fury inside them, and that wrath sometimes prevented them from bringing her what she wanted.

"Broc, where is Larena now?"

The winged Warrior shrugged and crossed his arms over his thick chest. "We know Larena and Fallon have been spending time together. There is the possibility that he took her back to his castle."

"Find out," she demanded. "I need to know whether Larena is alive. I need her in my army, Broc. Do you understand?"

He bowed his head. "Aye, mistress. I will depart immediately."

Broc left Deirdre, but instead of taking the stairs to the right, he turned left and walked down the long corridor before he found another set of stairs and descended into the darkness. He had once tried to count the steps, but had stopped at four hundred. Broc wasn't sure how far down the stairway went, but he knew it was several hundred feet below ground.

He paused when he reached the end and listened. There was a multitude of small chambers that were sectioned by bars. This was one of Deirdre's dungeons. It was a place where she put a man to break him. None who were put in the darkness came out whole.

Broc heard the mournful cries of women and flexed his shoulders, his wings opening partway. Druids, he surmised. He never understood how Deirdre continued to find them, but she did. It was her black magic and link to evil of course. Yet, part of him wondered if the rumors of Deirdre having a seer were true.

Each of the Druids would fight her, but in the end, Deirdre always won. Just as with Isla. The petite black-haired Druid was another of Deirdre's pawns. But then again, they all were.

The men in the prisons were either Druids, or those she thought could be turned into Warriors. There was only one here who was already a Warrior.

Broc turned right and wandered down the hallway. None of the prisoners rushed toward the bars. They stayed in the darkness, but Broc felt their eyes on him, felt their hatred for what he was.

He understood all too well about loathing and disgust.

About halfway down he found what he was looking for. Quinn MacLeod. The Warrior refused to transform for Deirdre. She had him beaten over and over again and kept him chained to the wall. The chains held him upright, and if Quinn couldn't keep his feet underneath him, his arms and shoulders would feel the brunt of the pain.

"What do you want?" came a muffled voice from the darkness.

Broc's keen eyesight saw Quinn in the blackness. The Warrior had blood oozing down the side of his face from a cut on his forehead. It looked as though one of his arms had been jerked out of the socket and a leg broken.

"They worked you over well," Broc commented.

Quinn chuckled. "Have you come to give me more?"

"Not this time, though I'm sure Deirdre will send me soon enough."

"Then what do you want?" Quinn's voice was laced with loathing.

Broc wondered how close Quinn was to transforming. Everyone knew Quinn's fury had ridden him for three hundred years. So much so that he hadn't been able to control his god. Yet, now in Deirdre's prison, he kept that anger on a tight leash, much to Deirdre's ire.

"Do you think you can withstand her?"

Quinn's nostrils flared as he glared at Broc. "I can. And I will."

Broc stared at the Warrior for a few more moments. "Maybe you can, MacLeod. Maybe you can."

FOURTEEN

Fallon woke to a pain in his chest like nothing he had ever felt before, and it wasn't from a wound. It was from betrayal. He couldn't even rejoice in the fact he was once more home. Somehow he had managed to fall asleep without giving in to his need for the wine.

He sat up and swung his legs over the side of the bed, his head in his hands. There was a throbbing in his skull that had nothing to do with wine, though he wished it were otherwise.

The darkness of the chamber told him it was night-time, though he had no idea how long he had slept. His exhaustion and loss of blood had pulled him into a deep sleep, despite the fact that his mind couldn't stop thinking of Larena and what she had kept from him.

He rubbed his chest, wondering why it ached so. The more he thought of Larena, the more the hurt spread.

It wasn't that he didn't understand why she hadn't told him. What hurt was that she hadn't trusted him enough to even tell him she had it. Did she think he would take it from her? She should have known him better than that.

We were only together a few hours.

Fallon sighed. It seemed as if he had known Larena for centuries, not hours. She had trusted him enough to show him she was a Warrior, but apparently she didn't trust him enough to tell him about the Scroll.

That was how it was in his life. There was never enough for him.

He pushed to his feet. He was tired of feeling sorry for himself. His self-pity had sustained him for three hundred years. No more would he allow it to rule his life.

There was a soft knock on the door before it opened and Cara poked her head inside. She smiled when she saw him standing. "Lucan was getting worried about you," she said as she pushed the door wider.

"How long have I slept?"

"Just a few hours. I set aside a trencher of food for you, even though Galen tried to take it."

Fallon found himself grinning. "I suppose Galen is eating us out of the castle."

"Just about," Cara said with a chuckle. "His appetite is never ending. I make two extra loaves of bread a day just for him. By noon, they're gone."

Fallon eyed his sister-in-law. "How have things been?"

"They've been good. Lucan has missed you, more than he's let on, but I can see it. He was lost for a couple of days with both you and Quinn gone, but he found his way."

"With your help."

Cara shrugged. "I do what I can, but Lucan is very stubborn. We're all glad you're back."

"I didna accomplish anything. The king wasn't there.

He prefers to rule Scotland from his palace in London. What has our country come to?"

She walked to him and laid a hand on his arm. "The world is constantly changing, Fallon. You and your brothers haven't seen it like I have. It will take you all a while to become accustomed to it."

"I fear one day Scotland will lose herself to England completely."

"Not as long as there are men like you and Lucan."

Fallon wrapped his arms around Cara and gave her a hug. "Thank you for everything, but most especially thank you for loving my brother."

She tilted her head up and kissed his cheek. "Loving Lucan is the easy part." She pulled out of his arms and walked to the door. "Are you coming downstairs?"

"Aye."

"She's doing much better, by the way, though she hasn't woken."

Fallon nodded before Cara left the chamber. He had been curious about Larena's recovery, but he hadn't been able to ask. As usual, his sister-in-law was able to read him easily.

He wasn't surprised to find a tunic and breeches laid out at the foot of the bed. Lucan knew him too well. Fallon changed out of his kilt before he headed below.

He stopped at the head of the stairs leading to the great hall and let his eyes take it all in. Lucan had built a bigger table. The other one was still in the hall with a blond Warrior using it. Hayden sat with both legs stretched out before him taking up the entire bench.

"Fallon," Logan called as he walked out of the kitchen and took the bench opposite Hayden.

Fallon waved to the youngest Warrior of their group. Logan's brown hair was damp, as though he had recently bathed.

"Finally," Lucan said as he waved Fallon to him. "Cara managed to save you some food from Galen's constantly empty stomach."

Fallon walked down the steps to the men's jesting with Galen. He stopped at the foot of the table where an empty chair stood. His chair. Another empty spot was on his left where Quinn should have been. He glanced to his right where Lucan sat.

Next to Lucan was Cara. On the other side of Cara was Galen Shaw. His dark blue eyes met Fallon's as he nodded. Across from Galen was Ramsey MacDonald. Ramsey was a man of few words, but his keen insight was useful.

Ramsey gave Fallon a welcoming smile, his gray eyes crinkling at the corners. Beside Ramsey was Sonya, the red-haired Druid who had come to them just weeks ago. Fallon then nodded to Hayden and Logan at the opposite table before he took his seat.

"I see you've made a bigger table," Fallon said to his brother. Much had been done while he was away, and he was anxious to see how far they had come on the castle.

Lucan laughed and glanced at Hayden and Logan. "There's enough room for those two with us, but they prefer to eat alone."

"I couldn't let Hayden eat by himself," Logan said. "Besides, I spent more time protecting my food from Galen than eating."

The hall erupted with laughter. Fallon looked at Hayden. The big blond Warrior had a hatred for *drough* that went deep, so deep he had threatened to kill Cara despite Cara's never undergoing the blood ritual that would make her a *drough*. Hayden and Cara stayed away from each other, but everyone knew the day would come when something was likely to happen.

Fallon waited until the chatter quieted down before he spoke. "I'm sure all of you know about Larena by now."

"I told them," Galen said.

Hayden leaned an elbow on the table. "Is she really a Warrior? Did you see her change?"

"I did," Fallon answered. "She has a goddess inside her, not a god, which is why I think the goddess chose a woman instead of a man."

"Do you know the name of the goddess?" Ramsey asked.

Fallon nodded. "Lelomai, goddess of defense."

"Hmm," Galen said. "What kind of powers does she have?"

Fallon thought back to the first time he saw her disappear. He had been dumbstruck that she had been able to do such a thing. It would definitely come in handy in a war. "She has the usual powers of sight and hearing, but she can make herself unseen."

"Do you mean to say she can make herself invisible?" Lucan asked.

"I do. I doona know much about her goddess, but apparently there are some differences. It could be because Larena is female, or because she has a goddess inside her. When we turn, it is just our skin and eyes that change. With Larena, even her hair changes."

"To what?" Logan asked.

"She shimmers." It was the best Fallon could do to explain it. "You can see every color imaginable on her, but it's muted."

Cara smiled and placed her hand over Lucan's on the table. "It sounds beautiful."

"It is." The words were out of Fallon's mouth before he could stop them.

"So what happened in Edinburgh?" Ramsey wanted to know.

Fallon shrugged. "The king wasn't in residence. He rules from London, so I wasn't able to speak to him. However, Lorena's cousin has the king's ear and sent him a missive. I'm hoping to hear something soon. If not, I may have to take a trip to London."

Hayden tapped his finger on the table to get Fallon's attention. "And the Scroll? Did you learn if it was real or not?"

Though he and Lucan might not take the ring from Larena, Fallon wasn't going to risk a chance that the others might discover her secret. Not yet anyway. "I learned nothing of importance."

Out of the corner of his eye, Fallon saw Lucan's brow furrow. He faced his brother and held his stare. "We'll get Quinn out."

"I have no doubt," Lucan said.

But Fallon knew he did. It was written all over his face.

FIFTEEN

Fallon walked along the battlements. The constant wind whipped his hair about. He stared out over the sea that churned in the darkness, the water reflecting the moon's glow.

It was a beautiful night, one he had wanted to share with Larena. Fallon knew he shouldn't feel betrayed, but he did. He understood all too well the need to keep secrets. Yet, he had imagined things were different with him and Larena since they were both Warriors. How could he have been so stupid?

It was her kisses.

It was everything about Larena from her sharp mind to the regal way she moved to the feel of her legs wrapped around his waist as he thrust inside her.

Maybe it was because he had seen Lucan and Cara fall in love before his very eyes, but Fallon had felt something deep for Larena and something strong, special. He had thought she felt it too.

"I knew I would find you here," Lucan said as he came up beside him.

"I wanted to see the water and smell the salt in the air." Though Fallon had missed his brother, he wasn't up for conversation just now. But if he knew Lucan, Fallon wouldn't have a chance to deflect any questions.

Lucan was quiet for several moments as if gathering his thoughts. "Was it difficult for you in Edinburgh?"

Fallon shook his head as he remembered. "I hated every moment of it. You cannot trust anyone, and the gossip is unbelievable. Everyone there is out for themselves first and foremost."

"Yet you survived it."

Fallon blew out a breath and braced his hands on the stone wall in front of him. "Barely. I wasn't there verra long."

"Larena helped you, didn't she?"

"Aye." There was no sense lying to his brother.

Lucan turned his back to the wall and leaned against it as his head swiveled to Fallon. "She told you what she was. That must have taken a lot of faith in you."

"She told me because she wanted me to bring her here and help protect her from Deirdre. I'd like to think she trusted me, but I think fear ruled her more than anything." Even as he said it, Fallon knew he was lying to himself. It had taken a great amount of courage for Larena to show him what she was.

"What happened there, Fallon? You've come back a changed man."

Fallon looked at Lucan and smiled wryly. "Worse?"

"Better. I think it was Larena's influence."

"Maybe," Fallon admitted. "I saw her and wanted her. I've never felt lust like that before. Every man in Edinburgh wanted her."

"What was she doing there?"

Fallon grinned. "She and her cousin, Malcolm, were there to look for information about Deirdre. She was tenacious and confronted me in my own chamber when she learned who I was."

Lucan chuckled then. "The beautiful woman whom you thought you couldn't have arrives in your chamber. I gather you didna resist her?"

"I tried, but in the end I didn't want to."

"Mother always told us everything happens for a reason."

Fallon looked back out at the water. He could hear the waves breaking against the cliffs. How many times had he stood in this exact spot and watched the water? So many times, and always it had soothed him. But not tonight.

"How old is Larena?" Lucan asked.

"A hundred, or thereaboots."

"I'm curious how Deirdre didn't know of her existence until now," Lucan said into the silence.

Fallon repeated Larena's tale, and when he finished, Lucan whistled long and low.

"She's been alone most of the time," Fallon said. "She's survived on her wits and courage, as well as her mistrust of everyone. Only recently has Malcolm accompanied her."

"Malcolm has put himself in an incredible amount of danger."

"He's a good man. You would like him. It's too bad he isn't a Warrior. I would have liked to have him fight with us."

Lucan crossed his arms over his chest. "I'm sure I would like him. Where is he now?"

Fallon wondered that himself. "I have no idea. There's no reason for him to stay in Edinburgh, so I assume he'll return to his clan. I told him he was welcome here any time."

"I still don't understand why the Warriors would want to kill Larena instead of bringing her to Deirdre. Deirdre would want to use Larena, not have her murdrered."

Fallon ran a hand through his hair and straightened. "I agree. I imagine we'll hear what happened once Larena wakes."

"I'm anxious to find out."

So was Fallon.

"You aren't going to ask her about the ring, are you?" Lucan asked.

"I told her we were looking for it and the reason why. She chose to keep the information from me."

"Ask her for it, Fallon. Tell her our plan. You saved her life, so she owes you."

He shook his head. "She doesn't owe me anything. How can we ask her to endanger many lives for Quinn? She doesn't know us, Lucan, so she cannot trust what we say as the truth. We will find another way. Using the Scroll as leverage was always going to be a gamble."

Lucan stared at him a long moment before he swore and pushed away from the wall. "The answer to everything is right before us. I think we should talk to Larena, tell her our plan, and ask her to trust us. God's blood! I cannot sleep with wondering what Deirdre is doing to Quinn."

Fallon looked toward the rolling hills and the mountains that were obscured in the darkness. For too long Fallon had been selfish, and he was doing it again.

Quinn needed him, and Fallon had promised himself and Lucan they would get their youngest brother out of Deirdre's clutches. Too much time had passed already.

"I know," Fallon said. "We will get Quinn out of Deirdre's hold. I can talk to Larena, but it's her decision. If she says nay, it's nay."

Lucan clamped a hand on his shoulder. "Agreed. She might have told you about the Scroll later."

"Maybe. It doesn't matter now."

Lucan started to walk away, his boot heels hitting the stones. Then he stopped and said over his shoulder, "If you care for her, Fallon, then fight for her."

Fallon thought about Lucan's words long after he left. He didn't deserve a woman like Larena, nor should she be strapped with a man that couldn't protect his family and friends.

He walked the battlements content in his solitude. The others must have sensed it, too, for they didn't speak when he passed them as they stood guard.

The one thing he couldn't deny was that he did care for Larena. He wanted her back in his bed. He wanted to kiss her sweet lips and feel her silky skin beneath his hands. He wanted to hear her call out his name as he brought her to fulfillment, and he wanted to fill her again and again and again.

If he had his way he would lock them in a chamber for days and make endless love to her, only stopping to eat. He wanted her head filled with him just as she consumed him.

Aye, he did want her. And he would fight for her.

* * *

Larena tried to stay in the confines of sleep. She didn't want to feel the pain anymore or see the look of grave concern on Fallon's face.

Fallon.

Just the thought of him made her heart quicken. She woke slowly, though she didn't lift her eyelids. Breathing evenly, she waited to feel the consuming fire that had raced through her blood. Instead, there was nothing.

She opened her eyes to find herself on her left side where the light from the nearby window reached the bed—a bed she didn't recognize.

"How are you feeling?"

Her gaze jerked to the chair near her and the large, dark-headed man with twin braids on either side of his temples seated there. He gave her a smile that reached all the way to his sea-green eyes.

A glance at his neck and the golden torc confirmed what she had suspected. She was staring at one of Fallon's brothers. "You must be Lucan."

He inclined his head. "I am. You had us all worried. Fallon especially."

Larena slowly sat up, hoping to see Fallon, but only she and Lucan were in the large chamber. No pain filled her body now. She licked her lips and looked around.

Directly across from the bed was the large hearth. A table with two chairs stood between the fireplace and the window. There was a small table on one side of the bed where a pitcher and cup sat. There were two chests on either side of the bed, and an old round shield with two swords crossed beneath it hung on the wall near the door.

"You're in Fallon's chamber, the master chamber," Lucan said. "Would you like some water?"

She nodded and watched him pour the liquid into the cup. She drank three cups before she sat back and sighed. The disappointment in not finding Fallon was great. She wondered where he was. It was silly, but she had expected him to be by her bedside

"Is there any pain?"

Larena was startled out of her thoughts by Lucan's deep voice. "Nay. Whom do I thank for saving me?"

"You mean besides Fallon?" Lucan smiled after he spoke, but she saw the hard light in his green eyes, eyes so similar to Fallon's.

She swallowed and nodded. "Aye, besides Fallon."

Before he could answer the door opened and a beautiful woman with chestnut hair and dark eyes walked to Lucan's side. She slid her arms around the Highlander's waist and smiled down at Larena.

"I hope my husband hasn't been rude," the woman said.

Lucan threaded his fingers with hers. "I would never dream of it."

The woman laughed and focused her eyes on Larena. "I'm Cara. We've heard so much about you. I cannot believe you're a Warrior."

"Thank you for helping to heal me," Larena said. The easy, open friendliness of Cara made her wary, but she liked the honesty she saw in Cara's dark eyes. "Fallon told me you are a Druid."

Cara looked at her husband, her brow furrowed, before she turned back to Larena. "Aye, I am a Druid. Are you hungry? I can get you some soup I made."

"That would be wonderful." She hadn't missed the look between Cara and Lucan. What were they keeping from her? And why?

Lucan kissed Cara and whispered something in her ear before he left. Larena shifted beneath the covers. She wore a different chemise, one that was clean and unmarred by blood and claw marks. Larena picked at the neckline as her thoughts moved to Fallon once more.

"Your chemise was ruined," Cara said as she took Lucan's seat. "I found another. It's not as nice as the one you wore."

"It's perfect," Larena said. "What I had in Edinburgh was for show only."

Cara rubbed her hands together nervously. "Fallon told us of your cousin and what you both went through. That sounds so dangerous."

"It was something I had to do, and Malcolm wouldn't let me go alone."

"Will he come here?"

Larena shrugged. "I don't know. I don't even know where he is now."

"I want to ask what happened during the attack, but I promised Lucan I wouldn't. He and Fallon have been waiting for you to wake so they can find out what occurred."

"Wh . . ." She stopped and cleared her throat. "Where is Fallon?"

She hated herself for asking, but she had to know. He had seemed like the kind of man that would have stayed by her side the entire time.

Cara chuckled. "He's been wandering around the castle since late last night looking at all the improvements. I know he was eager to get to work after the morning meal. I'm sure he will be here shortly."

There was a quick knock on the door before it opened again. This time a tall, slender woman with fiery curls walked in carrying a tray with a bowl of soup and some bread. She placed the tray across Larena's lap and offered a wide smile.

"Hello, Larena. I'm Sonya."

The name suited her, and Larena liked her instantly. She returned the smile. "The other Druid. My thanks for helping to heal me and for the food. I didn't realize how hungry I was until I smelled it."

"Don't let us stop you from eating," Cara said. "We're the only two females in the castle, so we tend to band together against the males."

Sonya laughed, the sound light and airy. It was evident there was a good bond between her and Cara. "So true," she said, and pulled another chair over beside Cara.

Larena listened to the two women as she ate. They kept up a steady stream of conversation, talking about nothing in particular, and it was obvious to Larena they were there to keep her engaged.

She finished the broth and put the last bite of bread in her mouth. She was ready to get out of the bed and into some clothes.

"Would you like some more?" Cara asked.

"Thank you, but nay," she said.

Sonya jumped up and hurried from the chamber. Larena watched her go, wondering what made the Druid leave so quickly. It wasn't long before Sonya returned pulling a wooden tub into the chamber.

She straightened and dusted off her hands. "We thought you might like a bath."

Larena nearly sighed at the idea of soaking in hot water. "That sounds like heaven."

"We'll start bringing the water up," Cara said.

After they left, Larena rose from the bed and walked to the window. She looked out to see cliffs of jagged rock that plummeted to the dark water below. The waves crashed and spray flew into the sky to shimmer in the sunlight. Larena imagined she could almost feel the mist of water. The smell of salt filled the air, and the breeze from the water cooled her face.

She couldn't wait to see the rest of the castle and surrounding land. Her bare toes squeezed against the cold stones beneath them. She turned and looked at the bed. Fallon's bed, she corrected.

Would she share the bed with him? Was that why he had put her in his chamber? Could she allow herself to become more attached to him than she already was?

When he had spoken of Quinn and their plan to rescue him, her hand had gone to her ring, ready to give it to him or anyone in need of rescue from Deirdre. Then she remembered the vow she had made to her clan and Robena. She couldn't forsake that vow, even if she did want to help Fallon, nor could she put everyone else at risk if the plan failed.

She touched her side where the wound had been, but there was no pain. When she lifted the chemise she found no scars either. It was as if she had healed as she always did. Yet, she knew the *drough* blood was supposed to kill her. Were the Druids at MacLeod Castle that powerful?

The door opened and Cara and Sonya entered carrying buckets followed by Lucan and another man with light brown hair and laughing hazel eyes. He gave a quick nod to Larena before dumping his buckets and leaving.

"That was Logan," Cara told her. "He's always smiling and jesting. I don't think there is anything that can get him down."

It took a few more trips before the tub was filled and the three women were left alone again.

Larena looked at Sonya. "I don't have a scar. Shouldn't the poison have at least given me a scar?"

Sonya hesitated and cast a glance at Cara. "You were all but dead when Fallon arrived here with you in his arms. I used magic, aye, but it wasn't enough."

"You needed blood," Cara said. "Lots of it."

"Blood," Larena repeated, confused. "So that's what saved me?"

Sonya nodded.

"Who gave the blood?"

Cara handed her a bar of soap and cleared her throat. "Do you need help?"

Larena shook her head and allowed her to evade the question. She wanted some time alone to think. And she wanted to soak for as long as she could in the water. Even now curls of heat rose from the tub, beckoning her.

"Welcome to MacLeod Castle," Sonya said before she left.

Cara grinned after the Druid. "I have a few gowns I've let the hem out of that should fit you."

"I don't want to take your gowns."

"Don't think anything of it. There are many gowns that were taken from the village after Deirdre killed everyone. I alter them as Sonya and I need them. I'll return with one as soon as I finish."

When the door closed behind Cara, Larena jerked off the chemise. She dipped her toe into the scalding water to test it, and then slid beneath it with a sigh.

Her hand went to her side. She had needed blood. But then whose blood was inside her now?

She thought of the attack from the two Warriors and the pain that had devoured her. The blackness had taken her soon after, but she remembered opening her eyes to find herself in Fallon's arms. His beautiful dark green eyes had been focused on her as he said her name over and over again.

Larena covered her face with her hands. She should tell him about the ring and what was inside. He wanted information about the Scroll. That was easy enough to give, but what if he asked for the Scroll? She would explain that as much as she wanted to give it to him, she couldn't. He would understand. Wouldn't he?

More disturbing than that thought was wondering if he would want her in his bed again after she confessed to having the Scroll.

SIXTEEN

Fallon looked out over the castle from the tower and smiled. He hadn't expected so much to have been accomplished while he was away. All but two of the towers had been restored, including the one he stood in now.

His heart hurt as he thought about returning the castle to its former glory. He could well imagine his father standing in the bailey with his arms crossed over his thick chest and his dark hair streaked with silver nodding in approval.

At least this was one thing Fallon had done right.

The sound of footsteps on the stairs announced the arrival of his brother even before Lucan stepped through the doorway.

"I've been looking everywhere for you," Lucan said, his brow furrowed.

Instantly Fallon thought of Larena. "Is something wrong with Larena?"

"Nay. She's woken."

Fallon let out a breath he hadn't realized he was holding. "Is Cara seeing to her?"

"And Sonya as well. Logan and I helped bring up water for her to bathe."

Fallon swallowed and turned his head away lest his brother see the flare of lust that spiked in him when he thought of Larena in the water. "Is she feeling well?"

"She seems to be."

He wanted to inquire if she had asked about him, but somehow Fallon kept his mouth shut.

"You need to tell her what you did for her," Lucan said.

Fallon nodded. "I'm sure I will."

"Are you going to fight for her?"

He faced his brother then. "She's mine to protect."

Lucan grinned and nodded. "Good. I like her. You need to go to her though. She's in a new place, and the only one she knows is you."

"I will go to her after the noon meal is finished. She is still resting, and I want an update from the others."

It was a lie. He wasn't ready to face Larena quite yet. But as Fallon walked down the winding stairs of the tower, he found he wanted to go to Larena right then and shake her for not trusting him. Then he would kiss her until she melted against him.

It had been so long since he had been around women that he had to remember to treat her like a lady, not some object that was his to claim. Still, the god inside him demanded Fallon declare her as his own, to mark her as his so no other man would dare touch her.

Just as he expected, when he and Lucan arrived in the great hall, the others were already at the table helping themselves to the food Sonya and Cara had prepared.

Fallon took his seat at the head of the table and filled his own trencher while listening to Hayden speak of going hunting that afternoon.

"I'll be down at the water fishing," Lucan said.

"Sounds good," Galen said. "Cara, could you make me another loaf of bread?"

Fallon found himself chuckling as the others groaned at Galen's request.

Logan threw his empty goblet at Galen but Galen easily deflected it. "Doona you ever get enough, mon?"

"Never," Galen said with a smile, before popping a piece of bread in his mouth.

There was a round of laughter that even Fallon found himself joining. The castle had missed such sounds, and he was glad to have them return. The men—and women—around his table weren't true family, but they were his family.

The MacLeods had given their vow to fight Deirdre and protect anyone in need.

It was his duty now to make the decisions. Fallon had always relied heavily on his brothers for their input, and that wouldn't change. The men sitting around him had proven their skill as warriors, and he valued their ideas.

Fallon waited until everyone was finished talking before he cleared his throat to get their attention. "We had a plan to break Quinn free of Deirdre. In order for it to work, we needed the Scroll and the spell that would bind the gods."

He paused and took a deep breath. "We doona have the Scroll, and we aren't likely to get it." Logan opened his mouth, but Fallon held up a hand for silence. "I have an idea, but before I get to that I want to finish."

Logan nodded his head and waited.

"Sonya has been a great tool in teaching Cara how to

control her powers, but neither of them knows how to bind our gods. Without that spell to bind Deirdre's Warriors, we will have one hell of a fight."

"I'm always willing to kill wyrran," Hayden said.

Galen scratched his chin and glanced around the table. "I don't like being outnumbered, but if we plan it right we could surprise them and use it to our advantage."

Fallon nodded. "I also believe that could work to our advantage."

Lucan put his elbows on the table and steepled his fingers. "What do you propose?"

"Has anyone seen the Scroll?"

Everyone shook their heads, as he expected.

"It is my understanding that neither has Deirdre."

Ramsey chuckled, drawing everyone's eyes to him. "I know what you're thinking, Fallon. I like it."

"Aye," Fallon said. "I propose that we make our own scroll."

Hayden cursed and rose from his seat to pace. Galen ran a hand down his face while Lucan studied Fallon with a steady gaze.

"Do you really think we can do this?" Lucan asked. "If Deirdre suspects it's false we'll never get Quinn free."

"Do we have another choice? I cannot stand the thought of Quinn in that dungeon another moment," Fallon said through clenched teeth. "I've waited, just as you asked. And I agree, it was for the best. She was expecting us immediately, and we've taken the time to try and learn something that will help us. But the simple truth is, we know no more now than we did when Quinn was taken. I'm through waiting, Lucan."

Ramsey leaned forward on the table. "I understand that, Fallon. He's your brother. You would do anything for him, but what if she's already broken him?"

"Then I'll fix him."

There was a moment of stunned silence and then chaos erupted as everyone spoke at once.

Fallon counted to ten before he slammed his hand on the table. "Enough!"

He looked at each man and woman at the table and took a deep breath. "All that matters to me is bringing Quinn home."

"And what if he's sided with Deirdre?" Galen asked. "Distance will not sever her hold on him."

Fallon fisted his hand and looked into Lucan's eyes. "I know Quinn. He will fight Deirdre with everything he's worth. If she has pulled him to her side, it's only with magic. We have Druids who can fight that magic."

Sonya shook her head sadly. "How effectively is the question. Deirdre's black magic is very powerful."

"I willna leave Quinn with Deirdre no matter what."

"I agree with Fallon," Lucan said. "Quinn comes back with us."

Hayden cursed and pushed his trencher away. "Quinn could be a spy."

"Any one of you could be a spy," Fallon stated. "Even knowing that we allowed you into our home. Why would I treat my brother any differently?"

Ramsey lifted his hand for silence as Hayden began to argue again. "Fallon has made excellent arguments, and even though I have my doubts that Quinn will be the same man he was before Deirdre captured him, we can do nothing else but bring him home."

Fallon gave a nod to Ramsey. One by one the others agreed. Now all Fallon had to worry about was getting Quinn away from Deirdre and whatever horrors he brought back with him.

Larena watched from the shadows on the floor above while Fallon spoke to the others. She had planned to stay in the bath soaking, but the need to learn about her surroundings was too great. And, if she was honest with herself, she wanted to find Fallon.

She had dressed in the simple blue gown Cara had brought to her chamber. To her surprise, it fit perfectly. Cara had also supplied woollen hose and several pairs of shoes. Larena had found a pair that fit, and after combing her fingers through her hair she had left Fallon's chamber.

It was the voices from the great hall that drew her down the corridor and the flights of stairs. Not wanting to be seen, she had kept to the shadows and observed the people below.

She wasn't surprised to find Fallon at the head of the table. He had a natural ability to lead that others recognized. She suspected that even if he hadn't been raised to be laird, he still would have been a leader.

Her gaze fastened on him and she watched as he ate and spoke to Lucan who sat on his right. There was an empty place to his left that she knew was saved for Quinn. That Fallon looked again and again at the empty seat told Larena just how desperately he wanted to have his brother back.

She tried to imagine how it would feel to have a sibling taken from her. As an only child, she found it difficult. She'd had friends, but the only other family she'd been raised with was her cousin Naill. He had been several years older than her and didn't want to be bothered with a girl.

It was a new experience to watch the way Fallon and Lucan interacted. They had many of the same mannerisms, and she expected Quinn had some of those same traits. It was really too bad Quinn had been taken. She would have liked to see all three brothers together.

Larena shifted her gaze to the only women in the group. Cara sat beside Lucan while Sonya sat across from Cara. They carried on their own conversations, but both listened aptly when the men began their discussion.

She recognized Logan sitting at a separate table. The big blond seated with him looked sinister, with his furrowed brow and hard eyes. She would keep her eye on him. Men who looked as he did sought out trouble, and she wanted no part of that.

With her attention back on Fallon's table she looked the other two men over. The black-haired one had his back to her, but after just a short observation she noticed that he didn't speak as often as the others.

The other man, with dark blond hair, had an easy way about him, but there was also something in his gaze that spoke of unnamed horrors he had witnessed.

All of them were Warriors. Larena had never been around so many. In truth the only Warrior she knew by face was Camdyn MacKenna.

The men below most likely knew she was a Warrior by now. How would they react to her? Fallon was the only person she really knew, and they had known each other mere hours. Had she made the right decision in asking him to bring her here?

Then she remembered the attack in Edinburgh. Deirdre had discovered her. Deirdre's reach seemed endless, and if Larena knew anything about Deirdre it was that the *drough* never gave up when she set her sights on something. And now, her sights were set on Larena.

It was good timing that Fallon had come to Edinburgh when he had. She would be dead now if he hadn't been there. She owed him her life.

She covered her ring with her left hand. She could repay Fallon by giving him the Scroll, but every time she thought of it, she grew sick to her stomach.

Robena had drilled into her mind endlessly how important it was for the Scroll never to land in Deirdre's hands. Everything Larena had fought for these last hundred years would be in vain if she handed the Scroll to Deirdre.

The change of tone below drew Larena out of her thoughts. She peered around the stone and listened as Fallon spoke. He was calm and in control, fully in his element in his castle. She loved watching him. He was amazing.

Larena wanted to go to him and kiss him.

She started toward him when she heard Fallon mention the Scroll. Her heart leaped into her chest when she heard him say he'd never intended to give Deirdre the real Scroll, only a fake.

Her fingers clutched her ring, ready to pull it off and show everyone the Scroll so they could copy the Celtic scrollwork that would let Deirdre know it was real.

But then she stopped. Fallon would want to know why she hadn't told him in Edinburgh.

Larena hated lying to him. Fallon had told her things she knew he had never shared with anyone else, but she couldn't do the same. There were some things, such as the Scroll, that the fewer people knew about them the better.

She took a deep breath and looked around the table to find Cara's gaze on her. Larena shook her head, hoping Cara would keep quiet. Cara gave a small nod of her head in acknowledgment.

Larena knew she should go down to the great hall and introduce herself, but she couldn't move. She turned away from the scene and leaned her back against the stone wall.

She had spent several years at the king's castle, but she had always kept herself separate from others. Her inability to trust, Malcolm would say. Malcolm had been her only link, and even then she hadn't allowed herself to become too attached to him since she knew she would leave him one day.

Now, below, there were six immortal Warriors. What the MacLeods had done by opening their castle was to create a family. The last time Larena had been part of a family they had scorned her and driven her from her home.

But she had to stay with Fallon. If Deirdre captured her, it would only be a matter of time before she discovered what her ring was.

Larena sighed. She would do as she always did then and keep her distance from everyone. It was the only way she could survive.

She turned to walk down the stairs and found Fallon before her. Her lips parted as she gazed into his handsome face. He always took her breath away, and the need to touch him, to feel his arms around her, was crushing.

She hadn't noticed before that he had traded his kilt for a tunic of deep red and leather breeches, faded with time and use, that were tucked into black boots. He looked more natural in this attire, and she couldn't say which she liked better, the kilted Fallon or the casual one before her now.

"How did you know I was here?"

He shrugged. "I smelled your scent."

A thrill went through her at his words, and she had to remind herself to keep her distance even though everything inside her cried out to be his.

"How do you feel?" The question was voiced in a calm manner, but the way his dark green eyes burned her body caused her blood to quicken.

"As if the attack never happened."

"Good." Fallon held out his hand. "Everyone is waiting to meet you, and I want to hear about the attack."

She placed her hand in his, and then stopped him when he would have turned away. "Wait. I . . . I need a moment."

"For what?"

"There are Warriors down there I don't know."

He regarded her silently for a moment. "My brother would never hurt you. He will protect you with his life. The others have proven their worth to me. They are here to put an end to Deirdre."

"I know." How could she explain it to him when she couldn't understand it herself?

"Come," he said with a pull of his hand. "Everything will be all right. Trust me."

Trust. It was just a word, but it was something she didn't allow herself to do. With Fallon, however, things were different.

She let him tug her onto the stairs. The conversation in the hall fell quiet as they descended. She swallowed, hating the eyes on her. It had been easy to blend in at the king's castle, but she wouldn't get that luxury here.

"Thank you," she whispered to Fallon.

"For what?"

"For saving my life."

He shrugged as if it meant nothing. There was something about Fallon that had changed. She couldn't put her finger on it, but he wasn't the same man she had shared a bed with in Edinburgh.

SEVENTEEN

Larena waited until she and Fallon had stopped by his chair before she pulled her hand from his grasp. She made herself look around the table instead of at the floor as she wished. With her hands clasped before her to help hide how they shook, she listened as Fallon introduced her.

"You've already met Lucan, Cara, and Sonya," Fallon said. "Next to Cara is Galen Shaw."

Larena smiled at Galen, noting he wore a kilt as if it were his second skin. His dark blue eyes looked her over before returning her smile.

"I've heard your name, Galen Shaw."

Galen's brows rose. "Have you now? And by whom?"

"Camdyn MacKenna."

"You've spoken to Camdyn?" Galen asked as he sat up straighter.

She opened her mouth to reply when Fallon asked, "Who is Camdyn?"

"A Warrior," Galen answered. "He prefers to keep to himself, but I left markings to let him know where I had gone."

Larena nodded. "He found them. He stopped by Edinburgh Castle several weeks ago and told me."

Galen laughed and slapped the table, clearly over-joyed with the news. "Camdyn is a fine Warrior, Fallon. He will be a great asset to us."

"Then where is he?" Lucan asked.

"He'll be here. Camdyn never breaks his word," Galen said.

Fallon pointed across from Galen. "That is Ramsey MacDonald. He's the quiet one."

"My lady," Ramsey said with a bow of his head.

Larena instantly liked the raven-haired Warrior. He didn't sport a kilt, but there was a fire in his gray eyes that only Highlanders had. "Ramsey."

"You've already met Logan," Fallon said, as Logan gave her a wink. "The hulking one across from him is Hayden Campbell."

Larena looked into eyes so dark they were nearly black. It was a startling contrast with his blond hair, but Hayden's eyes seemed to convey the idea of men-ace just as his demeanor did. "Hayden."

"Larena," Hayden replied in a cool, deep voice.

Fallon pulled his chair out and motioned for her to take it. "Sit, please. Would you like something to eat?"

"Nay." Larena took his chair, hating to be the center of attention. Fallon slid next to her in Quinn's empty spot. She tried to read the emotion in his eyes, but he had closed himself off to her.

She should be relieved. She had wanted to distance herself anyway, right? Then why did it hurt so badly?

You wondered if things would change once you reached his castle. Now you know.

Aye. Now she knew.

"Can you tell us of the attack on you?" Lucan asked.

Larena took a deep breath to help fortify herself. She didn't want to relive the attack, but there were things Fallon and the others needed to know.

"There were two of them. One of the Warriors had pale green skin and a nasty attitude. The other had dark blue skin and wings."

"Wings?" Lucan repeated, his brow furrowed. "Are you sure?"

Larena nodded. "I saw him fold them against his back. They were wings."

"Could it be the same one?" Cara asked.

Fallon lifted one shoulder. "I imagine it is. Did they both attack you?" he asked Larena.

"Nay, only the pale green one. They told me Deirdre wanted to meet me. When I asked how she found out about me, they told me it was the wyrran. One had gotten into the castle. I killed it, but apparently there was another watching and it saw me transform," she told Fallon.

"A wyrran? In Edinburgh?" Galen asked.

Fallon nodded. "Aye. It showed itself to a large crowd in the great hall. I went after it, but I lost it in the maze of corridors."

"That's when I found it," Larena said. "I chased it out of the castle and killed it."

Logan chuckled. "Impressive. Do you see many wyrran at the castle?"

"That was the first I'd seen at the castle," Larena said, unable to keep the smile from her lips. Logan's easy charm helped to ease her tension.

Sonya leaned forward. "Did you know you had been poisoned with *drough* blood?"

"I did. It was the winged Warrior who told me about the poison. He said Deirdre wanted me alive, so he suggested I find Fallon and have him bring me here."

"Why?" Hayden asked. "That doesn't sound like any of Deirdre's Warriors I have encountered."

Larena shifted in her chair and shrugged. "I couldn't say."

"I suppose they knew you were there from the wyrran as well?" Lucan asked Fallon.

Fallon ran a hand down his face before laying his palm on the table. "Apparently. They were counting on me to find Larena and bring her here to be healed."

"If you're correct, then they'll be coming for Larena," Ramsey said. "That means another attack, and this time Deirdre will send more Warriors."

Hayden rose from the table and cursed. "We won last time, but they'll know how many Warriors we have now. Deirdre won't make the same mistake again. And we're down one Warrior."

"Nay, you're not," Larena said as she rose to her feet. "I can fight."

Hayden's lip curled in a sneer. "Fallon said he saw you change."

"Do you think he lied to you?"

Silence greeted her question. Hayden moved toward her, and Logan and Galen rose to their feet.

"I believe Fallon, as we all do," Hayden answered. "But I want to see for myself."

Larena lifted a brow and glared at him. "I will want to see you transform as well. After all, being told you're a Warrior doesn't make it so, now does it?"

Logan chuckled and shook his head. He raked a hand through his light brown hair and returned to his seat. "She's got you there, Hayden."

She found Hayden looking at her with something akin to respect in his black eyes.

"Fair is fair," he said, a heartbeat before his skin turned a dark red. Small red horns poked through his thick blond hair to stand straight up. His claws were red and gleaming, and his lips peeled back in a grin, showing her his impressive fangs.

Larena looked Hayden over before gazing into his red eyes. "Horns?"

"I have the god of massacre within me. What can I say?"

"Thank you," she said. She glanced at Fallon to find him watching her. His gaze steadied her, reminding her of his presence.

Larena usually transformed without her clothes since she used her power and turned herself invisible, but that wasn't an option at the moment.

Once Hayden returned to his human form, Larena released her goddess and let the change overtake her. Chills raced over her skin as the goddess stretched inside her. Larena wiggled her fingers as her claws distended from them. The fangs filled her mouth, and she was careful not to cut her tongue or her lips.

"Shite," Galen murmured.

Logan cleared his throat twice before he could speak. "You can say that again."

Ramsey let out an appreciative whistle while Hayden bowed his head to her.

Larena glanced at her arm to see her skin shimmering as it always did.

Cara's dark eyes were huge with awe. "Even her hair. Just as Fallon told us. She's stunning."

With every eye trained on her, Larena fought the urge to fidget. Then Fallon was on his feet beside her. His hand brushed hers, and she had the absurd notion to intertwine her fingers with his.

"Will you show them the rest?" he asked.

In answer, she made herself invisible and heard the audible gasps from Sonya and Cara. The effect wasn't the same as when she'd done it for Fallon since she had been nude at the time. As it was, it looked as if there were nothing holding up her gown.

"Without your clothes, no one can see you, can they?" Ramsey asked.

"Nay," she replied. "I can go anywhere undetected."

One side of Galen's lips turned up in a smile. "Larena will be a great advantage against Deirdre."

Larena pushed her goddess back down and let herself return to normal. She resumed her seat, hoping the talk would turn away from her now.

But then Galen walked to her and transformed. She was so stunned that for a moment, she could only stare into his blinding green eyes. She'd always wondered why the entire eyes, even the whites, turned the color of the Warrior.

"I have the trickster god, Ycewold, inside me," Galen said.

She gazed at his dark green skin, but before she could speak, Ramsey took his place. Ramsey's skin was the color of deepest bronze, a beautiful contrast to his black hair.

Ramsey gave her a small bow. "I have Ethexia, the god of thieves, within me."

Larena clenched her hands in her lap. She had expected to have to earn her way into these men's worlds, but by showing her their god, they were telling her she was one of them.

Logan shoved Ramsey aside and grinned. "I have the god of betrayal, Athleaus, inside me." As he spoke, his skin changed to silver. With a wink from his silver eyes, he returned to his seat.

Then Lucan stood. He had already transformed, and he looked at her with obsidian eyes. "I am one of three. Inside me is part of Apodatoo, the god of revenge."

Larena wanted to ask him to wait before he changed so she could see more, but Fallon stood on her left and her attention shifted to him.

He stared at her for one heartbeat, two, then he transformed before her eyes. His skin, tanned from the sun, turned as black as pitch. Midnight claws stretched from his fingers, and fangs a startling white flashed at her through his lips.

His beautiful dark green eyes were gone, and in their place were eyes as black as the night sky. She rose to her feet and reached out to touch his arm. She had wondered what he would look like when he let loose his god, and she was awed.

"I am one of three." Fallon's voice filled the great hall, soft and commanding. "The god of revenge fills me."

Larena's fingers touched the golden boar head on Fallon's torc. She had fought many wyrran in her years, and had seen only a few Warriors before now. Yet, she had to say Fallon was the most beautiful, the most imposing Warrior she had ever seen.

"Thank you," she whispered and dropped her hand. Then in a louder voice with her eyes still on Fallon, she said, "Thank you. All of you."

Fallon's black gaze held hers captive. "You are one of us now. You have a home here."

A home? She hadn't had a home since she'd had to leave her father. Did she dare to hope for something she had dreamed of having for years? The answer was aye because the thought of leaving it all behind wasn't something she could consider.

Her eyes began to burn with unshed tears. She hadn't cried since she buried her father, so why did Fallon bring out her tears?

She blinked, and Fallon had leashed his god. Once more dark green eyes watched her. Larena couldn't help but think that a major change had just happened in her life, in the space of a heartbeat.

Fallon and the others were offering her a home with them. They would be her family. But could she allow herself to get close to them? Did she dare?

EIGHTEEN

Fallon wanted to pull Larena into his arms. He saw the vulnerability in her smoky-blue gaze, and it tugged at his heart in ways he never expected to feel about a woman.

He had been worried about how the others would react to having a female Warrior with them, but the men had shown their acceptance. He wasn't sure what he would have done had they acted differently. Whatever was necessary most likely.

All that was left was Larena herself. Fallon knew she feared Deirdre. Not because Larena had ever met the *drough*, but because of the stories of Deirdre's treachery. But was it enough to keep Larena at the castle?

Fallon motioned for Larena to keep her seat. He wanted her to get to know the others so she would feel safe, but more than that, he didn't trust himself to be near her just yet.

The memories of their lovemaking were still vivid in his mind, and his body yearned to have her once more. However, he knew she needed time. How much, he didn't know.

He turned and started toward the castle door when Lucan's voice halted him.

"Where are you going?" his brother asked.

Fallon paused with his hand on the latch. "To have a look around."

He pulled the door open and stepped into the sunshine before Lucan could ask more questions. Fallon felt the pull of his god, a pull he had heard more and more since he had stopped drinking the wine.

It never crossed his mind to deny his god. He ran and leaped onto the battlements, a smile on his face at finally doing what his brother had done for centuries, and surveyed the land. He'd denied the powers of his god for so long, that he found he quite enjoyed being able to do things that regular men couldn't do.

No MacClures had returned to claim the castle or their destroyed village since Fallon and the others had transformed and warned them never to return.

In a way, Fallon wanted the MacClures to return. They had dared to take his lands while he had been battling evil. He needed to fight and who better than the clan that had taken his lands and castle?

Most of the cottages in the village had either been burned or ripped apart by the wyrran and Deirdre's Warriors. Lucan had told him he and the other Warriors had taken whatever they could from the village and filled the castle with it.

There were a few empty chambers in the castle, but Fallon had the unshakable feeling there wasn't going to be enough room for everyone. They could pack more people into the castle if Warriors were to share chambers.

However, there was the village. It wasn't as close to the castle as Fallon would have preferred, but it was near enough. They could rebuild the cottages and Warriors could live there if need be.

He was deep in concentration, thinking about the village, when he felt a presence beside him. Fallon turned his head to find Ramsey there. The quiet Warrior gazed at the village as he leaned his hands upon the stones of the saw-toothed merlon while he braced a foot on the crenel.

"You did the right thing in bringing Larena here," Ramsey said. "We will need her."

Fallon blew out a breath. "I'd rather she didn't fight beside us. I know she's a Warrior and killed many wyrran, but she's only battled other Warriors once. And it nearly killed her."

"They cheated." Ramsey turned his gray eyes on Fallon. "And she willna like being coddled."

"I know," Fallon admitted. And he did. He had to acknowledge that she could take care of herself and allow her to do so, or he would lose her forever.

"You care for her."

It wasn't a question. Fallon stared into Ramsey's unwavering gray gaze a moment before he nodded. "I do."

"What do you want to do with the village?"

Fallon was surprised by the abrupt change of subject. "I'd like to rebuild the cottages and make them ours. We might need the room. No other Warriors have come as yet, and we still have a few chambers in the castle."

"But you think it would be to our benefit?"

"Aye."

Ramsey stared at the village for several silent moments. "What if the MacClures return?"

"We'll deal with that when it happens. We have bigger worries. No one else might come to fight us, but I'd rather be prepared."

"I agree," Ramsey and faced him. "Good thinking, Fallon. When do you want to begin?"

Fallon turned and looked at the castle. There was still much to do. "We finish the castle first."

"The third tower is nearly complete, and Hayden and Logan have begun reconstruction of the fourth."

Fallon listened to Ramsey, mentally checking off what had been done and what was left to do. "Good."

His gaze was drawn downward as the men walked out of the castle. Fallon jumped to the bailey, landing as softly as a cat. Ramsey followed close behind him.

"Cara and Sonya are showing Larena around the castle," Lucan said.

Fallon nodded to his brother then looked at each Warrior in turn. "I need every one of you to think about the stories you've heard of the Scroll. I want to begin making the replica immediately."

"All of us wanted to go after Quinn as soon as we found him gone," Galen said. "But you did the right thing."

Had he? Was securing the castle more important than getting his brother free?

"Deirdre willna harm him," Hayden said.

Logan shifted from one foot to the other and crossed his arms over his chest. "She wants you and Lucan also. She wouldn't dare hurt Quinn since she needs the combined power of all three of you."

"None of that matters," Fallon said, more tersely than he intended. He closed his eyes and breathed deeply. He knew the men were just trying to help, but they didn't understand the hopelessness and guilt that weighed so heavily upon his shoulders.

When Fallon opened his eyes it was to find Lucan

with his eyes on the ground. Fallon let out a sigh and said, "We've all been inside Deirdre's mountain. Some of us longer than others, but we know what goes on there. She willna kill Quinn, nay, but God only knows what she's done to him already. I shouldn't have gone to Edinburgh."

"Then you wouldn't have found Larena," Lucan said as he raised his gaze to Fallon. "With Larena's ability to turn invisible, she can get to Quinn better than any of us. We might not need the Scroll."

"And then what?" Fallon asked. "Larena won't be seen, but Quinn will. Do you think Deirdre won't keep Quinn near her?"

Ramsey, who had remained silent during the exchange, turned his head to Fallon. "Finding Quinn within the castle is important. Once we learn where he is being kept, we can plan our strategy, even if that does include using the fake scroll. If we can set it up so that you can reach Quinn, you can bring him back here before Deirdre has time to understand what's happened."

"And the rest of you? Am I to leave you to her?" Fallon shook his head. "I'm not saying the idea isna a good one. It could work, but the last thing I want is to leave someone behind. I don't ever want to go to Deirdre's mountain again after this."

Logan, who usually always wore a smile, turned bleak hazel eyes to Fallon. "I don't want to go at all, Fallon, but I know Quinn would do it for me. So I will face that evil bitch again if it means Quinn's freedom."

Fallon clenched his hands in an effort to control the emotion within him. As the rage at what Deirdre had done to them slid through his veins, his claws extended. He wanted to leave right now to rescue Quinn, but it would be rushing in recklessly. Their da had taught them better than that.

"Others will come," Galen said. "Larena told us Camdyn was on his way."

"Let's hope he gets here before we leave," Fallon said.

"I have a bit of talent for drawing." Ramsey spoke into the silence. "I was told the Scroll had the knotwork of the Celts around the edges."

"Aye," Hayden agreed. "I was told that as well."

Fallon nodded to the two men, thankful Larena wouldn't have to tell them about the Scroll she guarded. "Good. Get to work on that. Anyone else who knows anything about the Scroll either tell Ramsey and Hayden or go with them. The rest of us will finish rebuilding the towers."

He needed to do something with his hands, anything to occupy his mind. Quinn was gone and Larena was falling further and further out of his reach. He could see it in her eyes. Whatever had been between them in Edinburgh was fading, and if he wanted to keep her, he needed to think fast.

Quinn forced his legs to hold him up even though his body screamed in agony. He'd barely begun to heal before Deirdre sent Warriors to torture him yet again.

He had lost his boots and his tunic. His breeches were torn and ripped in so many places that they scarcely covered him. The only thing they hadn't taken from him was his torc. But not for lack of trying.

Quinn smiled, and then winced when his busted lip

cracked open again. The Warriors couldn't understand why the torc wouldn't come off, not even using their superior strength. They didn't realize the torc was made to never be removed, and apparently, some magic had been put into it as well. At least that was Deirdre's explanation to the Warriors.

Quinn didn't care as long as it got them to leave his torc alone. He was exhausted and weary. He wasn't sure how many hours or days had passed since he had been brought to the mountain.

All he knew was the darkness, the hunger clawing at his belly, and the constant anguish of his body.

The Warriors had begun standing outside his cell waiting for him to slump over in sleep. As soon as he did, they would unlock the door and come inside to begin hitting him. Quinn doubted if Deirdre knew what her swine were doing.

Part of him longed for death, to end the constant cycle of pain, but he couldn't do that to his brothers. He owed it to them to stay alive, for he knew they would come for him. No matter how long it took, they would come.

Quinn's eyes drifted shut and sleep claimed him almost immediately. He felt his knees begin to crumple, and he came awake with a jolt. He wanted to shout in anger and frustration, but he didn't dare. It would give Deirdre what she wanted.

He chuckled as he realized Deirdre had gotten him to do what his brothers hadn't in three hundred years. He was controlling his god. Though he didn't know how long he could continue. Every fiber of his being wanted to get his hands on the Warriors torturing him and rip them apart.

When he thought of killing them, his rage bubbled, and the god threatened to break free. Quinn fought against the rising tide of his fury and focused on his breathing and staying awake.

The Warriors outside his cell suddenly scrambled to their feet. Quinn watched with curiosity, because the only person who could make the Warriors react in this way was Deirdre. Yet, she hadn't been to see him in . . . well, a long time. She had said she wouldn't return until he released his god.

He forced his newly broken leg to bear some of his weight since his other leg was numb. Deirdre came into view, hardly giving her Warriors a glance, before the door was unlocked and she walked inside.

She took one look at him and spun around to her Warriors. "Who did this to him?" she demanded.

The three Warriors looked at the ground like little children who had gotten caught in a lie.

"Did I order him to be beaten again?"

One of the Warriors spoke an almost indiscernible, "Nay."

Quinn tried to keep his eyes open, but his broken leg sent pain shooting through him. He wouldn't be able to stand much longer, and then he would sag against his chains and pull his shoulder that was already dislocated.

His body could heal rapidly, but it was hard to keep up because of how much torture had been inflicted on him.

He heard Deirdre shouting, but couldn't make out

what she said. Hands grabbed him, and he yelled out as they wrenched his dislocated arm. When something brushed against his broken leg, the anguish was excruciating.

Quinn welcomed the blackness that swallowed him and took him from his living hell.

NINETEEN

Larena enjoyed her time with Cara and Sonya. Both women had welcomed her with friendly smiles and much laughter. Cara had told her how she and Lucan had met, and about their struggles against Deirdre.

She had even watched as Cara coaxed a plant to grow. Larena knew of the powers of the Druids thanks to Robena, but she had never known the Druids could make plants grow. It was fascinating, and the more Larena was around the Druids, the more she realized how important they were to the Warriors—and to mankind.

Sonya, it seemed, was very powerful for a Druid. She wouldn't tell Larena everything she could do, but Larena did learn Sonya's magic could aid in the healing of wounds.

Yet, when Larena asked whose blood had been used to help her, neither of the women would answer, and Cara had quickly changed the conversation.

Larena had let them. For some reason, they didn't want her to know whose blood was inside her. It was silly, but she had hoped it was Fallon's. Maybe it wasn't, and that's why the women wouldn't tell her.

The afternoon had flown by faster than Larena realized. She spotted Ramsey and Hayden in the great hall bent over a piece of parchment, their voices low. She knew they were working on the Scroll, and a part of her itched to aid them. But it was better if she didn't.

Instead, she went to the kitchen to assist Cara and Sonya with the evening meal. The men hunted and brought in whatever they could, from fish to fowl to boar to venison.

"It's never enough," Cara had said with a laugh as she kneaded more dough. "Galen eats as if he has two stomachs."

"Three stomachs," Sonya said with a nod. "His belly is never full. We had to begin hiding some of the food because he kept coming in here during the day to eat."

Larena joined in their mirth. She learned a great deal about each of the Warriors from the women. Logan had a habit of playing tricks on everyone, which helped to keep their spirits from sinking too low. Ramsey was often seen standing alone or walking the perimeter of the castle by himself.

Hayden kept his distance from Cara because of his deep hatred for *droughs*. Cara's mother was a *drough,* and Hayden suspected Cara would turn *drough* as well.

Lucan had easily stepped into Fallon's shoes while Fallon had been gone, and he was a calm, steady influence, just as Fallon had said. Galen was the one who seemed to have an answer for everything.

It had been so long since Larena had been around women with whom she could be herself that at first she wasn't sure how to act with Cara and Sonya. But the two quickly put her at ease with their casual banter, so that

Larena allowed herself to be pulled into their small circle.

Then came the evening meal. Larena hadn't seen Fallon except from a distance the entire afternoon. He worked longer and harder than the rest, and he was the last to come in to supper.

Larena tried to look away from his damp hair, but she wanted to run her fingers through the dark brown locks that had begun to show strands of burnished gold from being in the sun.

Everyone had their own places at the table. Larena didn't know where to sit, so she hesitated. She was about to join Logan and Hayden at the other table when Galen touched her elbow.

"There is plenty of room for you to sit between me and Cara."

She looked into his blue eyes, wondering if he had somehow read her mind. One blond brow lifted as he waited for her answer.

Larena glanced at the table to find Fallon watching her. "All right," she answered.

Galen fell in step beside her as she walked to the table and slid into the seat on Cara's right. Cara's smile was bright as she turned to her, and the small squeeze she gave Larena's hand was filled with genuine warmth.

"I meant to tell you earlier to sit next to me," Cara said.

Larena waved away her words. "Think nothing of it."

As they ate each Warrior gave an overview of what he had accomplished that day. Larena was surprised to hear that Fallon, Lucan, and Galen had completed the reconstruction of the third tower and moved on to the fourth.

"It should be finished in a day or two," Lucan said. "I

have a few more tables and chairs to make for the chambers as well."

Fallon nodded. "Ramsey? How did you and Hayden fare today?"

"As well as can be expected," Ramsey said after he swallowed a mouthful of food. "The knotwork takes time to create."

"It looks good," Hayden said. "Ramsey wasn't jesting when he said he had drawing skills."

"Excellent." Fallon scratched his chin as his brow furrowed. "How long do you suspect it will take to complete?"

Ramsey shrugged. "I didn't get as much done today as I would have liked, but now that I have the initial knotwork down, it should go faster." He looked at Hayden. "What do you think?"

"A week," Hayden said. "Maybe two."

Fallon sighed. "I was hoping for sooner, but I understand this isn't an endeavor you put together quickly."

"Then it has to be weathered," Lucan said.

Hayden nodded his head, blond hair falling over his shoulder. "I can take care of that. The process will take a day or two. The longer we let it go, the better it will look."

"Then I leave it in your and Ramsey's capable hands," Fallon said. He paused and pushed away his trencher to put his elbows on the table. His gaze passed over Larena and lingered for a moment. "I know I went to Edinburgh to ask the king for the castle and only the castle. However, I doona know how many people will come, or if any more will."

"More will come," Logan said. "I know they will."

"I suspect you may be right, Logan, but there are only a limited number of chambers in the castle. Now, we could begin to share chambers if need be, but I had another thought."

Lucan chuckled and nodded. "The village."

"Aye," Fallon said. "The village. The MacClures haven't returned, and I doubt they will. Not for years anyway. By then, we may not need the village. Many of the homes were burned or ripped apart in Deirdre's attack. There are only six left standing, and they aren't in good shape."

"I'll go tomorrow to have a look at them and make a list of what is needed," Lucan said.

Galen set down his goblet. "Good plan, Fallon. I like your thinking."

"Aye," Hayden said. "It's close enough to the castle to work."

Ramsey turned to Fallon with his intense gray eyes. "I told you earlier I agree with your decision."

"As do I," Logan said.

Fallon then looked to Larena. He hesitated a moment, then shifted his gaze to Cara and Sonya. "What do you two think?"

"I like the idea," Cara said. "Or we could also build some new cottages closer to the castle."

Lucan lifted his wife's hand and kissed it.

Larena felt a spurt of envy for the love they shared. They had been through so much and deserved the happiness they had found. She wondered, though, whether she would ever find such happiness, and if she did, whether her problems with trusting people would allow her to love?

"Sonya?" Fallon's voice cut into her thoughts.

The red-haired Druid licked her lips and shrugged. "I worry about who will live in the cottages. What if there's another attack?"

"There will be another attack," Fallon said. "Never doubt that. It's just a matter of when."

"Then who will live in the cottages? Warriors? What if more Druids come? Who stays in the castle and in the cottages?"

Hayden cleared his throat. "I'll give up my chamber to a Druid. After all, we're going to need them and they cannot protect themselves as Warriors can."

"I agree," Fallon said. "Does any Warrior have a problem with that?"

"Nay," they answered in unison.

Larena could have watched them all day. Fallon was wonderful to observe. He wanted opinions on his proposals, and he didn't hesitate to change his mind if it were necessary.

Before she knew it, people were rising from the tables. She helped Sonya and Cara carry the trenchers into the kitchen.

"Impressive, isn't it?" Cara asked once they were alone.

Sonya chuckled. "The change in Fallon is remarkable, I'll grant you that. He was raised to be a laird though."

"Still," Cara said with a shrug, "I like how he includes everyone. He didn't have to ask us what we thought, though I wish he had asked Larena."

Larena shook her head. "Why would he? I've only

just arrived. I got a tour of the castle today, but I haven't seen the village or been here during an attack."

Cara put her hands on her hips, her dark braid falling over her shoulder. "You're a Warrior. He should have asked."

"He will once Larena has seen everything," Sonya said.

"I wouldn't have had an opinion to give him," Larena hurried to tell Cara. "He knows that."

"Probably," the smaller Druid answered, and began washing while Sonya scraped the plates.

With the three of them helping, it didn't take long to clean up from the meal. Larena slipped away and hurried to the battlements. She wanted a few moments alone to think over everything that had happened since she had met Fallon. She had never been so confused by a man before, but then again, she had never met a man like Fallon MacLeod.

He filled her mind constantly, and her body burned for his touch. She had gone decades without him, but now, she couldn't go a few hours without needing him. What was wrong with her?

She looked over the moon-drenched land and the giant rocks that protruded from the ground to the cliffs and the sea below. Beyond the village, Cara had told her there was a forest where she had met Galen.

It was no wonder Fallon had longed to return. The place was majestic, just the sort of wild countryside in which a Highlander like Fallon would find refuge.

She took a deep breath and a whiff of orangewood filled her.

Fallon.

She turned her head and watched as he stepped from the shadows. Her heart raced, her blood heated . . . and her body hungered. She longed for him to reach out and touch her, to pull her into his arms and offer safety, as he had done in Edinburgh.

Instead, he stopped a few paces from her and gazed at her. "How are you faring?"

"Very well," she replied. "Everyone has been so kind, especially Cara and Sonya."

He nodded. "I'm glad to hear it."

Silence stretched between them. Larena grew agitated, not knowing what to say or what he wanted with her. She knew what she wanted, but she had told herself she couldn't have him anymore.

If he tried to kiss her, would she pull away? She didn't think she had the strength to tell him no, and she knew she didn't want to.

"You fit here," she said, to break the quiet. "You're a born leader."

"My father would be happy to hear you say that. I'm not so sure sometimes."

She heard the note of sorrow in his voice as he spoke of his father. She leaned her hip against the stones. "Your father would be very proud of you. Never doubt that, Fallon."

He narrowed his gaze as he studied her. "Why do you say that?"

"Because I see the way Lucan looks at you. There is pride in his gaze, and love. Whatever may have happened before, you've become the man you were supposed to be."

"If that were so, you wouldn't have nearly died."

He had spoken so softly she almost didn't hear his words. The impact of them slammed into her chest. "That wasn't your fault."

"I told you I would protect you." He shifted so that he stood in profile to her, the moon bathing one side of his face.

Larena studied him a moment as she fought the urge to touch him. "I chased after the wyrran, Fallon. There was always the threat that Deirdre would discover who I was. And never forget, I'm a Warrior."

He turned his head to look at her. "I know what you are, Larena. I have no doubt you can fight, but could you have held your own against two Warriors?"

"I don't know," she answered honestly. "It was my first time fighting a Warrior. Before it was always wyrran that crossed my path."

"Wyrran are different from Warriors."

"I've learned that the hard way," she murmured, and looked to the sliver of moon that hung in the sky.

He sighed and faced her. "Lucan trained Cara to fight against the wyrran. Maybe we should help you train against Warriors."

"If I had been able to use my powers—"

"Doona count on your powers," he interrupted. He took a step toward her and lowered his voice. "What happened should have taught you that lesson. Aye, your power to become invisible is a great boon, but there will be times you cannot use it. Wouldn't you rather be prepared?"

She knew what he said was true, but it was too difficult

to agree with him, to acknowledge that he was right. Yet, what else could she do? "Aye."

The heat of his gaze made her quiver. She fisted her hands to keep from reaching out to him.

Why not give in to the desire?

Because she feared the influence Fallon could have over her if her feelings for him continued to grow. And she knew they would. If she could only control her emotions as she did her goddess, she wouldn't worry about falling in love with him.

And if you already are?

She prayed she wasn't. There wasn't room in her life for love. Or a future.

Liar.

Larena turned and walked away from Fallon and his prying eyes. He saw too much, and she didn't want him seeing into her soul. If he did, he might see that she withheld important information from him.

And how she hated not telling him about the Scroll. She wanted to share it with him, to help him and the others create an imitation that would fool Deirdre. Her vow, however, prevented even that.

When she had repeated the words Robena told her, Larena had never dreamed she would be in a position like this. She had found it laughable that the vow had called for her to keep the information from everyone—including a husband if she chose to marry.

She had never thought to marry, much less find a man that made her think of the future. Fate, it seemed, had dealt her a hand she had to live with, whether she liked it or not.

Larena blinked back the tears that filled her eyes.

She hated the weakness those tears brought. She was a Warrior. She needed to remember that.

She stopped and leaned against the battlement wall, her fingers digging into the cool stone. She didn't know whether Fallon had followed her or not, and she hoped he hadn't. His presence jumbled her mind and put her emotions in chaos.

Fallon wasn't about to let her go that easily. Larena was his, and it was time she knew it. He lengthened his stride and caught up with her.

His hands itched to jerk her against him so he could feel all her luscious curves and taste the nectar of her mouth. Instead, he placed his hands on either side of hers and pressed against her back.

He breathed in her special scent as his heart thundered in his chest. Her decadent golden locks teased his skin as the wind lifted them from her back. She had left her hair unbound, and he wanted to plunge his fingers in its thick, silky length.

Fallon gave in and placed a kiss on the exposed skin of her neck. It was a quick kiss, but he heard her indrawn breath just the same. A smile pulled at his lips. She might play at being unaffected by his touch, but her body said otherwise.

He was a fool to tempt himself so, but when it came to Larena, he didn't think straight.

"Do you know how you make me burn?" he whispered near her ear.

A shudder racked her. Then, she turned to face him. Fallon didn't move his hands from the stones. He knew if he did, he would reach for her, and he wasn't going to give in. At least not tonight.

His gaze roamed over her face, from her gently arched eyebrows to her chin that lifted when she was being stubborn.

"Maybe it's your mouth," he continued, keeping his voice low. "The taste of your kisses is headier than any wine. Or maybe it's your hands. The feel of them on my body makes my blood boil. Maybe it's your legs and the way you wrap them around my waist as I thrust inside you. Maybe it's your body and the way my cock fills you."

He paused and leaned close to her. He let his mouth hover over the skin of her neck. Her pulse beat wildly and her chest rose and fell hurriedly.

"I thought you felt it, too, this thing that's between us." He blew against her skin before he lifted his head. "Was it bringing you here that changed things? If I had known you would become a different person, I would have kept us in Edinburgh."

Her lips parted and her gaze fell to his mouth. Fallon knew she wanted to kiss him, and God help him, he nearly gave in. But he wanted Larena to hunger for him with the same intensity that scalded him.

He didn't know what had happened, but she had distanced herself from him. Was it the ring and the Scroll within? Did she fear what he would do with that knowledge?

Anger replaced the desire heating his body. She had trusted him enough to let him bring her here, but he wasn't worthy of more than that?

Obviously, he was going to have to prove otherwise.

Fallon stepped back and dropped his hands. "Enjoy the evening," he said and walked away. It was the hardest thing he had ever done, but if he was going to claim Larena as his own, she had to accept the passion between them.

And he was going to see that she did. Even if it killed him.

TWENTY

Larena's legs crumpled as she watched Fallon walk away from her. She slid down the wall and rested her cheek against the stones to help cool her heated skin, skin that craved his hands, his lips.

Fallon brought out her passion so easily. Just a few words and the delicious timbre of his voice, and she ached to feel him. Her sex throbbed for the release she knew only Fallon could give her, but it was more than the physical pleasure he brought her. Being near him did something to her. She felt more like the woman she always thought she would be.

She had wanted to tell Fallon that he hadn't been wrong, she had felt what was between them. How could she not?

Her body trembled with the need to have him against her, on top of her . . . inside her. She might have thought she could detach herself from him, but her body wouldn't let her.

And her heart . . . her heart she would desperately try to keep safe, though she feared she might very well lose it to the laird of the MacLeods.

Larena rose on unsteady legs, the heat from her blood making her long to find Fallon. Instead, she took a deep, steadying breath and tried to slow her racing heart. The breeze stirred over her skin, reminding her of the warmth of Fallon's breath. Just thinking about it sent chills of anticipation down her back.

Denying the need for him seemed ludicrous. They had found a passion together that she had only ever dreamed of. Why not take what happiness she could find in his arms? Especially since she didn't know what the coming days would bring now that Deirdre knew of her existence and Fallon said an attack would come.

Larena spun around and hurried to her chamber. She had asked Cara to give her another one since she couldn't stay in Fallon's. Now she wished she hadn't.

Once inside her chamber, she stripped out of the borrowed gown and reached for the bowl of water.

Fallon shouldn't have been shocked to learn Larena had requested another chamber. But he was. It hurt more than he wanted to admit when he walked in and found no trace of her. It was true he rarely used his chamber, but he had looked forward to coming here all day knowing she would be sharing it with him.

Had he been wrong about the desire between them? It had been centuries since he had taken a woman, but he had thought he sensed in Larena something different, something that had always been unreachable, unattainable before.

He blamed it on Lucan and Cara. Lucan had given Fallon hope that he, too, could discover contentment in a life he had thought doomed.

Fallon gave up staring at the door waiting for Larena to come to him and fell back on the bed with a sigh.

He needed to face the fact that she didn't want him anymore. He wasn't sure what had happened, but he had an idea it had to do with her ring and the Scroll.

If it was, she would never tell him, but Fallon wasn't about to give up. He wouldn't take the Scroll from her or allow another to seize it. Unless she told him about it, however, he could never prove his intentions to her. It all came down to trust.

He had never had his worthiness questioned before. In his clan, it was a given he was honorable because of who he was. Yet, Larena had been alone most of her time as a Warrior. She learned early on not to trust anyone. So it was no wonder she didn't tell him about the Scroll.

Fallon wasn't sure how he would gain her faith, but he would do whatever was necessary. She was his to protect whether she knew it or not.

He shouldn't want her as he did. He knew nothing good could come of it. As much as he wanted to be the man his father had intended for him to be, Fallon had failed in every way possible. Everything he was doing now was to atone for the past, but nothing could make up for what he had done to his brothers.

And Larena? Did he dare to bring her close enough to him so that he could fail her too? He shouldn't want her to want him like he did. It would be much better for Larena if she found someone else. But the thought of another man touching her brought fury unlike any Fallon had ever experienced rushing through him.

He threw his arm over his eyes in an effort to find the sleep he knew wouldn't come. His mind was filled with Larena, Quinn, the Scroll, and the next attack by

Deirdre. He thought of the village and wondered if other Warriors and possibly Druids would come to the castle. He worried how he would feed them all, and most importantly, how he would protect them from Deirdre.

His head began to ache at the base of his skull. There were so many decisions to be made, so many lives to consider. It was one of the reasons he looked to Lucan as often as he did. Fallon might be the leader of their little group, but he wanted to hear what the others had to say and consider every angle.

He didn't know how long he lay there staring at the canopy of his bed. He knew before he smelled the lilies that Larena was in his chamber. His body recognized her in an instant, and the hunger that was never far filled him again.

Fallon sat up and found her standing at the side of his bed studying him. Her golden tresses fell around her naked body in wild disarray, hiding her lovely breasts from his gaze. He wanted to reach for her hand and pull her against him. But she had to come to him. She had to be the one to acknowledge the undeniable passion that pulsed between them.

"You didn't imagine it," she whispered. "There was something between us in Edinburgh. There is still something between us, Fallon."

"Yet you doona want there to be something, do you? What do you fear?"

She shook her head and licked her lips. "I don't want to want you, but I cannot stop the feelings inside me. I can't think when you're around me, but then when you're not, I find that I cannot think of anything but you."

Fallon was glad he had stripped out of his clothes. He didn't want to waste another moment without feeling his skin against her bare flesh. He fisted his hands in the covers and fought to keep his desire under control.

"You came to me," he murmured.

She smiled wryly. "My body, it seems, is yours to command."

"As mine is yours."

"Is it?" She leaned forward to run her finger along his leg.

He tried to swallow, but his mouth was dry. As her hand neared his crotch, his cock swelled, eager to feel her hands on him. "You know it is. I've been yours since I first saw you."

Her fingers cupped his balls and gently rolled them in her hand. "I'm not sure if I believe you."

Fallon was on fire. He couldn't form a coherent thought as her hands caressed him, building the flames that already threatened to burn him. He lay back on the bed, offering himself to her. "Tonight. I am yours."

"Good." Never releasing his balls, she climbed on the bed and straddled his legs. Her other hand claimed his cock as her fingers wrapped around his thickness. She stroked his length before gently rubbing her finger on the sensitive head. "Since the first time I saw you I've longed to touch you thus."

Fallon never wanted her to stop. His rod jumped when she ran a finger along the underside of his arousal. He was close to spilling, but he didn't care. Larena was with him and she was touching him. That was enough.

For now, at least.

Her hands knew just where to stroke, just how much pressure to apply to give him the most pleasure. Sweat beaded his skin and he clenched the covers in an effort to keep from grabbing her and throwing her down on the bed before he plunged inside her.

Fallon moaned and his eyes rolled back in his head when he felt her hair tickle his legs. Her warm breath washed over his cock, making it buck in her hands before it swelled even more.

And then he felt her mouth on him.

Fallon groaned and lifted his head so he could watch. Her soft lips fit around him as she took him deep in her mouth while her tongue stroked him. He had never felt anything so good, so wicked, in his very long life.

"Ah, sweet heaven, Larena, you're killing me," he murmured, his gaze fastened on her wet lips over his cock. His hands went to her head to grip her hair. He couldn't decide if he had reached for her to halt the exquisite pleasure or to make sure she never stopped.

But it became too much. He could sense his seed rushing up, and though the thought of spilling in her mouth left him dizzy, he wanted to feel her wet heat surround him.

Fallon lifted her and rolled her onto her back in one move. He leaned over her, his hands braced on either side of her head. Their gazes locked and held.

"You have no idea what you do to me," he said. He had to make her understand how important she was to him.

She smiled wickedly then. "I like the taste of you. I want more."

He moaned and clenched his teeth together. She was going to kill him.

Fallon decided she needed some payback and leaned down to take a nipple in his mouth. He stopped just short of his lips touching the tiny bud and flicked his tongue over it. He chuckled when her nipple hardened.

"Fallon," she said with a little cry.

He didn't keep her waiting. He covered the nipple with his lips and let his tongue twirl around the bud before nipping it with his teeth.

Larena's back arched and her nails scoured his back. He rubbed his cock against her sex and felt the moisture there, the readiness that told him she craved his touch.

"Shall I taste you as you've tasted me?" he asked against her breast as he kissed from one nipple to the other.

She tossed her head back and forth. "Please, nay. I need you. Now."

Just as he guided the head of his arousal to her entrance, she pushed at his shoulders until he rolled onto his back. He stared up at her with a smile as she once more straddled his hips and held herself over his cock.

He trembled with the aching need to have her, to bury himself in her heat and thrust inside her. But he waited. She tortured him by holding his rod in her hand, her sex hovering over him, giving him just the barest touch of her wet heat.

Fallon growled and tried to think of anything but the woman above him so he wouldn't peak. But she demanded all of his attention, and he couldn't deny her anything.

Inch by agonizing inch she lowered herself onto his straining cock. Fallon lifted his hips to bury himself deeper, but Larena kept in control. She was driving him daft with need.

And he loved every moment of it.

When she took all of him, he reached for her breasts and thumbed her nipples as she began to rock against him. With her mouth parted and her head thrown back as she rode him, she was the most beautiful sight he had ever seen.

Fallon never wanted to forget this moment, never wanted to forget the feelings that Larena brought out in him.

He pinched her nipples and rolled them between his fingers. She cried out, her hips moving faster as her tempo increased. He was so close to climaxing, but he wasn't ready for it to end. He was never ready for it to end when she was in his arms.

Larena's nails dug into his chest. She leaned forward and kissed him, rubbing her nipples against him. Fallon gripped her hips and ground against her, eager to bury himself deeper, always deeper, harder. She whispered his name and straightened as her hips once more rocked against him.

He moved his hand between their bodies and found her clitoris with his thumb. He stroked the swollen nub faster with each cry from her beautiful mouth until she was shaking with need.

She screamed his name and jerked. The first pull of her climax around his cock brought his own orgasm. Fallon held on to Larena as he surrendered himself to her.

His arms cradled her as she slumped against him, their bodies slick with sweat from their lovemaking. He could feel the thudding of her heart and realized it matched his beat for beat.

When he was at last able to open his eyes he looked into a face he wanted to see beside him every day for the rest of his life. The realization should have shocked him, but it didn't. His body had known Larena from the first. It just took his brain longer to catch up.

"Oh my," she murmured drowsily.

"Sleep. I've got you." He tucked her against him and kissed her forehead.

For once, everything was as it should be.

Deirdre wanted to kill the three Warriors who had dared to repeatedly torture Quinn, but she needed them. Yet, she could—and would—make an example out of them.

She had called the wyrran and other Warriors into the cavern that served as her great hall. The mountain had done a magnificent job of opening such a space for her, but then again, the stones couldn't ignore a command from her. They were connected, she and the stones, in ways that others couldn't understand.

Deirdre looked at the three Warriors behind her. They were held by magical chains from the floor and ceiling with their arms and legs braced apart. They had been stripped of their clothes as well.

One of the Warriors turned his head to look at her over his shoulder. She saw fear in his eyes, just as she wanted. They didn't know what she would do to them, and it was time they learned.

"These three have decided to take matters into their own hands with a prisoner." Her voice carried to all corners of the cavern.

She turned to the crowd. "I won't tolerate such impudence. You will obey me at all times in everything. Or you will feel my wrath."

Deirdre drew in a long breath and heard the crowd gasp as the strands of her white hair that dragged the floor rose around her and extended to a greater length. She glanced at the locks that had once been a striking golden color; as her power had grown, the color had disappeared.

Her hair, and her eyes, had a way of making people cower in fear. She smiled and faced the three Warriors.

"Never again will you disobey me. If you do, I will kill you. Do you understand?"

"Aye, mistress," the three replied.

Deirdre let her hair fly. Her hair was a weapon that could be used in many different ways. This time, she would use it as a whip, though she had killed with the strands before, as she would again.

Over and over her hair slashed the backs of the Warriors until their skin was shredded and blood dripped down their legs to the floor. Only then was her anger appeased.

Her hair fell lifeless to her ankles, no longer a weapon. She turned to a group of wyrran. "Leave them until they are healed. Then throw them into the Pit for a week."

The Pit was where she put people she wanted to break quickly, or die gruesomely. Only the strong survived in the Pit, but even then they didn't last long. Most realized it was futile to fight her and aligned with her or she had them killed.

Without another word, she strode from the great hall to the stairs that wound through the mountain. She had sent Quinn to her chamber to be bathed, and with merely a touch, she had ensured he slept through it all.

The door to her chamber opened as she neared it. As always, the wyrran sensed her presence. She glanced at James, who was still held by the rocks as his punishment as she walked into her bedchamber. She moved to the bed and looked down at Quinn. The dirt and grime from the dungeons no longer coated his skin and hair.

The material that had once been his breeches had been removed and a blanket now covered his lower body. Deirdre threw back the blanket and looked at the man who would share her bed, the Warrior who would give her the child she longed to have and who would fulfill the prophecy told to her long ago.

She had never wanted anything as desperately as she wanted Quinn, not even the power she killed for. There was something about Quinn that drew her. Nothing had ever been denied her, and Quinn wouldn't be an exception. He might not comprehend it now, but she could offer him the world and beyond.

Deirdre caressed his freshly shaven jaw then down his chest, which rippled with muscles, to his taut stomach and lean hips. Then she wrapped her fingers around his flaccid rod.

She could use her magic to make him want her, but she wouldn't have need of that. Once she showed Quinn the pleasures that awaited him in her bed, he would eagerly come to her on his own. Besides, if she used her magic, he could not impregnate her with their child, and she couldn't chance that, not after finally having him in her grasp once more.

"Sleep, my king," she whispered, and kissed his

cheek. "Your body needs to heal properly, and it won't do that if you wake to find yourself in my bed."

Deirdre continued to stroke his cock until it hardened. She smiled. This was just the beginning, and even though she wanted to climb atop him and lower herself onto his arousal, she wanted him awake when they joined. Awake, and willing.

"Do you like my touch? I know what brings you pleasure, Quinn. In my bed, you will experience delights beyond your imagining."

She kissed his chest and pumped her fist up and down his hard length. His hips rose to meet hers and his lips parted on a low groan full of need and desire.

The MacLeod brothers had kept themselves apart from other humans, and in doing so, they had denied themselves the physical release their bodies demanded and the insatiable appetites they experienced as Warriors.

His rod grew longer, thicker. She leaned over him and took him in her mouth. His hips rose off the bed, pushing himself farther into her mouth. She took all of him, moaning as he began to thrust faster. He tasted divine. She used her tongue to give him more pleasure and sucked him deep. All too soon his body jerked and his seed filled her mouth.

Deirdre ground her hips against his thigh and kissed up and down his cock. He was magnificent, and she couldn't wait to feel him inside her. It was too bad he was asleep.

Her need spiked as she gazed at his rod resting on his stomach now, still semihard from her caresses. She could give herself pleasure, but she needed something more.

Deirdre rose from the bed. "Find William," she ordered a wyrran. "Send him to the bathing chamber where I'll be awaiting him."

The wyrran scurried off to carry out her command. Deirdre undressed and moved to lie beside Quinn. Her body trembled to take his, to have his hard length on top of her. Yet she had to be strong. If she took him now, everything she had done, all the power she had accumulated, would have been for naught.

It infuriated her that she, the most powerful Druid ever, couldn't make the one man she wanted need her. This was the lone instance where her magic was useless.

In order for her to have the child that had been foreseen, no magic could be used on Quinn or the child would never be conceived.

Deirdre had thought breaking Quinn would be easy. She should have known he would fight her. But that was one of the reasons she had chosen him as her king.

The rage inside Quinn couldn't be denied for long. It was only a matter of time before he was hers. Lucan and Fallon could try all they wanted to turn Quinn away from her, but they would fail.

Then, all three MacLeods would be hers.

TWENTY-ONE

It was hours before dawn when Fallon woke to find Larena still in his arms. He watched her sleep for a moment before he allowed his hands to caress her supple body. Her body was lithe and her muscles toned, but she had the curves of a woman that could make a man hard just thinking about them.

He cupped a breast and ran his thumb over her nipple. The tiny bud hardened and strained toward him, as if seeking more of the pleasure he wanted to give her.

To his surprise, her lips moved against his neck, licking him. The feel of her mouth against him sent a bolt of desire straight to his cock. It thickened, straining to be inside her once more.

Larena moaned and reached between them to wrap her hands around his arousal. "Is this what you thought I came for?"

Fallon choked on a laugh. "Please tell me it is. Before you, it had been three hundred years since I had touched a woman. I canna think I can go another moment without taking you."

"Oh, my." She looked up at him. "Three hundred years? And I thought my eighty years was a long time."

"If you didn't come to take advantage of me, then why did you come? Naked, I might add?"

The spark in her smoky-blue eyes made his stomach clench. He enjoyed watching her, got pleasure from each mood that crossed her face. She was so expressive and alluring that he ached to claim her.

"Aye, I'm naked, my handsome laird. Should I cover up?"

"Don't you dare," he said, and held her when she began to pull out of his arms. "I'd love it if you never wore another stitch of clothing for the rest of your life."

Larena's laugh was beautiful as it filled the chamber. "My entire life? That could be a very, very long time, I might add. How about I don't wear anything for the rest of this night?"

"Oh, you'll wear something all right."

"Really?" she asked, raising her brows. "And what might that be?"

"Me." He slanted his mouth over hers and slipped his tongue between her lips. He loved the way she kissed and how she clung to him.

She ended the kiss and placed her finger on his lips. "I enjoyed pleasuring you earlier. May I do it again? I want to explore your body, Fallon. I want to learn what pleases you and gives you pleasure."

"The answer is you. You give me pleasure." None of the women he had ever taken to his bed had said those words to him. They liked how he pleased them, but not a one had ever asked how to satisfy him.

Her hands ran over his shoulders to his neck before her fingers intertwined in his hair. She tugged on his hair and ran her nails lightly over his scalp. It sent chills racing over his skin, but it also reminded him that he wore his hair longer than fashionable.

"I suppose I need to have my hair trimmed."

"Don't you dare," she whispered. "I love it just as it is. And I love this."

Fallon placed his hand over hers, which held the boar's head of his torc. "Do you?"

"It is from an era of a time long ago, but one you belong in. You are the essence of the Highlands, Fallon. Everything about you lets people know you're a true Highlander."

His fingers tightened on hers. He didn't know if she understood the significance of what she had said, but he did. She had helped give him back a piece of himself that had gone missing when Deirdre unbound their god. She helped him remember who he really was.

A Highlander.

Fallon rolled her onto her back as he kissed her deeply, showing her without words how much he wanted her with him. His lips left hers and traveled down her neck to her breasts. He ran his tongue around a nipple before softly nipping it.

She cried out, but Fallon wasn't nearly done. He moved to her other breast and flicked his tongue over the already hard bud before he closed his mouth over it and suckled deep.

He ached to be inside her, but he wasn't done pleasuring her. Fallon moved down her stomach, stopping along the way to kiss her navel and nip at her hips. He moved his arms beneath her hips to hold her steady before he bent and licked her sex.

Larena had never felt something so wonderous before. The moan was locked in her throat, her body unable to move as Fallon continued to move his tongue over her sensitive flesh. With his hands holding firmly on to her hips, she could do nothing but pray he continued the unbelievable pleasure.

She cried out when his tongue began to tease her clitoris. She could feel herself swell as her need grew. Her hands gripped his forearms and her hips rocked against him.

As if he knew she was close to peaking, Fallon took her clitoris between his lips and sucked. Her body bucked and she cried out his name as she convulsed with her orgasm, leaving her panting and her body still throbbing.

He continued to stroke her with his tongue until the last of the tremors left her. Then he rose up and flipped her onto her stomach. He lifted her hips into the air, and in one thrust, he seated himself inside her.

"Fallon," she whispered as her fingers clawed the linens.

Fallon knew just how she felt. He wanted to prolong their lovemaking, but he couldn't wait any longer. Fallon began to pump his hips slowly at first, then faster as her moans grew louder.

He loved to watch Larena as she peaked. And to know he had given her such pleasure made him swell with pride. He pulled out of her until just the tip of him was inside. Then he plunged inside her once more.

His need built fast as it always did when he was with Larena. He was able to keep it at bay while pleasuring her. It wasn't until he felt her body tighten around him in another orgasm that he lost control.

"Larena!" he yelled as his seed burst from him with a climax that left him dizzy.

The orgasm left him weak and sated. As he rolled them to the side, still deep inside her, he knew he would never grow tired of Larena's body and the satisfaction she brought him.

Larena woke in the warm embrace of Fallon's arms, their legs entwined and his face turned toward hers. Dawn was just breaking, giving off a faint light in the chamber through the open window so she could see his face. She couldn't remember the last time she had slept so soundly or had been so content. It was all because of Fallon, she knew.

Fallon, who had shown her just how much he desired her. She had felt it in his kiss, seen it in his eyes. He had held nothing back.

And last night, neither had she.

For once, she wanted to be the girl who had found a man who pleased her and made her feel like the woman she was. Fallon had given her all that and more.

A tear leaked from the corner of her eye and trailed over her cheek to land on Fallon's arm, which was cradling her head. She wished she could stay with him, just as they were, forever. But she knew better than anyone that nothing lasted forever.

Larena slowly pulled out of his arms and rose from the bed. More tears threatened, and she didn't want him to wake and find her crying for a future that could never be.

What made it worse was that she feared she had already fallen in love with Fallon. If he were to wake in that instant and ask her for the Scroll, she would give it to him and pray he didn't hate her for keeping it from him.

She reached out to stroke his face, but stopped before she did. He might wake and pull her back into his arms. She wouldn't be able to resist him then. She had never been able to resist him.

Take him. Take the future he offers.

And if he ever discovered what the ring on her finger was? He would hate her, and he would have a right to, despite the oaths she had taken. Fallon valued family and honesty. She could give him neither.

All they could share was the passion that neither could deny. She hoped it was enough because that was all she could allow herself to give him.

Larena took a step away from him toward the window she had come through the night before. She called forth her goddess then made herself invisible. For long moments she stared at him, half hoping he would wake.

When she could stand it no more, Larena climbed out the window. She returned to her chamber and transformed before she curled up on her bed and let flow the tears she had been holding back.

With the unbinding of her goddess, she had been surprised, scared, and more than a little excited. She hadn't comprehended the danger that lay ahead of her. Or the loneliness that would be her constant companion.

It was only after Robena's death and her father's murder soon afterward that Larena came to understand what her future held for her. She could trust no one.

Robena hadn't cared that Larena was a female Warrior. For all the Druid had known, there could have been other females. Nay, what Robena worried about was the Scroll. She had drilled that concern into Larena until it was all she thought about.

Larena wanted to take off the ring and toss it into a corner to forget it ever existed. She would throw it in the sea if she knew Deirdre would never find it. But Deirdre had a way of learning things that she should never know. Larena couldn't take that chance no matter how her heart ached.

Fallon pretended to be asleep until he could no longer smell Larena's scent. Only then did he open his eyes. He had hoped she would stay until morning so they could make love again.

Something was wrong. Larena had said nothing, but he had felt her eyes on him as she stood by the bed, could sense her longing. What had she been thinking?

She was used to being on her own and doing what she wanted. He didn't begrudge her that, but he wished he could wake up and find her still in his arms.

Fallon sat up and scrubbed his hands over his face. He wanted to think he had made some headway with Larena last night, but he wasn't so sure. She liked his touch, that much he knew. But was it enough to keep her by his side? Did he dare try?

As much as he wanted an answer, there wasn't one. He blew out a long breath before he rose from the bed and readied himself for the day. After dressing, he opened his door to find Lucan standing there with his fist raised to knock.

"Everything all right?" Fallon asked his brother.

Lucan sighed and glanced down the hallway. "Can I have a moment?"

Fallon stepped aside to allow him in. He shut the door behind Lucan and leaned against it to wait for his brother to speak.

Lucan stopped in the middle of the chamber and faced him. "Cara is worried about Larena."

"What about?"

"I wish I knew," Lucan said, frustration making his jaw clench. "It's all Cara could talk about last night. She kept saying Larena seemed agitated."

"I'm sure she is. She was attacked and almost died. She woke to find herself in a strange place with people she didn't know. She worried about how the Warriors would accept her. Larena has spent much of her hundred years by herself. And she doesn't trust anyone."

Lucan rolled his eyes. "That's what I told Cara, but you know my wife. She likes to fix things."

Fallon grinned. "She fixed you."

"Aye, she did."

"Tell Cara that Larena is going to need some time. I know how difficult it was for us to live with a god, but I cannot imagine what Larena has gone through as a female."

Lucan nodded and glanced at the bed. "Have you told her you know what the ring is, what she guards?"

"Nay, and I doona intend to. Leave it at that, Lucan." Fallon straightened from the door. "If she doesna want to tell me, then so be it. She must have her reasons."

"What if she's keeping something else from you?"

Fallon briefly closed his eyes and inhaled deeply. "She might be. She doesn't trust me."

Lucan's gaze narrowed as he studied Fallon. "You care a great deal for her, don't you?"

"My feelings for her are strong, I'll admit. I want her in my life. I cannot explain what it does to me to have her by my side."

Lucan moved to stand in front of him. "I'm glad you've found your woman, brother. You stood by Cara, so I will stand by Larena."

Fallon didn't miss the doubt in Lucan's eyes. "I know I haven't been much of a brother these last three hundred years. I've let you shoulder too much, and for that I can never apologize enough."

"Don't," Lucan said. "We've all had to deal with what happened to us."

"If I hadna been drunk, we might have been able to help Quinn. I'll always blame myself for that."

Lucan put his hand on Fallon's shoulder and squeezed. "You're a good man, and a fine leader. You've turned your back on the wine and taken charge of things. I trust your judgment, Fallon."

"Then trust me on Larena. I need her, Lucan."

Lucan held his gaze for a moment before he dropped his hand to his side and nodded. "I'll do as you ask, brother."

"Thank you."

"Come then. Let us eat," Lucan said, and strode to the door.

Fallon glanced at the bed and the rumpled sheets. An image of Larena on top of him, her head thrown back, flashed in his mind. He was determined to have her in his bed every night, even if he had to seduce her each time.

Sonya had already put out the food by the time he and Lucan walked into the great hall. Cara came out of the kitchen with three loaves of bread in her arms, a smile on her face, and her eyes twinkling as she gazed at her husband.

Galen strode into the hall from the bailey rubbing his hands together. He sat at the table and sniffed the air. "Warm bread and milk. I've been craving it all night."

Cara laughed and set an entire loaf in front of Galen. "Make it last longer and you won't have to raid the kitchen during the night."

He looked up at her and grinned. "I cannot help when I'm hungry."

Lucan and Sonya laughed as Galen broke apart the bread then quickly dropped it when it burned his fingers. Ribbons of heat curled from the two halves to disappear above him.

Hayden and Logan came in from the kitchen and filled their trenchers before taking their seats. Conversation filled the hall, bringing back many memories for Fallon.

He watched all of it with interest. When he and his brothers had first returned to find the castle in ruins, he had never thought it would be filled with laughter again.

It had taken nearly three hundred years and a coming war with Deirdre, but the stones were being put aright and people once more filled the castle. They were his family now, his responsibility.

Fallon had known what his role would be the moment he set aside the wine and began to make decisions. It still terrified him that he would make the wrong choice. Yet, no matter what, they followed him.

Cara set two slices of bread on his trencher and kissed his cheek. "I'm so glad you're back. It wasn't the same without you around."

He patted his sister-in-law's hand and smiled up at her. Cara had a good heart. She opened it to whoever needed her love and attention. There were few people like her in the world.

"Thank you."

Her smile faded and her dark eyes held his. "Trust yourself and your judgment, Fallon. We'll get Quinn back."

He forced a grin. She had always had the ability to read him and his brothers accurately, too accurately at times. "Of course we will."

"Now eat. You've a long day ahead of you."

Fallon waited until Cara had moved on before he lifted his gaze to Lucan. His brother's sea-green eyes were somber, but determined. Lucan had always had his back, and that hadn't changed.

"We go to the village today," Fallon said. "I know I wanted the fourth tower finished, but it can wait. Galen, you and Logan come with us."

Galen nodded and stuffed more bread into his mouth. "Are you expecting trouble?"

"Nay, but I'd rather be prepared."

Ramsey descended the stairs and took his seat. "Would you rather Hayden and I go as well?"

"I doona want to leave Cara and Sonya alone."

Sonya rolled her eyes and snorted. "You won't be far."

"I'll come."

Fallon's heart missed a beat at the familiar voice. He turned his gaze to the stairs to see Larena. Her hair was tied at the base of her neck with a lavender ribbon that matched her gown. He liked her in the simple dress. She wore it with as much ease and confidence as she had worn the fashionable dresses at court.

Larena had learned to adapt in ways Fallon and his brothers hadn't. They could take a lesson from her.

"If that would be all right," Larena said into the silence.

Fallon licked his lips and made himself stay seated instead of going to her and pulling her into his arms for a kiss. "That would be fine."

Larena descended the rest of the stairs and walked to the table. She once again took the seat between Cara and Galen. Fallon wanted her beside him in the seat that was saved for Quinn.

He had all the time in the world to woo her as he became the man he wanted to be. Fallon didn't like that it might take many years, but he was determined to have her in the end no matter how long it took.

It troubled Fallon that she refused to look at him as she ate. She kept her attention on Cara and Sonya. Occasionally, she would glance at Galen or Ramsey and speak.

Fallon had long since finished his meal and was talking to Lucan about building a few cottages closer to the castle when Larena looked up. Fallon met her gaze and saw the uncertainty in her smoky-blue eyes.

But doubt for what, he didn't know.

TWENTY-TWO

Fallon walked into the village with Lucan on his right and Larena on his left. Behind him were Galen and Logan. He stared at the destruction before him and swore he could hear the screams of the innocents who had died still ringing in the breeze.

The village had been so alive not that long ago, but Deirdre had seen it crushed in her efforts to find Cara. Now, only ghosts lingered in the empty streets and burned-down cottages.

At the far end of the village, tucked away and nestled in a grove of oak trees, was the nunnery in which Cara had been raised. Orphaned and unwanted children had found a home there with the nuns.

Fallon had often gone to the towers to watch them running through the village, their mirth reaching even the castle. There was nothing like the sound of a child's laughter. It was pure and simple and contagious, hitting a person square in the chest.

The village was eerily quiet now, and that disturbed Fallon more than the fire marks on the castle walls.

"Deirdre did this?" Larena asked when she came upon the first burned cottage. She placed her hand on the door hanging by one hinge.

Fallon nodded. "They killed everyone."

"Just as they did your clan," she murmured, and turned her gaze to him.

Fallon looked at her and saw the depth of her feeling. She hadn't known the villagers, but she felt the pain of their loss. The memories of his clan's murder didn't sting as badly as they used to.

He couldn't change what had happened to his family and clan, but he could make sure Deirdre didn't kill any more innocents.

Galen kicked at the remains of a door that lay in their path. "I wish I had been here for the first attack. Seeing this makes me want to find the Warriors and wyrran responsible and rip out their throats."

Lucan sighed. "If we had known Deirdre had sent her army, we might have saved some of them. As it was, we were trying to save Cara."

"Nay," Logan said, his usually cheerful voice hard and cold as ice. "It doesna matter how you try. You can't save them. Not when Deirdre is involved."

Fallon and the others turned to face the Warrior. Logan's customary smile and bright eyes were gone. He stared into the empty village as if he were seeing an image from his past, a past full of death and betrayal.

Fallon knew all the Warriors in his castle had a past. Some spoke of them, some didn't. Logan was one that kept his past to himself, but what Fallon was seeing now worried him more than Hayden's hatred for the *droughs*.

"Logan?" Fallon said carefully.

The young Warrior jerked as if slapped. His lips pulled back into a wide smile that didn't quite reach his eyes. "I think I want the first cottage. The thought of sharing a chamber with Hayden makes me gag."

Everyone chuckled at the jest, but Fallon knew something dark—and dangerous—lurked inside of Logan. Fallon recognized what Logan was doing. Instead of drowning in wine as Fallon had done, Logan teased and joked his way through the day. It was Logan's escape from his past.

Fallon was determined to pay closer attention to the young Warrior. He hadn't asked what had happened to Logan's family, and even if he did, he wasn't sure Logan would give him the truth. Maybe Hayden or Ramsey knew something. Fallon made a mental note to talk to the two Warriors as soon as he could.

Lucan nudged Fallon as Logan moved past them into the village.

"I know," Fallon said, answering his brother's unspoken question. "We need to keep an eye on him."

Galen stepped in front of Fallon, his gaze on Logan's retreating back. "We've all got pasts we deal with. They're like spirits that never leave. Whatever haunts Logan is his own to carry."

"Maybe so," Fallon said, "but I want him to know we're here for him."

Galen turned his head to Fallon. "Logan knows that. He wouldn't have come if he didn't. Right now, he wants what the rest of us want. He wants to fight Deirdre."

Lucan grunted. "I'm sure he'll get his wish again soon enough."

"Aye," Fallon said, and looked at Larena. "Deirdre willna have given up on Larena that easily."

"Not after having lost Cara," Lucan said. "Though I'm not sure she's given up on having Cara either."

Galen shook his head. "Deirdre doesn't give up on anything. If she wants something, she'll try again and again until she acquires it."

"Then we have to make sure she doesn't capture me or Cara," Larena said, before following Logan through the village.

Fallon grinned at her confidence.

Galen chuckled. "I don't think Deirdre would know what to do with Larena if she did capture her."

"I don't intend to find out," Fallon said. "Let's get to work."

They moved from cottage to cottage inspecting the damages and considering what would need to be rebuilt and replaced. Larena, Logan, and Galen began to haul out debris and pile it in the center of the village to be burned.

Of the twenty cottages, only five were salvageable. The others were beyond repair, just as the nunnery was. Fallon gauged the distance from the village to the castle.

It would be a good sprint to reach the castle gates, and that was if they were Warriors. The villagers had been afraid of MacLeod Castle and that was why the community had been moved so far away.

"It needs to be closer," Fallon murmured to himself.

Lucan came to stand beside him and dusted off his hands that were black from hauling burned wood. "I agree. The five cottages that can be restored are the farthest away from the nunnery, which helps us."

"Aye," Fallon said. "How many do you think we should build?"

Lucan looked over his shoulder at the remaining cottages. "Two. Maybe three. We can always build more if we need it."

Fallon didn't want to waste their time and resources building cottages that might not be used, but he also wanted to have them ready if they were needed.

Logan, Galen, and Larena walked up while passing a skin of water among them. Their faces and clothes were smeared black, and strands of Larena's hair had come free and stuck to the side of her face.

"What did you decide?" Galen asked.

Fallon pointed to the five cottages. "These five are the only ones worth rebuilding. We'll start on them first as we finish cleaning the village."

"And after?" Logan asked.

"Lucan has suggested two or three more cottages be built."

Logan wiped the hair that stuck to his sweat-stained face and looked about him. "Three would be good, but I think I might build a fourth. Also, when we're building, we should think about ways to secure the cottages."

Fallon raised a brow. "Secure?"

"Aye." Logan shifted his stance. "I agree that the Warriors should live in the cottages. We all know that Deirdre likes to attack quickly, and we saw how the traps we set in the castle slowed the wyrran to give us time to prepare."

"That's a good idea," Lucan said. "I hadn't thought of securing the cottages."

Fallon agreed. "Logan, can you come up with some ideas?"

Logan nodded. "I'll see to it."

"Good. Let's burn the rubble."

Lucan clapped his hands together. "I'll start gathering the wood I need to make the furniture."

"And I can begin reconstruction of the five cottages," Galen said as he accepted the water from Larena.

Fallon exhaled and nodded. It was all coming together. At least he would have something to occupy him as he waited for the fake Scroll to be finished and he could free Quinn.

He turned his head to look at Larena. She wiped the sweat from her brow with the back of her hand and laughed at something Lucan said.

After seeing her at court, he hadn't expected her to want to get dirty. But then again, she was a Highlander. He grinned. He couldn't help it. He liked having her in his life. She brought the sunshine with her. And, there was something about her presence that made him want to be a better man, a man his father would have been proud of.

Suddenly, her smile vanished and her eyes grew round. Fallon whirled around to find the winged Warrior landing several paces away from them.

In an instant, Galen and Logan had shifted into Warrior form. Fallon held up his hand to stop them. He wanted to know what the Warrior wanted before they attacked.

The dark blue Warrior looked at each one of them before he focused his gaze on Fallon. "Fallon MacLeod, I've come with a message from Deirdre."

"Who are you?" Fallon asked. The more he could find out about the Warrior the better. His father had always told him to know his enemies better than he knew his friends.

The Warrior folded his wings against his back. The tips could still be seen over his head and beside his legs and looked to be made of something that resembled leather. They were the same dark blue as his skin. "I'm Broc."

Fallon eyed the wings. "What is her message?"

Broc cocked an eyebrow, but refused to answer. After a moment he said, "Quinn is well."

"How can we believe you?" Lucan asked.

Broc shifted his gaze. "Ah, Lucan MacLeod. The middle brother. I know Quinn is well because I saw him before I came here."

"What does Deirdre want?" Fallon repeated. "Surely she didn't send you here for just a message when she knows we can kill you."

Broc smiled, flashing his long white fangs. "You can try to kill me. Many have. None have succeeded."

"I'll succeed," Galen said and started for him.

Fallon jumped in front of Galen and shoved him back. Fallon ignored Galen's roar of anger as the green Warrior flexed his claws. "Leave it for now," Fallon whispered.

Once Galen had fallen back, Fallon turned to Broc. "Is there more to the message?"

"Aye," Broc said. "She knows you will come for Quinn. It was why she captured him. She wants you to know that it is her wish to have all three MacLeods under her control once more."

"Never," Lucan ground out between clenched teeth.

Fallon fisted his hands as rage surged through him. He could feel the tingle of his skin and knew he was transforming, but didn't care. "We *will* come for Quinn. We *will* free him. And we *will* kill Deirdre in the process."

Broc shrugged. "It's been a long time since you were in her mountain. Do you forget the control she has over the stones? There is no way you can come into that mountain and free your brother."

"What about a trade?" Larena asked.

When Broc's gaze slid to her, Fallon bared his fangs and growled. Broc's knowing grin sent Fallon's rage soaring. The need to kill him and defend Larena made Fallon take a step toward Broc.

"I'm glad to see you have healed," Broc said.

Larena put her hand on Fallon's arm to halt him. "No thanks to your friend."

Fallon didn't want her talking to Broc. He didn't want her anywhere near the Warrior, but Fallon wasn't fool enough to tell her to leave. Larena was a Warrior, and Fallon needed to remember she had powers and could take care of herself.

Still, his protective instincts couldn't be contained.

"Larena," he growled in warning. There was only so much more he was going to listen to before he attacked Broc.

She glanced at him, her smoky-blue eyes silently beseeching him to trust her.

It was on the tip of his tongue to tell her he would trust her once she began trusting him. But he kept silent.

Broc grunted at her words, drawing Fallon's attention back to him. "James is no friend of mine. Deirdre was quite upset at what he did to you. If she didn't need her Warriors so desperately, I do believe she would have killed him."

Larena was thankful that Fallon had allowed her to speak to Broc. She could tell by Fallon's tense body and the way his skin changed from normal to black every heartbeat or so that he battled his urge to release his god and attack.

Before she could ask Broc more, the winged Warrior turned his attention back to Fallon. "Attacks will begin soon."

Fallon glared at Broc. "How do I know you speak the truth?"

"You don't, but you'll find out soon enough. Wyrran are on their way. Deirdre intends to keep you occupied here instead of forming a plan to free your brother."

Larena's stomach clenched in dread, and she looked between Lucan and Fallon. Lucan had already transformed, as had the others, and they stood waiting for Fallon to give the order to attack.

Fallon snorted and shook his head. "If that is Deirdre's plan then she needs time with Quinn."

"You've the right of it. She has plans for your brother," Broc said.

"Just whose side are you on?"

Broc smiled. "That is a question, isn't it?"

Then Broc's grin faded as he lifted his face to sniff the wind. In a blink, he leaped into the air, his wings spread wide. He flipped over backward and landed on the roof of a cottage, his fangs bared.

Larena saw the dagger sail through the air toward the spot Broc had just been. She ducked and felt arms come around her and jerk her against a hard body before being pulled to the ground.

Fallon.

When she raised her head it was to find a man with long black hair, his skin, fangs, and eyes the color of darkest brown.

"Shite," Fallon bellowed as he gained his feet. "Who the hell are you?" he demanded of the new arrival.

The newcomer turned his gaze from Broc to Fallon. "I'm Camdyn MacKenna."

TWENTY-THREE

Larena regained her feet, her blood pounding in her ears. She was startled to find her claws had extended without her knowing it. Her emotions were in a whirlwind, and if she didn't get control soon, she would be no help to the others when the wyrran attacked.

Unlike Fallon, Larena believed Broc. Why the winged Warrior would give them that information she didn't know, and didn't care. It gave them an advantage. And they needed every advantage they could get.

Broc didn't move from the rooftop. His gaze was narrowed on Camdyn, his growl of rage reverberating around them. Fallon and the others had their attention on Camdyn as well. It was the perfect time to ask Broc some questions she wanted answered.

Larena backed away from the men. Once she was clear, she ran and jumped onto the roof. Broc whirled around to face her, his fangs bared.

"What do you want?" he demanded.

"I want to know why you didn't attack me in Edinburgh."

He shrugged. "Why does it matter?"

"There were two of you. You could have easily overpowered me."

"My duties were to deliver James to the castle so he could subdue you. After that, I was to take you to Deirdre. My orders didn't include attacking you."

Larena studied Broc. His navy skin was so dark it appeared almost black. There was something in the way the Warrior spoke that made her realize he thought out each word carefully before he replied to anything.

"Did you know James had the blood on his claws before you arrived in Edinburgh?"

Broc's navy gaze sparked with anger. "Nay. Though it doesna surprise me. James thought the idea of a female Warrior ludicrous. He believed you would be weak and unable to fight. When you bested him, he couldn't stand it."

It was the reaction Larena always expected from Warriors. "And the *drough* blood? How did you know its reaction to us?"

"You've never been in Deirdre's prison or you wouldna be asking me that. Deirdre has ways of torturing that you've never dreamed of. She can stretch out pain for months and years until you're begging for death."

Larena swallowed at the cold loathing in his voice. She, like Fallon, wondered just whose side Broc was on. It was obvious he hated Deirdre, but why then didn't he escape from her as the others had? "And once James had *subdued* me? Why didn't you take me to Deirdre?"

Broc sighed loudly. He kept his attention on the men below him, but he glanced at her often. "I knew from the way your wound bled and the pain you were in that you needed help immediately. I can fly fast, but not fast enough to get you to Deirdre before you died."

"And you knew Fallon could?"

"Aye."

He said no more, and Larena had to bite back her groan of anger. She opened her mouth to ask another question when the first wyrran came out of nowhere to land beside her on the roof.

Larena didn't hesitate to transform. She was used to fighting naked while she was invisible, but there wasn't time for that. And her skirts hampered her.

Fallon shouted her name, but she couldn't answer him as a second wyrran joined the first. Larena jumped back to dodge claws as the second bit her leg.

Larena let out a shriek of fury and sank her claws into the chest of the wyrran that had bitten her and ripped out its heart. The first wyrran gave an ear-piercing scream, but before she could kill it, Broc ripped its head off.

"Stay vigilant," he urged before he flew away.

Larena wasn't able to watch him as more wyrran poured into the village. She took a step to jump from the roof and heard the distinctive sound of wood cracking. In the next heartbeat, she was falling through the roof to land with a thud on the ground.

Her head jerked up as the door was kicked in and Fallon came into view. Dust swirled around his black skin, making his fangs gleam.

"Are you all right?" he asked as he helped her to her feet.

She nodded. "Just dazed. I can fight the wyrran."

He hesitated and she saw he was warring with himself to let her stay and fight or to order her to leave. There was no way she was going to run off, not when she could help. And they didn't have time for an argument.

When Fallon took her hand and turned toward the door, Larena gave a sigh of relief. She knew it was ingrained in Fallon to protect women, but she wasn't just any woman. She was a Warrior. And she would prove it to him.

Larena spotted the wyrran coming for Fallon before he did. She pivoted and leaped in front of the yellow-skinned creature. All around her the sounds of battle filled the air. The screams of frustration and pain from the wyrran, and the bellows and roars of anger from the Warriors. It was so deafening she couldn't hear herself think.

Her claws sank into the wyrran's neck, the sickening sound of flesh giving way and blood splattering on her hands and arms reminding her how easily life could be taken away.

Larena didn't stop to ponder it though. She extracted her claws from the dead wyrran and turned to look for another. Her eyes scanned the village to find Galen and Logan with the last two wyrran. The Warriors made quick work of the evil yellow beings.

"Where are the rest of you?" Logan asked before he threw back his head and let out a loud roar, blood coating his silver skin.

Galen and Lucan were grinning at each other like young lads who had just felled their first deer. Camdyn stood off by himself and already had reverted to his human form, but even he had a gleam of satisfaction in his dark eyes.

Only Fallon stared down at the dead wyrran in silence. His black skin, claws, and fangs melted away as if they had never been. Larena walked toward him and pushed her goddess back down. He raised his head as she approached, and one side of his mouth lifted in a smile.

She loved that lopsided grin. "What is it?"

Fallon shrugged. "I canna help thinking over Broc's words. I hesitated to believe him about the wyrran. Why would he tell us, do you think?"

"I'm not sure. When I was on the roof with him, he killed a wyrran that was about to attack me."

"Interesting," Fallon murmured. "It would be nice to have a spy in Deirdre's mountain, but I know nothing of Broc."

"And you cannot chance trusting him."

Fallon nodded. "The attack is making me reevaluate everything he told me however. I think we need to heed his words, or at least be prepared for any event."

Larena cupped his jaw and smiled. They stared into each other's eyes, lost in the moment. It was shattered by the arrival of Ramsey and Hayden.

"What in the name of all that's holy happened?" Hayden demanded.

Logan clapped him on the back and smiled. "Wyrran attacked. After we had a visit from one of Deirdre's Warriors named Broc. Then, Camdyn arrived and tried to kill Broc. It was very interesting."

Larena chuckled when Hayden sent a murderous glare to Logan.

Hayden cursed long and loud. "I missed an opportunity to kill wyrran?"

"Doona worry," Fallon said. "I have a feeling you'll get your chance again soon enough."

The teasing ended when Galen walked to Camdyn and held out his arm. The men clasped forearms and exchanged a few whispered words.

Galen turned to them, his lips peeled back in a wide smile. "I'd like to introduce Camdyn MacKenna."

Larena remained by Fallon's side as Galen named each of them off to the newest Warrior. Camdyn was tall and thick shouldered. He didn't bother to wear a saffron shirt beneath his kilt, and despite being a Warrior, he had several daggers attached to his waist and one in the top of each boot. She guessed a few others were hidden as well.

When Camdyn turned his dark gaze to her, she smiled in greeting.

"Camdyn," Fallon said. "Larena told us of the message you gave her."

Camdyn nodded. "Aye."

"That was some time ago. Where have you been?"

"Around," was all Camdyn said. He turned to Larena. "It is good to see you again."

"You as well," she said.

Fallon scratched his jaw. It was obvious by the way Galen had greeted Camdyn that they were friends. Galen trusted him, and Fallon would as well. But first, he wanted some answers.

"Around? Around where?"

Camdyn shrugged a meaty shoulder. "I wanted to make sure what Galen said about you MacLeods was true."

"You spied on us," Lucan said.

"I did," Camdyn admitted. "Galen wouldn't have left

the forest unless he had found the MacLeods, but Deirdre's treachery knows no bounds. I needed to be sure it was really you," he said to Fallon.

"And are you?" Fallon asked.

Camdyn gave a curt nod. "I am. I intended to make myself known today, but then I sensed a presence. I stayed hidden to see what it was."

"Broc," Galen said.

"Aye. The winged Warrior," Camdyn agreed.

Ramsey stepped forward then, his gaze scanning the skies. "Where is Broc?"

"I don't know," Fallon said. It might have been the way Ramsey looked to the sky, or the way he asked about Broc, but Fallon had an idea that Ramsey knew the Warrior.

"Let's get back to the castle," Lucan said. "If I don't return soon to let Cara know I'm all right she'll have my head."

Fallon nodded and everyone started back to the castle but him. Larena hesitated, but he waved her on. He wanted to be alone when he spoke with Ramsey.

"Ramsey," he called. "May I have a word?"

The Warrior stopped and slowly turned to face him. "I suppose you want to know about Broc?"

Fallon glanced to make sure the others were far enough away. "Aye. You know him?"

"I do. I met him in Deirdre's dungeons."

He wasn't surprised that Ramsey answered honestly, but how much he would tell Fallon was yet to be determined. "How long did you know him?"

Ramsey shrugged and looked away. "The entire fifty

years she held me. He was already there when I arrived. You lose track of time in that mountain."

"I know. Why didn't he escape with you?"

"Escape is not what you think about after a while." Ramsey's gray gaze slid back to Fallon. His eyes had hardened and his lips thinned with his memories. "You only think about surviving the next round of torture, wondering if you're going to break and align yourself with her."

"Is that what Broc did?"

"I doona know."

Fallon considered Ramsey's words for a moment. There was a connection between the two men. He wasn't sure how strong it was, but it bore investigating. Ramsey could be a spy for Deirdre. God knew she had enough of them. "You've given me your advice many times since you've arrived, Ramsey. Your mind is quick and your suggestions good. I wonder, though, have I trusted you too quickly? Are you spying for Deirdre?"

Ramsey's skin shifted from normal to bronze in a blink. "I should kill you for suggesting I'm loyal to that evil bitch." He inhaled and gained control of the anger that had caught him unawares, as Fallon had intended.

"It is your job to make sure we can be trusted," Ramsey continued. "If I were in your place, I would ask the same questions. I tell you now, the answer is nay. I'm not spying for Deirdre. I want to see her dead."

There was no deceit in Ramsey's gray eyes. He spoke the truth, and Fallon believed him. "I had to ask."

"I know. It is what makes you a great leader."

Fallon hadn't expected praise. He liked Ramsey,

and the thought of him being a spy had turned Fallon's blood cold. "The things Broc said made me wonder just whose side he's on. He has helped us several times. He killed a wyrran to save Larena today, and he told us of the attacks."

"He told you of the wyrran attack? Why?"

"I have no idea. Then he told us Deirdre is doing it to keep us occupied so that we can't make plans to free Quinn. Lucan guessed that she is doing it to give her more time with Quinn."

Ramsey raked a hand through his hair. "I doubt she would have wanted you to know that information. For whatever reason Broc told us, we need to heed him."

"I've already assumed as much. Do you think he could be swayed to join us?"

Several moments passed before Ramsey responded. "I wouldn't count on it."

It wasn't the answer Fallon wanted, but until he spoke to Broc and asked, he wouldn't know for sure. Fallon didn't know if Broc would return to give him that chance, but he had a feeling he might. Whatever motivated the winged Warrior to help them would probably make him come back again.

TWENTY-FOUR

After the excitement of the morning with Broc, Camdyn, and the wyrran, Larena was ready for a quiet afternoon. Camdyn had been introduced to Sonya and Cara and was now helping with the cottages while the three women sat in the great hall.

"I cannot believe the wyrran attacked." Cara stuck her needle in the gown she was mending with force and yanked it out the other side. She shook her head and sighed. "I should have been there."

Sonya smiled and smoothed the material of the tunic she was sewing. "I think I would have liked to see the men fighting. And you as well, Larena."

With a grunt Larena settled in her chair. "I didn't do that well. I'm not used to fighting in my skirts."

Cara put down her sewing, her forehead furrowed. "What do you wear then?"

"I usually use my powers to become invisible and fight naked."

"Now that's something I imagine the men would like to see," Sonya said with a giggle. Her amber eyes twinkled with merriment, and soon Cara joined in her laughter.

Larena smiled despite herself. "Fallon pointed out

to me that there won't always be time to use my powers, and he's right. Especially when I'm fighting Warriors. I've depended on my powers for too long."

"What will you do?" Cara asked. "You could learn to fight in your skirts as I do."

"I could, but since as Warriors we jump and leap while we fight, the skirts will hamper me."

Sonya threaded her needle. "Well, it's not as if you can wear breeches."

Larena jerked upright, a sudden thought occurring to her. "Why not? The Celts did. Their women wore trousers and fought right alongside the men."

"We aren't in ancient times," Cara said. "I don't know if the men will approve."

"I don't care if they do," Larena said as she rose to her feet. "I need to be able to fight, and I cannot do that in a gown." She swallowed and looked at each of the women. She didn't normally ask anyone for help, but she needed Cara and Sonya. "Will you help me?"

Cara and Sonya exchanged a look before slow smiles spread on the women's faces. "Aye," they said in unison.

"Good," Larena said as relief swept through her. "Let's get started. We have no idea when the next attack will be."

Sonya tossed aside her tunic while Cara finished her last stitch and gently set the gown out of the way.

"I can't wait until Fallon sees you in breeches," Cara said with a chuckle. "He's going to be speechless."

Larena certainly hoped so. Not that she was doing anything to gain his attention.

Or at least she tried to convince herself that she wasn't.

Deirdre checked Quinn's injuries as she did several times a day. He was healing nicely. His body had needed the rest, and she liked having him in her bed. Every night she nestled against him and slept.

It was the first time she had ever let a man spend the entire night in her bed. And Quinn would be the last as well.

Her long nails that she filed to a sharp point traced up Quinn's bare leg to his hip. Whenever she was in the chamber with him, she took off the blanket so she could look her fill at his beautifully sculpted body.

He had lost weight in her dungeons, as they all did. But she would see the muscle put back on his bones soon. For now, it was enough just to be with him.

One of her pets scratched at her door before opening it. The wyrran let out a hiss, letting her know she had a visitor. Deirdre rose and rubbed behind the wyrran's large ears.

"Thank you," she said. "Let's go see what Dunmore has brought us this time."

Deirdre walked out of her private chambers to a set of stairs that led to a long corridor where her throne room sat. She opened the door to find the tall, hulking form of Dunmore. He had come to her as a young man eager for power, and through the years she had continued to give him more and more authority.

"Mistress." He bowed low, his dark curls falling over his high forehead. "You grow more beautiful each day."

"Such flattery." But Deirdre smiled.

She had always liked Dunmore. He had lines around his eyes now, but his body was still firm with no fat visible. He knew how to take care of himself, and as a man who had shared her bed, he knew how to pleasure a woman.

He also didn't mind a woman being in charge, nor did he hesitate to carry out her orders. Just the sort of man she needed to round up the Druids.

Dunmore pushed aside his red cloak and placed his hands on his hips, his feet braced shoulder width apart. "I found them. They were living in caves and starving."

"How many did you bring me?"

He glanced at the floor, his black eyes troubled. "Twelve in all. Two of the old women didn't make the trip."

"You are harsh with them," Deirdre said.

"As you've told me to be."

She smiled. "Go on."

"One of the young ones, a lad of about seven summers, escaped. We chased him, and just as we were about to catch him, he jumped off the side of the mountain."

"It appears my reputation precedes me." Deirdre walked to a silver chest that sat on a table near her throne. The chest was unadorned except for intricate knotwork in a beautiful design all over the chest. The knotwork had been infused with spells to keep anyone but her from touching the chest since it housed coin and jewels.

Deirdre opened the lid and lifted a small velvet bag. She tested the weight of the coins within before she turned and tossed it to Dunmore. "Once again you've done well."

He tucked the bag into his belt and bowed. "It is my wish to serve you."

"My seer has told me of another group of Druids that think they can hide from me." One of her greatest finds had been the seer, and Deirdre put her to use whenever she could.

"Tell me where to find them, mistress, and I will bring them to you."

Deirdre walked to Dunmore and tapped the cleft on his chin. "These Druids won't be as easy to find. They use magic to cloak themselves. There is one I want above the others. A young woman with turquoise eyes. You won't mistake her. She has . . . information I need."

"I've not failed you before. I willna now." His eyes glittered with determination, his jaw set.

She studied the man before her. Neither Dunmore nor his family had Druid blood or gods in them. Yet, he had proven to be a wonderful talent. She had intended to kill him for daring to seek her out, but she had sensed in him a thread of evil that she worked to her benefit.

"Nay, Dunmore, you won't fail me because you know how much I want these Druids. And because you like the influence I give you. Return with the girl and I will reward you with wealth beyond your imagining. Bring other Druids with her, and I'll make it worth your while."

Once Deirdre relayed where the Druids were hiding, he gave her another bow and left. She watched his retreating back. If Dunmore failed, she would skin him alive and use his bowels to choke him. She had to have this Druid named Marcail.

Fallon wiped the sweat from his face with the sleeve of his tunic. The clouds had begun to gather just after noon, shielding most of the sun. Rain was in the air, and he wanted the roof Larena had fallen through fixed before it began.

"Almost done," Logan called down from above him.

While Fallon had worked, his mind replayed Broc's visit and all he had been told. He hoped Broc hadn't been lying when he said Quinn was all right. Just thinking that his youngest brother might be suffering was like a noose tightening around his neck.

He prayed Quinn stayed strong while in Deirdre's mountain. Quinn had been so perilously close to losing it before Cara had come to their castle. And seeing Lucan and Cara's obvious love for each other had just made things worse for Quinn.

Not once since the deaths of his wife and son had Quinn ever spoken of them. Fallon and Lucan had bowed to Quinn's wishes and didn't ask questions. So, when Quinn confessed that he had never loved his wife, Fallon couldn't have been more stunned.

He had thought their union was one born of love. Quinn had fooled everyone, including himself. Fallon wanted the best for his brothers, and each of them deserved the kind of marriage their parents had had. He didn't want Quinn settling again.

Fallon rubbed his neck as he felt the ache that settled at the base of his skull every time he thought of Quinn.

Quinn was strong. He would know they were coming for him.

"Hold on, little brother," Fallon whispered.

"Finished!"

Fallon looked above him. Logan had repaired the hole so well it was hard to determine where Larena had fallen through. Fallon walked out of the cottage and nodded to Logan as he jumped to the ground.

"Well done."

Logan shrugged and dusted off his hands. "It was an easy task. I used to have to repair my family's roof."

Fallon waited to see if Logan would speak further about his past. It was a rare occurrence when any of them spoke about the time before they had been turned into Warriors.

When Logan said no more, Fallon piled more pieces of shattered beds, chairs, and tables on the fire. Most everything had already been burned, and by the end of the next day, the rest would be gone as well.

"Things are moving well," Lucan said as he walked up with Galen and Camdyn. "Already the village looks better."

Fallon handed his brother a water skin and looked up at the dark clouds coming their way. "We have six more cottages that need to be torn down and burned. The rain may delay things."

Lucan drank deeply before offering the water to Camdyn. "The rain willna bother my work, and if need be, I can work with you in the rain removing the cottages."

"Nay, work on the construction of the furniture," Fallon said. "Logan and I can handle the rest."

"And I can help," Camdyn added.

Fallon nodded to the most recent arrival. A glance at his brother told Fallon that Lucan liked Camdyn, which was good. The more Warriors they had to fight against Deirdre the better.

"It looks like Broc has returned," Galen said.

Fallon turned around to see Broc flying toward him with something in his arms. The way Broc flew as if he were injured gave Fallon pause. Without a word to the others, Fallon started running toward Broc.

The winged Warrior was flying low, barely missing the tops of the trees. He landed heavily as Fallon came to a stop in front of him.

"He's hurt bad, but not dead," Broc said, and laid Malcolm on the ground between them.

Fallon noticed the cuts and blood on Broc as the others fanned out behind him. "What happened?"

"I saw him being beaten."

"By whom?"

Broc rubbed his eyes with one hand while he flexed his other shoulder. "It doesn't matter."

But it did. Fallon waited while Lucan knelt beside Malcolm then nodded that the man was still alive.

"Why did you help him?" Fallon asked.

Broc's gaze met his. "Malcolm is an innocent. He is neither Druid nor Warrior. There was no need to harm him."

Fallon was taken aback by the anger in Broc's barely controlled voice. Then he noticed the injuries on Broc's body. Not all the blood on him was Malcolm's. "He helped Larena. In some people's mind, that is enough to condemn him."

"Not in mine."

Fallon blew out a breath. "Thank you."

Broc said nothing as he jumped in the air and flew away once more.

"I'm not quite sure what to make of him," Lucan said of Broc's retreating form.

Fallon shook his head. "Me neither. Let's get Malcolm to the castle. Larena will want to see him."

But when Fallon bent down to lift Malcolm he noticed the extent of his injuries, including the bone protruding from Malcolm's arm. Fallon met Lucan's gaze and sighed. Malcolm's arm hung at an awkward angle, and Fallon feared trying to use his powers to move him to the castle and what it might do to Malcolm's arm.

"Logan, I need you to find Sonya and bring her here. Tell her we have an injured man she needs to see to immediately. Lucan, find Larena."

Lucan rose to his feet, his face grim. "What will you do?"

"I'm going to move Malcolm into a cottage. We cannot treat him out in the open."

Camdyn moved to stand at Malcolm's feet. "I'll help you carry him. The more of us that hold him the better."

"I agree," Galen said.

"Then Logan needs to stay," Lucan said. "I can get Sonya and Larena."

"Hurry," Fallon urged his brother.

Lucan spun on his heel and ran toward the castle. Fallon wiped his hand down his face and looked at Malcolm. He could barely recognize his face.

"All right," Fallon said after a moment. "I want to

take him to the cottage we just repaired, Logan. The bed was still intact, wasn't it?"

Logan nodded. "Aye, and there are a couple of chairs that also hadn't been destroyed."

"Good. I want us to lift and move him carefully. He's unconscious, and I'd like for him to stay that way for the time being."

"Will Sonya be able to set his arm?" Camdyn asked. "It looks dreadful."

Fallon swallowed the bile that rose in his throat. "I honestly don't know."

The four of them lifted Malcolm with the care they would have shown an infant. Their steps were slow and measured as they walked to the cottage. Thankfully, it was the closest one.

Malcolm groaned in pain when Fallon stumbled over a rock and jerked. Fallon wanted him on the bed and some of the blood washed away before Larena saw him.

"The door is narrow," Logan said. "Camdyn, you go first, but step carefully over the threshold. Once he's through, Galen, you go next."

Camdyn eased through the door with Malcolm's feet. Galen had some trouble getting through, but after they angled Malcolm's body, he was able to walk into the cottage. Logan was next as he squeezed through the doorway without bumping Malcolm once.

Fallon had Malcolm's shoulders and easily stepped through the door, then turned to lay him down when they spotted pieces of the roof on the bed from when Larena fell through.

"Hold him." Logan moved with efficient speed as he cleaned off the bed and pulled back the covers.

It took all of them to lay Malcolm down without incident. Fallon straightened and jerked his head to the door when he heard a startled gasp and found Larena gripping the doorway so tightly her knuckles were white.

Larena's face crumpled, but she didn't cry, not that Fallon would have thought less of her had he seen the tears.

"What happened?" she asked in a strangled voice.

Fallon's heart ached for the pain that seemed to swallow her whole. "Broc brought him to us. He said he found Malcolm being beaten."

Her eyes lifted to his, and he saw the stark anguish in their smoky-blue depths. "Who would do this to him?"

"Broc didn't say, but I think it was Warriors."

"Could Broc have done it?"

Fallon shook his head. "It was my first thought. Until I saw Broc's own injuries. Nay, Larena, he fought to get your cousin free."

"Oh, God," she said and put her forehead to the doorway. "His arm, Fallon."

"I know. Sonya has great magic. She will do all she can." He just prayed it would be enough.

Larena took a deep breath and straightened from the door. That's when he noticed she no longer wore a gown but breeches and a tunic. The buttery soft brown leather encased her slim legs like a second skin. His mouth watered at the sight.

A tunic of blue had been altered to fit her, showing off her full breasts. Though the tunic hid her waist and most of her hips, Fallon still saw the swell of her buttocks.

He licked his lips and bit back a groan. He had never thought he would be reduced to such a state by the image of a woman. But then again, he had never imagined a woman such as Larena.

Her gaze dared him to rebuff her. Fallon didn't like the idea of her walking around in breeches, especially given the fact that both Camdyn and Logan were as thunderstruck as he was.

"You said I couldn't depend on my powers," she said. "You said I needed to learn to fight without them."

"So I did," Fallon murmured. She had taken his argument and used it against him. "I'm not used to seeing a woman in breeches."

She looked down at herself and stubbed the toe of her boot on the ground. "It feels odd, but I can move much better when I'm fighting."

Malcolm groaned and everyone forgot Larena's attire and focused on him.

"I knew this might happen to him," Larena said as she walked to Malcolm and placed her hand on his forehead. "He always said he would fight and die by my side, even though he doesn't have my powers."

"He is a good man," Fallon said.

Larena nodded. "I will never forgive myself if he dies."

"He won't die," Logan said. "Sonya is coming, and she will help him."

Fallon prayed Logan was right. Malcolm looked ghastly but Fallon knew from personal experience that Sonya's magic for healing was great.

A moment later Sonya, Cara, and Lucan walked into the cottage. Sonya didn't say a word as she went to Malcolm and began to inspect his injuries.

Fallon moved to the door where the other men had gathered. He crossed his arms over his chest and watched as the three women bent their heads over Malcolm.

Moments stretched into hours as they wiped away the blood again and again. Fallon and Lucan took turns getting more water for the women to wring out the blood-soaked cloths.

An eternity later, Sonya straightened, her hand on her lower back. "His arm is broken and dislocated. If I don't get it back in place and set the bone correctly, he won't be able to use his arm, regardless of the magic I use. Once his arm is done, I'll see to the other wounds."

A Highlander needed both arms. A clan looked to their laird for strength, courage, and wisdom. Without all three, they wouldn't follow him. And even though Malcolm had enough courage to overcome losing an arm, his clan wouldn't care.

Fallon walked to Sonya. "What do you need me to do?"

Her red hair was plastered to the side of her face, and her amber eyes held a wealth of misery. "Hold him. It's going to take all of you, I'm sure."

Fallon motioned the other Warriors over, and each set their hands on Malcolm to hold him down.

"I'm going to pop his shoulder back into position first," Sonya said.

She licked her lips and with a twist and a yank, put the joint into place. Malcolm yelled, his back bowing from the pain.

Sonya glanced up at Fallon. "Get ready," she advised everyone. "The bone has gone through the skin and he's going to fight."

"Can't you just use magic?" Logan asked.

Sonya glanced at him and shook her head. "If only it were that easy, Logan. Magic isn't the answer to everything, especially for mortals who hold no magic within them."

As soon as Larena touched his arm near the break, Malcolm's eyes flew open. He bucked and tried to break from their grip, his bellows of pain filling the cottage. Fallon and the other used all their strength to hold him steady so Sonya could set the break.

Cara took Malcolm's injured hand in hers and held it. Larena caressed his brow and whispered words into his ear that Fallon couldn't discern.

Malcolm's eyes were crazed, his breathing ragged. Already his wounds had begun to bleed again.

"Hold him," Sonya yelled when Malcolm gave a vicious yank.

"Forget his other injuries," Fallon said to the others. "Just hold him. Sonya will deal with everything once his arm is set."

With that, the other Warriors clamped down on Malcolm until he could barely move. He screamed in agony when Sonya pulled his arm to get the bone back under the skin.

Sweat beaded Fallon's brow as he imagined the pain that filled Malcolm. No one let up their hold until Sonya had set the bone.

"He's passed out," Larena said.

Fallon looked down to find that Malcolm was indeed unconscious again. He released his hold and stepped back. The others did the same, but Camdyn left the cottage.

Once he saw how pale Larena was, Fallon brought her a chair and made her sit. Then he wrung out a wet cloth and gave it to her so she could wipe Malcolm's brow.

Sonya gave him a nod, letting him know that she had everything under control. Fallon left the cottage to seek some fresh air. The smell of blood clung to the air in the cottage, reminding him of his clan's murder.

"Is he going to be all right?"

Fallon turned his head to find Camdyn leaning against the outside of the cottage. Camdyn's hands shook as he brought them to his face to brush away a strand of hair.

"I think so," Fallon answered. "We won't know about his arm until the break has mended. Sonya will use whatever magic she can to heal him."

Camdyn shifted his stance. "I had an uncle, a big bear of a man, who had his arm crushed when a tree fell on him. He had been respected and revered in the clan until that accident. Afterward, people wouldn't look him in the eye. He didn't give up living though. He learned to use his sword with his left arm, but when the time came for battle, they wouldna let him fight."

"What did your uncle do?"

"He stayed behind as they demanded, but their actions hurt him more than the loss of his arm ever did. My aunt was a good woman, and loved him despite his missing arm."

Fallon looked to his castle and frowned. "Malcolm is supposed to be laird of his clan."

"God help him then," Camdyn murmured.

Fallon pinched the bridge of his nose with his thumb and forefinger. Camdyn had the right of it. If Malcolm couldn't use his arm, his clan wouldn't want him. He would have nowhere to go.

After all Malcolm had done for Larena, Fallon couldn't let him wander Scotland. They would make a place for Malcolm at the castle.

"We'll help him," Fallon said. "He'll stay here with us."

Camdyn's head swiveled around to him. "You are the man everyone says you are. I'm sorry you didn't get to be laird of your clan, Fallon, but I'm glad to have you lead us."

Fallon didn't know how to respond to Camdyn. In the end, he gave the man a nod and walked away. There was work to be done, and he was doing no one any good just standing around.

TWENTY-FIVE

When Larena left the cottage night had fallen. The women had agreed to take turns watching over Malcolm. Larena had taken the first watch, and Sonya had come to relieve her. Malcolm slept soundly, his chest rising and falling regularly, but Larena was still worried.

She wasn't sure what Sonya had done or what kind of magic she had used, but whatever it was, it was healing Malcolm well.

Sonya had assured her she would send for Larena if Malcolm woke, but Larena expected him to sleep the night through. And so did Sonya by the way she readied for the night.

A shadow moved at the edge of the cottage and Larena caught a whiff of orangewood.

Fallon.

She walked to him, and when he opened his arms she didn't hesitate to accept his embrace. She laid her head on his shoulder and closed her eyes.

"If Broc hadn't found him . . ."

"Don't," Fallon whispered. "Broc did find him, and Sonya has healed him as best she could."

Larena nodded. "He will have many scars from the claw marks."

"Did you see his hands? He fought back, Larena. Even though they were Warriors, he fought back."

She blinked through the sudden rush of tears. "I thought once I left Edinburgh he would be all right."

"I don't think he was in Edinburgh. I told him if he ever needed anything that he was welcome here. I think he was on his way to the castle to see you." His strong hands took hold of her shoulders and pulled her away from him. "There is something else."

She couldn't see his eyes because the moon was behind him, but she heard the concern in his voice and saw the frown that marred his forehead. "What is it?"

"If for some reason Malcolm isn't able to use his arm as he should, he's welcome to stay here. You know his clan willna take him as their laird if he isn't whole."

"You would open your home to him?"

"I would."

She was stunned at his gesture. Fallon constantly amazed her. "Why?"

"Because he stood by your side when the rest of your family wouldn't. Because he put his life in danger to help you. Because he was your friend, and because he trusted me to help you."

"Fallon," she whispered, her throat clogging with emotion.

His mouth descended on hers, cutting off anything else she might have wanted to say. When his lips moved over hers expertly, teasing and coaxing her, she touched her tongue to his. He groaned and crushed her to his hard chest.

Larena never wanted to leave his arms. In his embrace she felt as if nothing could ever harm her, that she was protected and . . . loved.

Love.

It was a word she didn't say and never considered. Unless she thought of Fallon.

The last person who had loved her was her father, and he had been taken from her. Robena had cared for her and had been proud the goddess had chosen her, but Robena hadn't loved her. Nay, Robena had a job to do, and that's all that had mattered to the old Druid.

Love wasn't an emotion Larena could allow herself to feel. It opened her up to the pain she never wanted to experience again. It was better to close herself off, and keep her distance.

Are you so sure now that you've met Fallon? He could offer you much more.

Larena pushed such thoughts from her mind as Fallon deepened the kiss. His hands cupped her buttocks and held her as he ground his arousal against her.

All the breath left Larena's body. She clung to Fallon's thick shoulders and surrendered to the passion that unfurled low in her belly.

"My God, Larena," Fallon whispered. He kissed down her neck and bent her backward over his arm. "I want you. I *need* you."

She shuddered at his words then cried out when his teeth grazed her nipple through the tunic. Pleasure rippled through her like lightning. She lifted a leg and wrapped it around his waist.

The night air, filled with the smell of the sea, swirled around them. The moon and stars twinkled above while the water crashed against the cliffs. All around them death and destruction ruled, but in each other's arms they could find serenity.

"I need you too, Fallon," she confessed. "I need you desperately."

Wordlessly, he lifted her until her legs wrapped around his waist, and then he carried her behind the cottages. He pressed her against the hut and ground his cock against her.

Larena moaned and moved her hips. She was grateful for the privacy since she knew other Warriors were keeping watch and she didn't want them seeing the passion that was hers and Fallon's alone.

"This would be easier if you were in a gown," he growled.

Larena chuckled. "Just as it would be easier if you were in a kilt."

"I'll keep that in mind next time," he murmured against her neck as he nuzzled her skin. "You have no idea what the sight of you in the breeches does to me."

She reached between them and tugged his tunic up his chest, and then over his head. "Tell me."

"It makes me want to mark you as mine."

She trembled at his words. She wanted to be marked, and to be marked as his.

Their hands were frantic to rid themselves of the clothing that separated their bodies. Before the last piece of cloth hit the ground, they were in each other's arms once more.

Larena plunged her fingers in Fallon's dark locks as he lifted her once more. She wrapped her legs around his waist and moaned when his rod brushed against her sensitive sex.

"Please, Fallon," she begged. She had to have him inside her. Only he could make her forget the world around them and make her feel as if they were the only two people on earth.

His hands gripped her hips, holding her above his cock. She didn't look away when his gaze caught hers. Larena let herself drown in the exquisite green of his eyes.

He lowered her onto his shaft with one thrust. She tried to move her hips, but he held her steady. He filled her completely until the tip of him touched her womb. Only then did he allow her to move.

Larena locked her ankles together and buried her face in Fallon's neck as his hips began to shift. Each thrust brought him closer, took him deeper . . . and touched her heart.

She didn't know if it was seeing Malcolm dying before her eyes, but she felt raw, exposed, and she needed Fallon in ways that she couldn't put into words.

He hadn't asked questions. He had merely offered himself, as if he knew she would need him.

Larena kissed Fallon's neck as her need rose with the quickening of his hips.

"Ah, God, Larena," he ground out.

She kissed him again, letting her tongue trace along his skin. He moaned deep in his throat as his fingers dug into her hips.

Her hands shifted to his shoulders as she fought to hold onto him as her climax built. She gasped and sucked against his neck as her orgasm engulfed her.

Larena was blinded by the intensity, her body convulsing with the delicious waves of pleasure. Fallon continued to plunge inside her, drawing out her climax.

"You're mine, Larena. Mine."

She jerked, her mouth opening on a silent scream of bliss as his fangs sank into her neck and brought on another orgasm.

By the time she could open her eyes, Fallon was kissing the spot he had bitten. She knew without looking that he had marked her. She should be upset, but she wasn't. She was elated.

"Mine," he whispered just before he jumped them into his chamber at the castle.

Fallon couldn't believe he had given in to his desire to mark Larena. Feeling her body clench around him, knowing the anguish she felt at finding Malcolm, and the excitement he had experienced when she had come to him had been too much.

In the dark of night, she was his. Whether she would be in his bed when the sun rose was another matter. He had told her she was his, but in his heart he knew he didn't have her. He never would either unless she gave her heart to him.

Fallon jumped them to his chamber and laid her on the bed before he crawled in next to her. She turned to him and rested her head on his shoulder. His mind was full of her. Even the beating of his heart was for her.

Lucan had asked him if he cared for Larena. Fallon wasn't sure just what emotion was within him, but his feelings for Larena grew daily. She had no idea that she held him in the palm of her hand, and it was probably better if she didn't.

Not even knowing she kept the truth of her ring and her knowledge of the Scroll from him could dampen his feelings. She had her reasons for keeping her secret, and though it hurt that she didn't trust him, he tried to understand.

He let his fingers caress down her back. He wanted to clasp her to him and never let her go, but let her go he would. Chaining her to him would only make her want to leave.

Fallon knew in the end he was going to have to do the impossible. He was going to have to let Larena go.

He closed his eyes as a wave of pain swallowed him. The thought of not seeing her smoky-blue eyes every day, of not watching her lips form her breathtaking smile, or feel her hands on him, left him in a cold sweat.

"God, give me strength," he whispered.

Broc flew southwest once he left the MacLeods. He had taken too much time. Deirdre would be in a rage when he returned, but he had one more stop to make.

The wind pushed him along toward his destination. He saw the great stand of trees well before he reached them. The massive forest was home to many creatures— and Druids.

He dropped down next to the loch and transformed back into the man he was. It was the only time he pushed his god aside, the only time he allowed himself to remember the man he used to be. It brought too many memories, but he had to make this stop.

Broc ran his fingers through his too long hair and used the loch to wash the blood from his body. Malcolm's blood, and his own. His injuries had healed, but Larena's cousin probably wouldn't be so lucky. He straightened and wished he had thought to bring a tunic.

"Broc?"

Her sweet voice drifted to him from the trees. She emerged with a basket in one hand and her skirt in the other. The pale brown strands of her hair lay unbound around her.

"It *is* you," she whispered. "I thought you might never return."

He hadn't intended to return. He had promised himself on his previous visit nearly six months ago that it would be his last. It was getting too dangerous for the Druids. But he'd been unable to stay away.

"I cannot stay long, Anice. There are evil people looking for you and the other Druids. You must stay hidden as I told you."

Her smile never faltered as she walked to him. She dropped her basket and raised her hands to his face. "How I've missed you. I worry about you endlessly."

"I'll be fine," he said, and tried not to slap her hands away. She was a sweet girl, but she didn't always listen when it was important. "Did you hear me? You and the other Druids need to stay concealed."

"We've used our magic. Even my sister added her magic to ours before she left."

Broc stilled at the mention of *her*. She was the real reason he was here, the reason he couldn't stay away. His heart pounded like a drum in his ears. "Sonya left?"

Anice cocked her head to the side, her eyes narrowed as she regarded him. "She said it was important, that she was needed elsewhere. She said it was to aid those who fought against Deirdre."

Broc turned on his heel and ran his hand down his face. His heart pounded in his ears as his mind raced with possibilities.

He remembered when he had brought the two small girls to the Druids. He had continued to look in on them through the years. Neither of them knew his role in their escape from Deirdre, and he intended to make sure they never knew. He would have to answer too many questions about what had happened to their parents.

Sonya didn't know of him at all. He hadn't wanted Anice to know either, but she had caught him spying on Sonya. Broc had been desperate for another's touch. He should have pushed Anice away. Instead, he had taken her as his lover, but his gaze was always on Sonya.

He faced Anice again and tried to ignore the hurt in her eyes. "When did Sonya leave?"

Anice shrugged. "What does it matter? She will be all right, as she always is."

"When, Anice?" he demanded.

She shrank away from him, her brown gaze wary for the first time. She had no idea what a monster he really was or how many people he had killed. If she did, she would never have offered her body to him.

"Almost three months ago."

Broc struggled to breathe. *Three months?* Sonya could be anywhere. She might need him. Didn't she know it wasn't safe for Druids to wander Scotland? "Where?"

"She said she was going to the MacLeods."

Broc clenched his hands, unsure if he had heard Anice correctly. Sonya had been at the MacLeods' the entire time and he hadn't known? He needed to see for himself that she had made it to the castle, and the Warriors had allowed her inside. If there was one place he could believe Sonya was safe, it was with the MacLeods. For the time being.

"Anice, listen to me. Deirdre's magic has grown. She is finding Druids that have been hidden for years. The magic you and the others have used might not be enough." He wanted to tell her everything, of the Warriors and what Deirdre was after, but he didn't have time.

She swallowed and jerked her head in a nod. "You won't be returning, will you?"

"I cannot chance it. It's too dangerous. For both of us."

"I thought we had a future together."

Broc glanced down at the ground. He regretted using Anice, but he could not let her think they shared something. "There is no future with me."

Tears fell unheeded down her face to drop onto her chest. "Godspeed, Broc."

He waited until the forest had swallowed her once more before he dropped his head into his hands. It had never been his intention to hurt Anice. A moment of weakness had caused him to welcome her into his arms, and he would pay for it the rest of his life.

As for Sonya, she was his responsibility as well. He

had made sure Anice never spoke of him, so he didn't have to worry about Sonya telling the MacLeods anything.

Broc turned and raced away from the forest before releasing his god and taking flight. He would do whatever it took to keep the two Druid sisters away from Deirdre. Whatever it took.

TWENTY-SIX

Fallon waited until the door shut behind Larena before he opened his eyes. He had hoped what they had shared the night before would keep her by his side in the morning, but he had been wrong.

As much as he wanted to, he hadn't stopped her from leaving. With a sigh, he rose and dressed, but instead of heading to the great hall, Fallon went looking for Sonya.

He had seen the way she'd stiffened when Broc's name was spoken. It couldn't be mere coincidence that she also knew Broc. There was something about Broc's appearance and his helping rescue Malcolm that kept niggling at Fallon.

"Morning, brother," Lucan greeted him.

Fallon stopped in the corridor. "Morning. How is Malcolm faring?"

"Well. Larena is with him now. I've taken Cara to bed. She's exhausted."

"Good," Fallon said. "I'm glad to hear he's mending well. Have you seen Sonya this morn?"

"Aye. She's on the battlements. Is something wrong?"

Fallon hesitated. He saw the question in his brother's

sea-green eyes. "I don't know yet. She reacted at the mention of Broc's name."

"And you want to see if there is a connection," Lucan finished. "Aye, I would as well. Do you think she knows him?"

"Could be. Anything is possible. We know nothing of Broc other than what Ramsey has shared with us."

Lucan leaned a shoulder against the wall and crossed his arms over his chest, his gaze thoughtful. "Broc is a mystery. I'd like to talk to him myself."

"Stand in line, brother."

Lucan chuckled before he dropped his arms and pushed off the wall. "I expect a full report later."

Fallon shook his head as his brother walked away. Gone was the bleakness that had lurked in Lucan's eyes for too many years. Lucan was once more the man Fallon had known before the murder of their clan. Now, if only everything else could be as it once was.

When Fallon walked onto the battlements he found Sonya, just as Lucan had said. She stood with her back to the sea. Her hands gripped the stones tightly, her concentration palpable.

"Are you listening to the trees?"

She turned her head to glance at him. "I can barely hear them. I'm too far away. Every once in a while I will catch a word, but not enough to make sense."

"Have you always lived in the forest?"

"For as long as I can remember."

Fallon kept his gaze on her as he leaned an elbow on the stones. "What of your family?"

"My parents are dead and have been for many years.

All I have left is an elder sister who likes to spend her days picking wildflowers."

"Were you born with the Druids?"

She shook her head. "Nay. From what little I was told when I questioned the Druids, we were brought to them when I was just walking and my sister barely older."

"Interesting. What do you know of Broc?"

Finally, she turned to face him. Her amber gaze was steady as she met his eyes. "What makes you think I know anything?"

"You flinched yesterday when his name was spoken."

Sonya sighed and looked down at her hands, but not before he saw a flicker of emotion. "My sister spoke of a Broc, a man who would visit her on occasion. She would often speak of their future together, but when I questioned her about him she wouldn't tell me more. After a while, she quit talking about him altogether."

"Do you think it's the same Broc?"

She shrugged and looked into his face. "Fallon, my sister is a gentle soul. She is a good person, but the evil in the world does not trouble her. Anice thinks she can stay in the protected grove and keep away from Deirdre and any wickedness that could threaten her."

"But you don't?"

"Nay," she admitted softly. "I don't. I tried to convince the other Druids to leave, but the grove has been their home for too long. They feel safe there."

Fallon blew out a breath. He was troubled by what he had learned. "Can you convince the Druids to come here?"

"I doubt it. I told them of the warning the trees had

given me, but they held firm to staying in the grove. I tried to get Anice to come with me, but she said she couldn't leave. For all I know Broc is someone she made up. She was always going out into the forest alone. I would see her talking to herself, carrying on conversations with people that weren't there."

"I'm sorry, Sonya."

She waved away his words. "There's nothing to be sorry for. I gave them the warning."

"Surely you don't want your sister in Deirdre's hands."

Sonya's gaze burned him. "Of course not. But I cannot force the Druids to leave. I told them where I was and begged them to come here should something happen."

"Let me send Warriors to them."

"You would never find them."

Fallon straightened and reined in his growing ire. "Then you take a couple of Warriors and find them."

"I wish I could, Fallon, but I cannot leave. It's not just Malcolm that needs me. The trees told me I had to come here and stay, that if I leave MacLeod Castle, Deirdre will find me. And before you think me a coward, know that if I end up in Deirdre's hands, the location to Druids that have evaded her will be known."

"I would never think you a coward, Sonya. You forget I've been in Deirdre's mountain. I've seen what she can do. You are right to want to stay away from her, but we need to get the Druids here before she does find them. And she will eventually."

She sighed and nodded. "I will try to send a message through the trees if I can."

Fallon covered her hand that still held the stones in a

death grip. "You did all you could. Let me and the others help you for once."

"Thank you." Her lips quivered as she smiled.

Fallon left her on the battlements and walked to the hall. He glanced at Ramsey and Hayden who sat at the other table looking over the fake scroll. Fallon slid into his seat by his brother and blew out a breath.

"That bad?" Lucan asked around his mouthful of food.

Fallon was glad the other Warriors weren't in the hall. He was still sorting out all Sonya had told him. "The group of Druids Sonya lived with are in danger." He reached for some food and began telling Lucan everything he'd learned.

When he was finished Lucan whistled long and low. "I hope she can send the message. I cannot believe the Druids would think they were safe in the forest. No one is safe from Deirdre, not even here, but at least with us they stand a chance."

"The grove is known to them. I can understand not wanting to leave a magical and protected place."

"And Broc?" Lucan prodded.

Fallon tore off another piece of bread and rested his forearms on the table. "Sonya doesn't know if he's real or not."

"Is there something wrong with her sister mentally?"

"Sonya didn't say as much, but I think there might be."

Lucan drained his goblet and set it on the table. "I guess we'll have to wait and see about Broc then."

"I suppose so. I was hoping to learn something about him, but I know less than yesterday."

"By the way," Lucan said, and leaned close to Fallon.

"I found your and Larena's clothes this morning in the village. I folded them and put them in her chamber."

Fallon inwardly cursed. He had forgotten all about their clothing. "I appreciate it."

"Have you two resolved anything?"

Fallon shook his head. "I don't know that we ever will, Lucan. I would give her anything she wanted, but each morning, she leaves my bed with the sun."

"Give it time. I see the way she looks at you. There is something there, Fallon."

Larena wiped Malcolm's brow and silently willed her cousin to wake. She worried about his arm and how it would affect his future, but deep inside she knew she was running from the memories of her night with Fallon. She had stared at her neck in the mirror for a long time that morning still surprised to see his mark on her.

Her hand went to her neck and the bite that was now covered by her tunic. She wondered if Fallon was angry to find her gone once more that morning. How could she explain that staying to see him wake up was a step she couldn't take? Not yet anyway.

She knew her time with Fallon was running out. If she didn't give herself to him, she would lose him forever. Fallon had offered her everything. What had she done? She had kept part of herself from him, but more than that, she hadn't trusted him with the truth about the Scroll.

Larena put her head in her hands as she felt the tears threaten again. How she hated to cry. Ever since she had met Fallon the tears had been nearly unstoppable.

He deserved the truth. All of it. If he hated her for it,

then so be it. As a Highlander and laird to a clan, he should understand the weight of a vow.

Her decision to tell him made, she lifted her head and wiped her eyes. She needed to find Fallon before she changed her mind. She could help Ramsey and Hayden with the scroll so they could fool Deirdre completely.

But as she turned to leave, she heard her name whispered.

Larena whirled around to find Malcolm looking at her through his one good eye. She smiled and reached for his hand. "Hi."

"Hi," he murmured, and licked his cracked lips.

She reached for the cup of water and raised his head to help him drink. Once he was finished she wiped the water from his chin and brushed a lock of blond hair from his eyes.

"How are you feeling?"

He grunted. "Like. Hell."

"I know, but you're going to get better. You're at Fallon's."

Malcolm's brow furrowed, and she saw the questions forming in his mind.

"Not yet, cousin," she said. "You need to rest. There will be time enough later for answers."

"All right."

"Are you in pain?"

He nodded as his eyes drifted shut.

Larena squeezed his hand. "I will get you something. Rest easy."

When she turned around Sonya was in the doorway.

The Druid's amber gaze was troubled, but she quickly schooled her features and smiled.

"He woke?" Sonya asked.

"Aye, and he's in pain."

Sonya strode to the bed. "I'll mix some herbs in his water. It will ease his pain and allow him to rest."

"Thank you."

The Druid looked at her. "There's no need to thank me. This is what I do, the gift I was given. I will continue to use my magic to speed his healing."

Larena glanced at Malcolm once more. "Thank you anyway. If you ever need *anything*, Sonya, I will help you."

"It is good that you've come here. This is where you belong," Sonya said.

Larena let Sonya treat her cousin and left the cottage, strangely content at the Druid's words. She looked at the castle against the blue of the sky. She imagined it must have been magnificent in its former glory with the towers reaching to the clouds and the air filled with the MacLeod war cry.

The only evidence now of the massacre was the gray stone that was marred from the fire and the one tower yet to be rebuilt. The castle didn't house the MacLeod clan any longer, but if Fallon had his way, the land would be filled with people once more.

Druids and Warriors who dared to stand against an evil such as Deirdre would gather on this land and face the greatest battle of their lives.

"Larena!"

She turned to find Galen, Logan, and Camdyn holding up a large post.

"We need you," Galen called.

Larena glanced at the castle. Her confession to Fallon would have to wait.

Broc steeled himself, as he always did, before he walked into the mountain. Ten steps inside and he could hear the screams from the dungeons below. Those screams would haunt his dreams for eternity.

Though he wanted to find his own chamber, Broc knew he had to see Deirdre first. There would be a punishment for him, he was sure. Deirdre didn't like to be kept waiting.

Broc took the narrow stairs that wound up the mountain. When he reached the top, he turned left and walked down the corridor.

There were times he could have sworn the stones were alive, that they could read his thoughts and feel his hatred. He had been a part of Deirdre's army for so long now that he should be used to it, but he knew he never would be. The mountain was an unholy place, a place where wickedness thrived and built with each passing day.

He nodded to the two Warriors guarding Deirdre's door. They knocked and announced his presence. Broc heard her shout a response through the thick rock of her door.

As her double doors creaked open, Broc cleared his mind of everything but the MacLeods. It was a trick he had learned early on, and one that had saved his life countless times.

The first thing he did was look to the spot where

Deirdre had been holding James prisoner in the rocks. The Warrior lifted eyes full of hate and anger to Broc.

"Where have you been?" Deirdre demanded as she walked into the chamber.

Broc glanced at the doorway she had just passed through. He glimpsed her bed and a man's feet. He knew without a doubt it was Quinn. Was Quinn there because he wanted to be, or was Deirdre keeping him chained to her bed? Broc sighed inwardly. He wouldn't get to talk to Quinn again now.

Deirdre's white brows rose. "Well?"

"I stayed behind after the attack to see what Fallon and the others would do," he lied.

The ends of Deirdre's white hair twitched and rose from the floor. He had felt the sting of her hair before, and he had watched her strangle enough people with it to know that whenever she called for its use, it wasn't good.

"Did you tell Fallon everything I told you to?"

Broc bowed his head. "Of course, mistress. Every word." And then some, but she didn't need to know that.

"And Larena? Did you see her?"

"I did. She is alive."

Deirdre let her gaze run slowly over him. "You've been loyal to me a long time, Broc. I've never questioned your allegiance, but don't be late again or there will be punishment."

Through the bile that rose in his throat he continued to play her fool. "My apologies, mistress. I thought you would want to learn that they are rebuilding the village."

Deirdre's colorless eyes narrowed. "Is that so? Interesting, Broc. Very interesting." She started back toward her chamber, dismissing him, when she paused. "A group of Druids has been brought in by Dunmore. Help the others with the interrogation."

Broc's heart pounded in his chest and sweat beaded his brow. More Druids? How was she finding them? And how much longer before Anice and her Druids were discovered? "As you wish."

She paused, and with nary a word, the stones that held James released him. The pale green Warrior dropped to the ground and rubbed his arms and legs where he had been held. He gave a bow to Deirdre, and then stomped out of her chamber.

When Deirdre disappeared into her chamber, Broc turned and woodenly walked out of the room. The last thing he wanted to do was see the Druids tortured and killed, but he had no choice.

Broc turned the corner from the doorway and found Isla in his path. The *drough* was petite, barely reaching his chest, with long raven locks and ice-blue eyes that seemed to see straight through a man.

He didn't understand why Deirdre hadn't killed Isla like the other Druids. Isla rarely spoke and no emotion ever flickered over her face. Her eyes were as dead as Broc's heart.

"Isla," Broc said as he started around her.

"Did you see them?"

He paused as her softly spoken words filled the hallway. "See who?"

"The MacLeods."

"Aye. Deirdre had a message for them."

"They will come for their brother, Warrior, and the battle will be bloody. Many will die."

Her whispered words reverberated in his head long after she walked away.

TWENTY-SEVEN

It wasn't until the afternoon that Larena was able to get away to find Fallon. All day she had thought over what she would tell him—and how.

She didn't want to see the anger and hurt in his eyes, but she could no longer hold back the truth. What she had with Fallon was special, so special that she was willing to break her vow.

It had taken her too long to realize how much she needed Fallon, or maybe she had known all along but was too afraid to admit it. Regardless, she would right the wrong she had done to him and pray he still cared enough about her to hear her out. She would trust him with her greatest secret. It was going to be the hardest thing she had ever done, but she felt it was the right thing to do.

Somehow, she wasn't surprised to find Fallon on the beach. He stood on an outcropping of rocks gazing out over the water. Waves crashed around him, spraying him with droplets, but he never moved.

He was like a statue as he stood on the boulders—a handsome, dangerous Highlander whom she loved with all her heart.

That love was like someone had lifted her into the

clouds and allowed her to soar. Suddenly, there were possibilities she had never dreamed of. All because of Fallon and the love he had given her.

For long moments she watched him, mesmerized by the sight of him. In all her dreams, she had never imagined finding someone as honest and wise and good as Fallon. He was a man worthy of a great woman. Larena wasn't that woman, but she couldn't let go of him either.

If he wanted her, she was his.

Of a sudden, he turned his head and looked at her over his shoulder. His green eyes burned into hers.

Larena stepped off the path and walked toward him. She navigated the rocks easily in her breeches and boots, and when she looked up, Fallon was beside her, his long dark locks blowing in the breeze.

He held out his hand, and she didn't hesitate to take it. His warm, strong fingers closed over her hand as he led her farther against the cliffs, away from the sea.

"I'm surprised to see you here," he said.

Larena blew out a shaky breath. She had never been so scared in her life as she was at that moment. "I need to talk to you." She paused, unsure now that she faced him. "Why are you here?"

"I come here to think," he said as his gaze once more returned to the water. "My father used to bring me and my brothers down here to fish. We would talk of nothing or of important things. Always the sea has given me peace."

She looked at his profile and swallowed. "I can see that it does. You belong here, Fallon."

He turned his eyes to her. "And you, Larena? Where do you belong?"

"Nowhere. Everywhere. I have no home."

"You could have a home. Here. With me."

Her heart fluttered at his words. Unable to meet his gaze, she lowered her eyes to the ground and released his hand. "I have something to tell you. You won't like it."

"Tell me anyway."

She squeezed her eyes shut and pulled the ring off her finger. "This ring was given to me the day the goddess was unbound in me. It has been in my family since the first Warriors came into being."

When he said nothing Larena looked up. Fallon's face was impassive, his gaze fixed on her face.

"I made a vow that night that I would not speak of the ring . . . or why I wore it for any reason. For over a hundred years I've never taken it off. Until now."

She held out the ring and waited for him to take it. His fingers grasped it and brought it closer to his face to inspect it.

"Do you see the dark spot inside the stone?"

Fallon nodded. "I do."

Larena's hands shook as she raised them over the ring. She whispered the words Robena had taught her, words she thought she'd never use. There was a flash of light, and then the Scroll rested in her hands.

She brushed away a tear that fell onto her cheek and held out the Scroll to Fallon. "I should have told you. You trusted me."

He didn't take the Scroll as she expected. Instead, he handed her back the ring. "Put the Scroll away, Larena."

"You don't want to see it?" It was the one thing he

had sought for the release of his brother. She didn't understand why he wouldn't want to look at it. "You will need it for Quinn."

"I've known what the ring was, as well as what was in it, since the day I brought you here."

Larena stumbled backward, his words like a fist to her stomach. Her hands clenched the ring and Scroll. "What?"

"Sonya recognized the ring. She told me."

Larena returned the Scroll to the stone before she slid her finger between the gold confines of the ring. She wasn't sure what to say as her mind reeled from his words. He had known. *He had known!* "I see. You never asked me about it."

"The decision to tell me was yours. I couldn't push you into it, just as I can't make you stay in my bed with the rising of the sun."

"That's not fair, Fallon." She had come to him to release her heart only to learn he had known what she hid from him. He had still opened his arms to her, still marked her as his. He should hate her.

He grunted and raked a hand through his hair. "Life isn't fair. I've lived three hundred years alone, and most of those years are a blur thanks to the wine. It wasna until I met you that I truly lived. Can't you see how much I want you?"

"I do see it. It's the reason I came to tell you of the ring. I want to be with you too, Fallon."

"Nay, you don't."

He said the words so softly, that for a moment she wasn't sure she heard him correctly.

"But I do."

He shook his head, his eyes so full of sadness that it made her chest ache. "You want me when you need me, but the rest of the time I'm not worthy. I doona blame you. I'm not worthy. Not yet anyway. You've been alone for so long that you've gotten used to keeping everyone at a distance, and I'm . . . well, I'm a drunk who still fights the call of the wine. And I've got a lot to make up for."

His words stung more than she cared to admit. "You think you know me, but you don't."

"I know you better than you realize. You say you want me, but how much, Larena? How much do you desire to be with me? Will you be my wife so that we can spend the rest of our lives together? Or is it just enough that I share my bed with you each night?"

A lifetime with Fallon. The thought brought a thrill racing through her veins, but once the delight ebbed, she couldn't stop the worry of one day being alone again.

"Why can't what we have right now be enough?"

He took a step toward her, his face lined with grief. "Because I want more. I *need* more."

All her dreams of sharing time with Fallon crumbled around her. "I'm sorry. I can't give you what you need." She started back toward the castle, craving some time alone to mourn the love she had found . . . and lost.

"You can," he shouted after her. "You're just too scared!"

She spun around to face him. "You know nothing."

"Oh, but I do, Larena Monroe." He stalked toward her. His lips were pressed in a flat line and his jaw was clenched. Anger replaced his grief and gave his face a hard edge. "You're scared of being alone, afraid that there might be someone you can count on. You're terrified of putting your heart and soul in my hands for fear that I will leave you."

Her knees threatened to buckle. Each word was like a slap in the face, worse because they were true. She turned and ran away, ignoring Fallon as he shouted her name. Larena didn't stop until she found herself in a tower. She huddled on the floor in the small chamber and let the tears come.

No longer did she hold back the misery and loneliness she had ignored for too long. Fallon had ripped open her despair and it stared at her, demanding she acknowledge it.

But she couldn't.

Fallon cursed himself for ten kinds of a fool. He shouldn't have said those things to Larena. He knew he would have to handle her with care, but his temper had got the best of him when she said she couldn't give him what he needed.

He watched her race away from him, his heart breaking into a million pieces. He knew then he had lost her for good. The pain that ripped through him was worse than when he had lost his family and his clan.

Fallon fell to his knees from the weight of it. He threw back his head and spread his arms wide as he bellowed his anguish.

But even that didn't help.

He dropped his chin to his chest and covered his face with his hands. Everything he tried to fix, he only made worse. Look what had happened to Quinn. And now Larena.

He wasn't fit to lead himself, much less an army of Warriors if he couldn't win Larena. The rage that came over him was swift. His skin tingled with the change, but he didn't try to stop it. There was no stopping it now.

Mayhap not ever.

"Fallon?"

He jumped to his knees when he heard Lucan speak his name, but he didn't face his brother. "Leave me."

"I doona think so." Lucan continued to approach him. "What happened? I saw Larena run into the castle."

Fallon threw back his head and laughed, the sound hollow even to his own ears. "I've lost her, if she was ever mine to have."

"Tell me," Lucan urged, as he came to stand in front of him.

Fallon shook his head. "I need to be alone right now."

"We need you."

"Don't," Fallon bellowed. He turned his back to his brother. "You doona need me. You can lead these men, Lucan."

"Nay, Fallon. Please don't leave. I've already lost Quinn. I cannot lose you as well."

Fallon looked at the cliffs before him. He had failed Lucan too many times before, he wouldn't do it again even though every fiber of his being demanded he disappear and never return. "I'll be back, Lucan."

He bounded up the cliffs, not wanting to hear what his brother said in response. His heart hammered with exertion as he leaped from cliff to cliff and then raced over the rolling hills. He didn't rest or stop until his feet could no longer carry him.

Fallon fell to the ground and rolled onto his back, his rapid breaths burning his lungs. He used his arm to shield his eyes from the setting sun and gazed into the vivid blue of the sky.

He wished he knew where he had gone wrong with Larena. He wanted her back in his arms again, wanted to hold her sweet body and smell her delicious scent of lilies.

But he had lost her.

He ground the heels of his hands into his eyes, trying to erase the image of Larena's beautiful face from his mind. But Fallon knew that not even death could expunge her.

She was a part of him, just as his god was. Now and forever.

TWENTY-EIGHT

When Larena cracked open her lids the sky was gray. She wiped at eyes that were itchy and swollen from her tears, but she didn't care. Nothing mattered anymore.

She climbed to her feet and walked to the window. She hadn't cried so much since her father had been murdered and she had been truly alone for the first time in her life.

Hours had gone by while she was sunk in her misery. She was supposed to relieve Cara to look after Malcolm, but she had forgotten her promise while her heart mourned.

Just thinking of Fallon brought a renewed wash of pain in her chest. She wasn't sure how she was going to continue day after day with such anguish. She didn't know if she could. The pain she had felt at her father's murder was nothing compared to the ache within her now. This pain could never be soothed and would never leave her. Time might dim it, but all she would have to do was look at Fallon to see what could have been.

I cannot stay here. But I cannot leave. What am I to do now?

Larena blinked as her vision blurred with more

tears. She would face one thing at a time. Right now she would concentrate on Malcolm. He needed her.

She hurried from the tower. She was tempted to use her power so no one could see her, but she had been a coward for too long. Fallon had made her see that.

As she descended the stairs into the great hall she saw Ramsey and Hayden still bent over the parchment. Without a second thought, Larena extracted the Scroll from the ring and walked over to the men.

"Here," she said, and handed the Scroll to Ramsey. "This will help."

Ramsey's gray eyes narrowed as he looked from her hand to her face. "What is that?"

"The Scroll. I'm its keeper. I trust you will guard it with your life."

Hayden swore beneath his breath, and Larena felt the tears threaten again.

"I'm sorry. I should have told everyone, but I had taken an oath that I would never speak of it."

Ramsey reached for the Scroll and held it reverently between his hands. "There's no need for you to apologize, Larena. You can trust us."

"Just make sure our scroll is authentic enough to fool Deirdre. We need to get Quinn back. Fallon needs him."

"We won't let it out of our sight," Hayden promised. "You have our word."

She blinked her eyes to stop the seemingly constant tears and hurried from the castle. Every instinct within her told her not to trust Ramsey and Hayden, but she had to learn to do just that.

By the time she reached the cottage where Malcolm

was, she had dried her tears and gotten her emotions under control.

Larena opened the door to find Cara sitting next to Malcolm's bed with her sewing in her lap. The Druid looked up and beamed. The smile faded as she looked into Larena's face.

"Is everything all right?" Cara asked as she rose to her feet.

Larena forced a grin she didn't feel. Cara had always been so kind. Larena didn't wish to burden her with problems that weren't hers. "Everything is as it should be. I will sit with my cousin now."

Cara watched her for a few tense moments before she gathered her sewing. She paused as she opened the door. "If you ever need to talk to someone, Larena, I'm here for you."

The hated tears pricked her eyes. Larena hadn't intended to speak, but suddenly words poured out of her mouth. "It's been a long time since I've had a friend. Thank you, Cara."

"It is I who should thank you. You've helped Fallon in ways Lucan and I could never dream. I don't know what happened between you and Fallon while in Edinburgh, but he came back a changed man. Lucan says he's the man he was before their god was unbound."

Larena sank into the chair, her breath lodged in her throat. Had she helped Fallon? She didn't think so. Fallon would have become that man again without her. "I wish I could take credit, but Fallon has always been that man. He just needed to see that he could do it. He's a natural leader."

"You care for him a great deal, don't you?"

"I'm afraid it's much more than that."

Cara closed the door and hurried to her. She dropped down on her knees and took Larena's hands in her own. "You love him?"

"Aye, and I fear I've lost him."

Cara smiled gently, her dark brown eyes full of genuine warmth. "The MacLeod brothers are unusual, I'll give you that, but they are good men. Fallon cares for you, that much is obvious. You didn't see the look on his face when he arrived here with you in his arms. He had thought you were gone. He was like a madman, Larena. I've never seen such desolation before."

"Really?"

"He stayed with you the entire time Sonya healed you. His hand never left yours."

Larena glanced at the ceiling, praying Cara was telling her the truth. "He wasn't there when I woke. I thought . . ."

"There is something I'm going to tell you, something that Fallon doesn't want you to know. If Lucan knows I told you, he'll be very angry with me."

"What is it?" Larena had to know now. "I won't tell them."

Cara stood and blew out a breath. "Do you remember us telling you that you needed blood?"

"Aye."

"Fallon is the one that gave it to you. He wouldn't allow Lucan or any of the other Warriors to give you their blood. He wanted only his in your veins."

Larena's composure crumbled. Cara's image swam

with the tears that filled Larena's eyes, and the agony of exactly what she had lost. "I've been such a fool. Why didn't he tell me?"

Cara reached down and ran a finger over the milky-white stone on Larena's hand. "Because of this. He was hurt deeply that you hadn't told him."

"I told him today. I had no idea he already knew, but I had made a vow, Cara."

"He understood that."

Larena blew out a breath. "I cannot lose him now that I've just found him."

"If I know anything about the MacLeod brothers it's that they will come around. Give Fallon a little time."

Larena rose to her feet and wrapped her arms around Cara. "Thank you. Thank you so much. I didn't know just how lonely I was until Fallon brought me to his castle and gave me a family."

"You won't ever be alone here, Larena." Cara stepped back and wiped away the tears from Larena's cheeks. "Regardless of what happens, I will always be your friend and sister."

Larena smiled as Cara left, but her chest still felt as if her heart had been ripped from her. She reached over and took Malcolm's hand, needing his strength. She wished she could heal him as Sonya had done, but all she could do was sit and pray.

She studied the arm that had been broken so severely and ripped from the socket. Malcolm had made her think he was as strong as she was, but she should have known better. Leaving him hadn't been the answer. She should never have allowed him to associate with her in the first place.

"Don't."

Her gaze jerked to his face to find his blue eyes staring at her. "You can open both eyes now," she said with a smile.

"Don't."

"Don't what?"

"Don't think it was your fault this happened to me."

She sighed and dropped all pretenses. Malcolm had always gotten to the heart of any matter. It was what made him the man he was. "You nearly died because you've been seen helping me."

"Because I wanted to."

She smoothed away the hair from his forehead, thankful there was no fever. "I cannot wait to tell you everything. There are Druids here, Malcolm. One of them healed you. She's wonderful and amazing."

A shadow of a grin lifted the corner of his lips. "Indeed."

"And Warriors. Besides Fallon and his brother Lucan, there are five other Warriors here, including Camdyn."

"So he made it."

She nodded. "He did. Everyone has been here to see you. Are you still in pain?"

"A little. It's manageable. Tell me. Are you really in love with Fallon?"

"You were awake, I take it?"

"I was."

She sat back in the chair and clasped her hands in her lap. "I don't want to be, but it appears that Fallon has captured my heart. And the trust I never thought I would be able to give again."

"He's a good match for you, Larena."

She smiled despite the pain still in her chest. "Is he?"

"You couldn't have a better man at your side."

Larena wholeheartedly agreed. She was about to ask him about the attack he had endured when his eyes shut. With a wry grin, she let him drift back to sleep. There would be plenty of time to talk later. For now, he needed to get well.

She shouldn't have been as surprised as she was to see how rapidly he recovered. Whatever Sonya and Cara had done was, indeed, magical. It was the only explanation.

As for Malcolm's arm, Larena could only hope for the best.

She settled herself in the chair and leaned her head back. Her eyes closed as she let her mind wander to Fallon and the affection he had freely given her. She thought of the future, really thought about it, and pictured Fallon by her side.

There would be happiness with him, and love unlike anything she could dream of. But first, they would have to deal with Deirdre before they could have that future.

Yet, Lucan and Cara were doing it. There was no reason she and Fallon couldn't either.

Fallon came awake with a start. Something had moved near him, something that wasn't a part of nature. He kept perfectly still in the dark and listened. He had no idea where he was, and he'd been in such a rage, he hadn't paid attention to his surroundings.

His father had taught him better than that. Yet, he'd had to do something to control the fury or it would have taken him down a path he might never have recovered from. Even now, as he thought of Larena and how he had lost her, the anger shifted in his chest and threatened to burst forth again.

He cracked open an eye and saw the branches of a tree swaying to his right. He tried to remember the direction he had run. He had run north, away from the castle. But how far north?

He tensed as he heard a twig break in the silence. The usual sounds of the night weren't there, only the eerie, unnatural stillness.

And then he knew.

Wyrran.

Fallon opened his eyes further to get a better look. His advanced hearing could pick up the tiniest sound, letting him know the wyrran were close. Too close.

Fallon rolled to his side and jumped to his feet in one smooth movement. He leaped behind the nearest tree just as he spotted the first wyrran loping through the forest. He began to hear the clicks and soft shrieks that were synonymous with the creatures. There were dozens of them as well as Warriors. Fallon had to warn the others for he knew they were going to attack his castle.

His skin tingled as he unleashed his god. He ran his tongue over his fangs and sank his claws into the bark of the tree. There was no way he would allow the wyrran to capture Larena or harm anyone else at his castle.

A single Warrior walked while the others ran alongside the wyrrans. Fallon kept his gaze on the winged Warrior as he came to a stop beside him. Fallon tensed, waiting to be attacked.

Broc turned his head and his eyes locked with his.

Fallon waited for the Warrior to alert the others. Yet, Broc did nothing. After a moment, he shot into the air and spread his wings.

Shite!

Fallon didn't know what to think anymore. He didn't understand why Broc hadn't told the other Warriors about him. Deirdre would have had yet another Mac-Leod brother, and Lucan would have been on his own. But Fallon didn't have time to wonder about it.

He focused his thoughts on the great hall, gathering all his power around him. In his next breath he was back at his castle standing beside one of the tables.

"Damn, Fallon," Hayden said as he leaped from his seat at the table. "What is it?"

"Wyrran are coming. Gather the others and prepare. Where is Lucan?"

"Here," his brother said as he jumped from the floor above to the great hall. "How many?"

"Too many. Get the women and head to the dungeons. Guard the Druids, brother."

Lucan gave a curt nod. "And you?"

"I'm going to try to give you some time."

Hayden moved to stand beside him. "I'll come with you."

Cara raced down the stairs, her face white with fear. "Sonya and Larena are in the village tending to Malcolm."

Fallon cursed, torn between going to Larena and heading off the attack.

"Go," Ramsey said as he strode to the castle door, his skin turning bronze as he transformed mid-stride. "I'll make sure Sonya and Malcolm are safe."

With one last look at his brother, Fallon put his hand on Hayden and flashed them both to a spot of land away from the castle and village, but close enough that they could get back if needed.

Fallon jumped onto a rock that rose out of the earth like the fist of an ancient god. He seethed with anger at Deirdre's attack and his ire for not having Malcolm moved to the castle sooner. Malcolm and Sonya couldn't battle against the onslaught of evil coming their way.

And Larena.

He closed his eyes and wished he were beside her. She was a Warrior, but he was used to protecting women. She was his woman. He was a Highlander, and Highland men always sheltered their women.

"Larena," Fallon whispered.

"She'll be fine," Hayden said.

Fallon looked at the red-skinned Warrior that had taken up position on an outcropping of rocks to his left. Smoke rose from the tips of Hayden's horns and his fingers.

Fallon didn't pretend to not understand Hayden. "I pray you're right."

"Ramsey and the others will get Malcolm and Sonya to the castle. We'll have the most fun though." Hayden's fangs gleamed in the moonlight as he flashed Fallon a smile.

Fallon nodded. He longed to sink his claws into a wyrran, to tear a Warrior's heart out. His god lusted for blood, and Fallon was going to give it to him this night.

"Here they come," he murmured.

Hayden crouched down, his arms spread to the side

and his claws ready to slash. Fallon glanced at the sky and saw Broc soar above them. Was the winged Warrior heading to the castle to try and take Larena?

Fallon didn't have time to worry about it as the wyrran and Warriors came into view. He threw back his head and let out a war cry any MacLeod would have been proud of. Hayden's howl of rage rose to meet his.

The first wyrran jumped next to Fallon, and he lifted it over his head and then slammed the small yellow body on the stone. The wyrran's head smashed against the rock and split open.

Fallon barely had time to kick it out of the way as two more wyrran and a Warrior descended on him. He glanced at Hayden to see he was shooting flames from his hands. Fallon had no idea the red Warrior could call fire to him as his power.

Fallon grunted as a punch landed in his gut. He rammed his elbow into a Warrior and then slashed his claws across the Warrior's arm. Fallon grinned before he kicked a wyrran in the face.

An ear-piercing shriek filled the air as the wyrran went sailing off the boulder onto the ground to be trampled by its kin.

Fallon bit back a cry as the second wyrran raked his back with its claws. As he fought against the pain, the Warrior moved to stand in front of him and grabbed both of Fallon's arms to hold them out to his side. Fallon recognized the blue-skinned Warrior from his previous attacks on the castle.

"You cannot beat us," William said. "To fight against the inevitable is useless."

Fallon grinned before he sank his fangs into the Warrior's neck. Blood flowed through his mouth and over his chin. He gagged at the metallic taste of it, but wouldn't let go, even when the Warrior jerked against him.

Once his arms were free, Fallon plunged his claws into William's sides. Fallon ignored the pain caused by the wyrran that continued to claw his back and legs. All his focus was on the Warrior and killing him.

Suddenly, the blue-skinned Warrior wrenched backward, blood gushing from the bite wound on his neck and the five cuts on either side of him.

Fallon spat out the blood and turned to the wyrran behind him. He wrapped his hands around the wyrran's head and, with a yank, snapped its neck. Fallon roared into the night, his god, Apodatoo, demanding more blood, more death.

When he looked around, Fallon saw that the other Warriors and wyrran were ignoring them and heading toward the castle.

"Fallon, they've reached the castle," Hayden shouted. *Larena!*

Fallon leaped to Hayden's boulder and grabbed his arm as they jumped to the village.

TWENTY-NINE

Larena leaped from her chair as Ramsey burst into the cottage. One look at his bronze skin, claws, and fangs, and she knew something was wrong.

"What is it?" Sonya asked from the kitchen.

Ramsey glanced from Malcolm lying on the bed to Sonya. "An attack. We need to get you and Malcolm to the castle. Now."

"If we move him, we chance ruining his arm forever," Sonya argued as she rushed to the bed.

Ramsey strode to Malcolm's side and bent to lift him. "If we don't, he's dead."

"Where is Fallon?" Larena asked. "He can take Malcolm and Sonya in an instant."

Ramsey's Warrior bronze eyes held hers a moment, the silence filling the cottage. "Fallon and Hayden went to slow the attack."

"Just the two of them?" Her heart dropped to her feet. *Oh, saints.*

Malcolm grunted as Ramsey lifted him in his arms. Larena looked to her cousin's face to find him watching her. He nodded his head, and Larena knew what she had to do.

"Go with him, Sonya," Larena said.

Ramsey turned to her. "What are you planning?"

"I'll make sure you get Malcolm and Sonya to the castle. There's no time to argue, Ramsey. Go!"

When he didn't move, she called forth her goddess and sighed as the tickle of release stole over her skin a heartbeat before she changed.

She pushed past Ramsey and ran out the door into the village. The shrill cries of the wyrran could be heard, but it was the vicious roar that gave her pause. She knew without seeing him that it was Fallon who had given that bellow.

A shiver of dread and anxiety raced through her. What was approaching them wasn't the occasional wyrran she would fight and kill. These were hoards of wyrran and Warriors who were coming to take her to Deirdre.

"Never," Larena vowed as she flexed her claws.

She flicked one of her fangs over her lower lip as she walked from the village to stand between it and the castle. There was movement from behind her and she turned her head to see Galen, Logan, and Camdyn, all transformed with their gods, on either side of her.

"Make sure Ramsey gets to the castle with Malcolm and Sonya," she told Logan.

Logan glanced at the approaching attack. "I'll be back," he promised before he ran after Ramsey.

Larena's heart pounded in her chest while her blood drummed in her ears. She wondered where Fallon and Hayden were and if they were all right.

Please, God, keep Fallon safe.

Deirdre wanted Fallon, so there was a chance Fallon had been captured. Larena's blood ran cold at the thought. If Deirdre had somehow managed to imprison Fallon, Larena would do whatever she had to do to ensure he was freed. Whatever it took.

"Are you ready for this?" Galen asked from her right.

Larena shrugged. "Ready or not, it's coming."

"I've been itching for a fight," Camdyn said. "Let them come."

"Aye," she agreed. "Let them come and try their worst."

Galen grinned at her and shifted his shoulders. "It's going to be a bloody night."

No more words were spoken as the wyrran came into view.

Larena had never seen so many at once. For a heartbeat, she thought about running. And then she remembered who she was—what she was—and she stood her ground as her goddess came alive within her.

A glance over her shoulder showed her Ramsey and the others had gotten through the castle gate. She let out a sigh and faced the horde before her.

She joined Camdyn and Galen as they let out a roar. With one swipe of her claws, she beheaded the first wyrran that got close to her.

Larena pivoted and ducked a meaty fist she saw aimed at her face. When she straightened, she brought her own fist up between the Warrior's legs and punched him in the groin.

The Warrior cupped his hand around himself and fell to his knees. Larena took the opportunity and kicked him in the face. She reared back with her claws, but before she could behead him, Galen's arm came out of nowhere and did it for her.

"Behind you," he shouted.

Larena whirled around in time to catch a wyrran as it leaped at her. She fell back, the fall slamming her head onto the ground. The plunge momentarily stunned her, but it was enough for another wyrran to join the first as they began to use their claws on her.

Pain ripped through her as her chest and stomach were torn to shreds. She jerked her knee up and knocked one of the wyrran over her head. The second she grabbed by its arms and pulled, yanking the arms from the sockets with a loud pop and making them useless. She then rolled over on top if it and broke its neck.

Just as she stood, the first wyrran tried to attack her again. This time, Larena held out her claws and the creature impaled itself on them.

She flung the dead wyrran away and turned around. Only to find Fallon and Hayden now fighting with them. Fallon turned his head, his gaze meeting hers. Time slowed as awareness sizzled around her. With Fallon by her side she could face anything.

To her surprise, she saw Hayden using fire. That shock was short-lived as the earth trembled beneath her. She cast a look around to find Camdyn calling up the ground around them and using it as a weapon.

The wyrran and Warriors sent by Deirdre stopped in their tracks, staring at the wall of earth that separated them from Larena and the others.

"I cannot hold this forever," Camdyn shouted. "They are using their powers to break the wall."

Fallon's lungs felt as though they were on fire. He glanced at the Warriors around him, noting their wounds and the blood that coated them. His gaze came to rest on

Larena last. Her tunic was torn and barely hanging on her shoulders. Her iridescent skin shimmered like a beacon in the darkness, and all he wanted to do was take her in his arms and make sure she was all right.

"We cannot win this," he said. "There are too many of them."

"Malcolm is in the castle with Sonya," Galen told him.

Fallon nodded. "Good. We'll hold them as long as we can here."

"So they don't get the Druids," Larena finished.

There was a whoosh of air, and then they heard the flap of wings. Fallon looked up to find Broc hovering above them.

"This attack wasn't to kill," Broc said. "It is to capture as many of you as we can. Especially the Druids."

"Why are you telling us this?" Fallon demanded.

Broc glanced at the castle. "They are my reasons, MacLeod. I cannot tell you more."

Fallon's mind raced as Galen cursed. He waited until Broc had flown away before he ran a hand through his hair. They were outnumbered, and it was only a matter of time before someone was taken.

"We need to hide," Fallon said. "Camdyn, can you hold the wall for a little longer?"

The Warrior nodded, his focus on the wall of earth before him, his hands raised in front of his face. "I'll make sure it holds."

"What do you plan?" Galen asked.

"We need to hide, and not in the castle. Somewhere they won't expect to look," Fallon answered.

Hayden moved to stand near Camdyn. "Do what you need to, Fallon. I'll stand with Camdyn and ensure that any wyrran or Warrior that tries to break through this wall is burned."

Fallon turned to Larena, intent on taking her first, but she shook her head, her glorious iridescent locks moving around her.

"Nay. I have my own power, Fallon. I'll stay invisible if I have to. Get the others."

Fallon cursed. She was right, of course, but that didn't mean he liked leaving her. He grabbed her and planted a swift kiss on her lips. "Stay safe."

"I will," she promised.

With a sigh, Fallon turned to Galen. "You first, Shaw."

"Shite," Galen murmured, and clenched his jaw.

Fallon didn't give him another moment. He flashed himself and Galen into a cave in the cliffs. As soon as they were there, Fallon jumped to the dungeons of the castle.

"What's going on?" Lucan asked, his brow furrowed.

Fallon shook his head. "No time. Will explain later. We're leaving."

He needed to take more than one at a time, but he was afraid he'd fail. Yet, there wasn't a choice. He gathered Malcolm in his arms and nodded to Sonya. "Put your hand on me."

As soon as she did, he jumped them to the cave. Galen was there to take Malcolm and then Fallon was gone again. It took a matter of moments to get Lucan, Cara, Ramsey, and Logan to the cave, but it felt like an eternity.

By the time Fallon arrived back to Camdyn and Hayden, he couldn't see Larena. He prayed she was somewhere safe. Camdyn's wall of earth, though, was crumbling around them.

"Larena," he shouted. "To the cliffs. I'll find you there."

He didn't wait for an answer, but put his hand on Hayden and Camdyn and jumped them to the cave.

Fallon slumped against the cave wall, his body exhausted from the constant jumping with more than just himself. He straightened from the stones and started to leave when Lucan walked toward him.

"You need to rest."

Fallon nodded. "I just have to find Larena. She doesn't know the cliffs."

"She used her power then?" Lucan asked.

"Aye. I told her to meet me on the cliffs. I have to find her."

"Go then."

Fallon closed his eyes and took a deep breath before he jumped again. As soon as he stood on the edge of the rock face near the castle, he fell to the ground and watched as the wyrran and Warriors ran to fill the castle and the village. They would destroy what had been rebuilt, but it could be fixed again. All that mattered was that everyone was safe.

He was surprised to find no evidence that Camdyn had broken the earth and used it as a wall. It was as if it hadn't happened.

"Larena," Fallon shouted.

There was no answer. He didn't know where she was or if she had heard him tell her to meet him at the cliffs.

"Larena!"

With the wyrran screeching and the Warriors bellowing their fury, none of them could hear him. And at the moment, he wouldn't have cared.

"Larena."

"Here, Fallon. I'm here."

Fallon looked around and felt a hand on his arm an instant before she came into view. "Thank God," he said, and jerked her into his arms. "Are you badly injured?"

"I'm all right. Now."

He pulled off his tunic and handed it to her so she wouldn't arrive naked in the cave. As soon as she had it over her head, he jumped them.

"Thank the saints," Cara said when she caught sight of them.

Fallon wasn't ready to release Larena, but there were things he needed to see to. He pushed his god down and watched the black fade from his skin. The others had all transformed back into men as well.

"Is that everyone?" he asked.

"Aye," Ramsey said. "We're all here."

"Galen filled me in," Lucan said to Fallon. "What did they do when the wall of earth came down?"

Fallon ran a hand down his face and sank onto a stone. "It gave them only a moment's pause. They're in the castle and the village now."

Logan groaned. "Those bastards will destroy everything we've built."

"It can be rebuilt," Fallon said. "I'll keep rebuilding it to prove to Deirdre that she cannot stop us."

Larena dropped to her knees in front of Ramsey, her eyes wide and her skin pale. "The Scroll? Where is it?"

Fallon's heart missed a beat at her words. "You gave him the Scroll?"

Her stricken face turned to him. "I wanted to help."

"I have it," Ramsey told Larena, and pulled it from his tunic. "I wouldn't have left it, or the fake, for them to find."

"Thank you."

Ramsey paused before he gave the Scroll to Larena. "Have you ever read the names?"

She shook her head. "Nay. Why?"

Ramsey glanced at Fallon, a wealth of meaning in that one look. "No reason."

But Fallon knew better. Ramsey had seen something, and Fallon wanted to know what that was.

When the Scroll was once more in Larena's ring, Fallon breathed a sigh of relief. "We escaped this time, but it might not work again. They'll learn about the caves eventually."

"Then we need to find somewhere else," Sonya said.

Hayden growled. "I'm a Warrior, Fallon. I don't like hiding."

"Neither do I," Fallon said, and got to his feet. His next words would have to be chosen wisely, or he could lose the group of men—and women—he had come to rely on. "Do you think I like running away from Deirdre? I'd rather fight to my death, but they weren't here to kill, Hayden. They were here to capture us. Would you rather run away, or be back in Deirdre's mountain?"

Hayden turned his head away and refused to speak, which was answer enough.

"What the hell are we going to do?" Lucan asked. "Deirdre has more wyrran than we could kill, and even if we did manage to kill all of them, she would just make more."

Fallon watched as Lucan pulled Cara's trembling form into his arms. Sonya sat beside Malcolm, who had been laid on the ground. The other Warriors waited for Fallon to respond, but it was Larena's smoky-blue eyes that he sought.

She gave him a small nod of encouragement. Fallon swallowed and crossed his arms over his chest. Her strength and belief in him gave him the fortitude he needed.

"We've all vowed to fight against Deirdre. Tonight hasn't changed my mind. I will stand against her until there is no breath left in my body."

The others mumbled agreement.

"I doona know what Deirdre's plan is next, but beyond a doubt, my next step is to get Quinn out of her clutches. I'm not going to wait another moment. I'm leaving in the morning. My fight to get Quinn back is my fight. I'm not asking any of you to come with me."

"That's a hell of a way to speak to us," Galen said, his voice as cold as the north wind. "I came to you, to your brothers, to defeat Deirdre. That includes helping get Quinn free. So, I'm going with you whether you want me or not."

One by one, the other Warriors stepped forward and pledged themselves to him. Fallon was overcome with emotion. He clenched his hands, afraid to speak.

"I always told you, brother," Lucan said. "But you never listened. I would follow you into hell itself."

"I'm afraid that's just where we're going, Lucan," Fallon murmured.

Larena rose and came to stand in front of him. "You saved me from death with your blood. You brought me here to protect me from Deirdre. You gave me . . . hope. Is there any other place I would be but by your side?"

He didn't know how she knew it was his blood in her veins, but it didn't matter. "I cannot bring you near Deirdre. I would die if she imprisoned you."

"But she won't. Do you forget that I can be invisible? I'm your best advantage at getting into the mountain and finding Quinn to let him know we've come to rescue him."

"She's right," Cara said. "As much as I hate to admit it, she's right."

Sonya blew out a breath and licked her lips. "The truth, Fallon, is that you're going to need all of us. If someone is injured, you'll need me to heal them."

"Nay," Lucan bellowed. "You and Cara aren't going anywhere near that damned mountain. If one of us is injured, Fallon can jump them back to you. Besides, we cannot leave Malcolm by himself."

"Lucan is right," Fallon said before Cara or Sonya could argue. "I'm risking too much by bringing Larena and the other Warriors to Deirdre. But with every drop of Druid blood, especially the Demon's Kiss around Cara's neck," he said, motioning to the vial that held the *drough* blood of Cara's mother, "Deirdre's power grows."

"I can help," Cara argued.

Fallon nodded. "And you will, but from the castle. We will be injured, and it will take both you and Sonya to aid us."

Cara relented after Lucan whispered something in her ear. Fallon shifted his gaze to Sonya to see her defeated expression, but she nodded in understanding.

"Good." He lowered himself to the rock and leaned against the wall behind him. He had never felt so tired or drained in his life.

A small, tender hand touched his face. Fallon turned toward the contact, needing to feel Larena's skin against his.

"How are your wounds?" he asked.

She shrugged. "They've healed."

"We got away this time, but we might not the next."

"We'll deal with that when the time comes. You did well tonight, Fallon. Never doubt that. It was quick thinking getting us away from the attack and somewhere they couldn't find us."

He grunted, unsure her praise was warranted. "I thought my heart would leap from my chest when I saw you fighting. You were magnificent."

"So were you."

He opened his mouth to tell her he was sorry for earlier, but she moved away from him, retreating to a corner by herself.

Maybe it was for the best, Fallon told himself. There were too many ears listening, and the things he had wanted to say—the things he *had* to say—were for Larena only.

Fallon rose and walked to Sonya, who hadn't left Malcolm's side. He knelt by the Druid and nodded at Malcolm. "How is he?"

"He was doing better before he had to be moved." Her hand hovering over his broken arm, she sighed. "I had to make him sleep he was in such pain, Fallon. He wanted to help fight, and I fear he would have if I had not done something."

"You did the right thing. Larena would have both our heads if something happened to her cousin."

Sonya shrugged and tugged a strand of fiery hair behind her ear. "I fear what the damage this night has done to his arm. It has begun to swell again. My magic can only do so much."

"Do what you can. That's all we can ask of you."

She licked her lips and turned her amber eyes to him. "Is it enough? My healing abilities have always been great and exceeded what most Druids are able to do, but I fear that the one day I will really need my magic, it will fail me."

A stab of fear jabbed in Fallon's heart. "Did you have a vision of this?"

"Nay, just a . . . sense of what is to come."

Which meant a vision, but Fallon wasn't going to argue with a Druid. "Have you joined Cara's magic with yours for Malcolm?"

"We were just about to do that again when you returned. I will see it done now."

Fallon moved away as Sonya motioned for Cara to join her. He stood to the side and watched the Druids work. Though he couldn't see the magic move from their hands to Malcolm's body, he could feel it.

There was a distinct change in the air, a crackle almost, that alerted a Warrior that magic was near. In a powerful Druid like Sonya, a Warrior could sense what she was before she spoke.

Cara had been different because she hadn't known she was a Druid and hadn't developed her magic. Now that Sonya had begun training her, Fallon could sense the magic growing in his sister-in-law by the day.

They were fortunate to have two Druids with them, and every Warrior there would do everything they could to protect them from Deirdre.

Fallon sighed and made himself as comfortable as possible. It would be a few hours yet before the wyrran and Warriors gave up looking for them. Meanwhile, he would plan his attack on Deirdre.

THIRTY

Deirdre wanted to kill something, to rip her army limb from limb and display their heads on pikes atop her mountain. How could her Warriors, her wyrran, not have captured at least one from MacLeod Castle?

"You should have seen what Fallon can do," William said. "One moment he's standing in front of you, the next he's half a league away."

Deirdre tapped one long nail against her leg. "So, he's finally learned of his power. I wondered when he would figure it out."

She couldn't help but speculate on what Lucan's and Quinn's power would be. Had their god given them the same power, or did each of them have something different? She would have to keep her eye on Quinn so he didn't just poof out of her mountain.

"Broc," she said as she turned to her only winged Warrior. "What do you have to say in all of this?"

He shrugged a dark blue shoulder, his wings brushing the two Warriors on either side of him. "You've underestimated them, mistress. Another has been added to their ranks. Camdyn MacKenna."

Deirdre blew out a breath. "I'd had such hopes for Camdyn. It's too bad he's aligned against me. The only saving grace in this awful day is the group of Warriors seized on their way to MacLeod Castle."

"How many?" Broc asked.

There was something in Broc's tone. He had been the one to spot the small group, and had told her, but she couldn't stop the niggle of doubt in her mind. "Only four. One died when he was given too much *drough* blood in his wounds."

She walked to Broc, the other Warriors moving away from him. Her long nail trailed down his bare sculpted chest to his flat stomach then to the waist of his breeches.

"Your idea to use a small amount of *drough* blood to incapacitate them was brilliant, Broc."

He looked at her with his midnight-blue eyes and shrugged. "I am here to serve you."

"So you are." She hadn't taken Broc to her bed, and if Quinn wasn't lying in that bed now, she would be tempted to taste the winged Warrior for herself. As it was, it would have to wait.

"Continue to keep watch on the MacLeods," she ordered Broc, and stepped away before she ran her hand over his cock to see how fast she could arouse him. "Return tomorrow to bring me news."

"As you wish, mistress."

Maybe the doubt she felt wasn't about Broc but another Warrior. She would have to keep a closer watch on her men. After all, if Broc had broken away from her, he wouldn't have given her the location of the Warriors on their way to the MacLeods.

Nay, Broc was hers. All hers.

* * *

Minutes ticked into hours. The rain had come and gone in a quick burst. The waves drowned out any sounds that might be coming from the castle, but Fallon had waited as long as he could. Dawn would be upon them soon, and he wanted everyone back in the castle.

He nodded his head toward the mouth of the cave, indicating that Lucan should follow him. Fallon started for the entrance only to find Larena standing there, her arms wrapped around herself.

His tunic hung to the middle of her thighs, and the breeze lifted the hem and molded the fabric to her curves. The sight of her bare legs made all the blood rush to his cock so fast the world started spinning.

She had loosened her hair from its braid so that it fell around her in golden waves. He itched to sink his hands in the silken depths and bury his face in the thick strands so he could inhale her natural fragrance of lilies.

Fallon walked to her, unable to stay away. She didn't take her eyes from the water. She stared at the churning depths as if mesmerized.

"What is it?" Lucan asked.

Fallon jerked his attention from Larena and turned to his other side where Lucan had come to stand. "I'm going to go take a look and see how many are still in the castle."

"Let me come with you."

"Nay. I willna be long. I just want a quick look. Everyone is tired, and I want them back in their chambers as soon as we can get them there."

Lucan sighed. "Just be careful."

Fallon waited until his brother walked away before he glanced at Larena. "Are you all right?"

"It's beautiful up here," she murmured. "All I can hear is the sea and the wind. I had no idea we were so far up the cliff."

"I used to see this opening when I swam in the sea. I always wondered what was in the cave. When we came back here from Deirdre's, it's the first place I went. I spent a lot of time here trying to calm my mind and prepare myself to be the man my brothers needed me to be. It didn't work."

She turned her head to him then. The moon's reflection off the water showed in her smoky-blue eyes. "I can see why you came here. Just imagine how you would have been without this cave."

"True enough, I suppose."

"Hurry back," she whispered.

Fallon wanted to pull her into his arms and kiss her. He wanted to drown himself in her touch. Having her so close was the sweetest torture a man could endure.

He wasn't sure where they stood. After their argument, there had been the attack and no time for them to talk. He knew she still desired him, but that didn't mean she wouldn't push him away. And it was that thought that stopped him from reaching out to her.

He unleashed his god and jumped to the castle before he could change his mind and kiss her.

Fallon cursed under his breath as he saw a handful of Warriors and several wyrran milling around the castle and the village. A large fire burned in the village, and he suspected it was a cottage.

Though he should get back to the cave, there was something in his chamber he wanted. He jumped to his chamber to find it not only empty, but undisturbed.

Either the wyrran hadn't made it to his chamber yet, or they hadn't felt the need to destroy it.

"Unlikely," he said.

Fallon strode to the largest of his chests and threw open the lid. He pushed aside his tunics until he found the smaller ornate chest within. He lifted the small box and held it in his hands, staring at it for long moments.

The last time he had looked inside had been over three hundred years ago. He had never thought to open it again, but as soon as he had met Larena, he had wanted to get back to the castle and find the coffer.

Fallon slowly opened the lid and looked at the piece of jewelry within. His stomach clenched at the thought of Larena wearing it. He knew in that instant how deep his feelings for her went.

He lifted the gold from its resting place and tucked it in the waist of his breeches. It took only a moment to put everything back as it was, and then Fallon jumped to the cave.

Larena wished she and Fallon were alone. She needed to tell him he had been right, that she had been scared. But not anymore. Not as long as she had him.

She wasn't sure when she had stopped being frightened, only that the emotion that had been with her for years was suddenly gone.

Before Fallon had left, she'd thought he was going to kiss her. She'd seen the longing in his eyes, but he hadn't. Her disappointment had been almost too much to bear. She hoped she hadn't ruined things between them forever. She was ready to get on her knees and plead with him if that's what it came to. She'd do anything as long as she could have him for her own.

Her hand lifted to touch the mark he had given her. His mark.

"Cara told me of your conversation," Lucan said as he came to stand beside her.

Larena had expected to hear from Lucan eventually. She didn't look at him, just kept her gaze on the sea below. "Have I lost Fallon?"

There was a long silence during which Larena thought he wouldn't respond. Then Lucan sighed. "When we were growing up I used to watch my brother with women. They flocked to him because of who he was and the power that he would someday have as laird of our clan. He was always good to the women, but not once did I ever see him look at one as he does you. There is hunger and need and something even deeper in his gaze. Only for you."

Larena's heart raced, her hope growing. She turned to look at Lucan only to find him watching her.

"You cannot lose Fallon because he cares too much for you. If you want what he has to offer, tell him. He needs you."

"And I need him," she confessed. "I need him more than I thought possible."

Lucan's hand landed on her shoulder to give her a brotherly squeeze. "Both of you are strong individuals. Together, you can do great things."

"Like you can with Cara?"

"Even more because of the man Fallon is. He's a leader, Larena. He needs a strong woman by his side whom he can lean on."

Larena placed her hand over his and smiled. "I'll be that woman if he'll have me."

No sooner had Lucan walked back to Cara than Fallon reappeared in the cave. Larena listened as he told of the few Warriors and wyrran left wandering the castle and village. She glanced back at the sea and the waves rolling onto shore.

She didn't want to wait to talk to Fallon but leaving the cave was chancy. However, it was a chance she was willing to take.

Her skin heated as it always did when she felt Fallon's gaze on her. She gave him a smile over her shoulder before she dove out of the cave.

Fallon ran to the mouth of the cave and watched as Larena dove headfirst to the rocks below only to roll in a ball and land as softly as a cat crouched on her feet.

"God's teeth," Hayden murmured.

Someone whistled, and that's when Fallon realized everyone had crowded around him. His blood heated and surged when Larena straightened and walked to the edge of the water, throwing off his tunic in the process.

"That's one hell of a woman," Logan said.

Galen, who stood next to Fallon, punched Fallon in the shoulder. "You're one lucky bastard, MacLeod."

Fallon chuckled. Then he met his brother's gaze. "Aye, I am."

He jumped from the cave, landing not far from Larena's spot. She was already in the water when Fallon jerked off his boots and breeches. He laid the gold gently on top before he walked into the sea.

Larena stood looking at him, the waves rolling

around her, lifting her up before releasing her once again. Fallon didn't take his eyes off her as he moved through the water. He fought against the tide that tried to push him back to the beach.

It wasn't until he stood before Larena that he allowed himself to breathe. There was so much to tell her, so much to say, he didn't know where to begin.

"You were right."

Her words surprised him. "About what?"

"I was scared. Everyone I have ever cared about left me. It would have been worse with you because you're immortal."

Fallon took her hands in his and pulled her against him. He rested his cheek on her forehead and just held her. "Don't you understand? You have my heart and my soul, Larena. They are yours to do with as you want. I could never leave you."

Her arms wound around him, holding him as if there were no tomorrow. She trembled, whether from the cool water or his words, he didn't know.

He pulled away from her and looked into her beautiful eyes and knew the feeling within him was love. "I cannot promise that we won't fight, that there won't be days you won't want to smash my head in. But I can promise that I will love you always and do my best to make you laugh at least once a day. I can promise that my life will be devoted to you and giving you everything you could want to make you happy."

"There is only one thing I want."

"Tell me. It's yours."

A tear fell from her eye to roll slowly down her cheek. "You, Fallon MacLeod. I want you."

Emotion clogged his throat, making it difficult to speak. "I love you," he whispered, just before he placed his lips on hers.

He drank in her heady taste, drowning in everything that was uniquely hers. Her hands delved into his hair, and he moaned in response.

The waves pushed her into him, rubbing her body against his in ways that only stoked the fire in his blood. He grasped her hips and held her above his hard, aching cock.

"Take me, Fallon. I'm yours. I'll always be yours," she murmured.

He lowered her until he was seated to the hilt. She leaned back into the water, her hair floating around her like a sea of gold.

Fallon groaned her name as she rotated her hips. Pleasure flooded him, turning his veins to molten lava. The sight of her luscious breasts with water floating around them and her nipples already hard was too much to take.

He leaned down and sucked a delicious bud in his mouth. Her nails raked his shoulders when he gently bit down on the hard peak and ran his tongue back and forth over the nub.

"Fallon," she screamed, her back arching.

He wanted her too desperately to hold back the flow of his desire. As much as he longed to lick every inch of her, his body wouldn't let him now.

Fallon withdrew from her only to thrust long and deep. Again and again he pulled out and plunged within her, harder, faster. She matched his tempo, their gazes locked.

Her mouth opened on a silent scream as her slick walls convulsed around him. Fallon continued to pump inside her, trying to draw out her orgasm as long as he could before he threw back his head and filled her with his seed.

Fallon's body jerked with the force of his climax, but Larena was there, her arms wrapped around his neck as she smoothed the hair from his face.

"You keep surprising me," she whispered in his ear before she bit down on the lobe.

Fallon trembled and ground his hips against her. He was still buried inside her, still hard. "It's you. You do this to me."

"I love you."

He pulled back until he could see her eyes. He knew she cared for him, that much was obvious by her earlier words, but he hadn't expected to hear her declaration of love.

"Larena . . ."

She placed her finger on his lips. "I tried to deny it, but the feeling continued to grow. I love you more than life itself, Fallon MacLeod. I'll take the fights and the laughter and however many years we have together, as long as I have your love."

"Ah, God, Larena. You'll always have my love."

He carried her to the shore were he sat with her on a boulder.

"I know I shouldn't have left the cave, but I needed to talk to you."

Fallon shrugged and intertwined his fingers with hers. "If any wyrran saw us, we'll take care of them."

"I endangered the others."

"Most of them are Warriors still eager for battle. It will be all right."

She turned her head to him and smiled. "I think I will want to take midnight swims often."

"I agree." Fallon stared at the stars above him in a sky that had turned from black to light gray. Everything was almost as it should be. "Only Quinn is missing."

"We'll get him back," Larena said, and kissed his shoulder. "Quinn will be back with you and Lucan where he belongs."

Fallon blew out a breath. "I hope you're right."

To his surprise, Larena sat up and tugged on his arm. "I've missed every sunrise with you. I'm not going to miss another."

Fallon jumped from the boulder. "Stay right there." He hurried to put on his breeches and boots. He hid the gold beneath the tunic she had discarded before her swim.

He walked back to her and handed her the tunic. Her forehead furrowed when she felt the gold through the fabric.

Fallon waited with bated breath for her to find it. When she pulled the golden torc from the folds of his tunic and stared at it, he thought he would die of anxiety.

Her eyes shifted to him. "A torc with a boar's head."

"It matches mine. I had it made before Deirdre destroyed my clan, in the hopes of one day giving it to the woman I would spend the rest of my life with."

Larena caressed the torc lovingly. "You want me to have this?"

"I want you to marry me."

"Fallon, are you sure?"

He laughed. "You're the one thing I am sure of. Say you'll be my wife, Larena."

"Oh, aye, Fallon," she said with a wide smile. "If you want me, you can have me."

He pulled her off the boulder and into his arms. "I want to get married immediately. I want everyone to see the torc."

"Your mark wasn't enough?" she asked with a chuckle.

"I need to bind you to me any way I can."

She leaned back and kissed him. "You already did with the most powerful thing you could. Your love."

EPILOGUE

Larena blew out a nervous breath and touched the torc that now rested around her neck. The weight of it felt right against her skin, as if it should have been there long before. The bailey was filled with the Warriors and Druids she now called her family.

"Are you sure?" Fallon asked her.

Larena raised a brow at him. "If you ask me that again, I swear I will have to beat you."

He smiled, but she saw the worry in his dark green eyes.

"I won't do anything reckless, Fallon. We just got married. Now, let me do what I need to do to find Quinn."

Fallon ran a hand through his hair and briefly closed his eyes. "I pray I'm doing the right thing. I'll never forgive myself if someone gets taken or hurt."

"We will heal," Lucan said. "Now, let's get moving before Cara comes up with a good reason to go with us."

Larena glanced at her new sister-in-law, who stood on the steps of the castle together with Sonya. Cara's eyes were clouded with apprehension, her hands fisted at her sides. Larena couldn't imagine being left behind, so she understood Cara's feelings.

Next to Cara was Malcolm. She still couldn't believe what Ramsey had told her and Fallon just the night before. Not even seeing the Monroe name on the Scroll helped things.

She had foolishly thought she was the Monroe Warrior, but it seemed her goddess came through her mother's family. It took seeing her mother's maiden name and the Monroe name for it to finally sink in.

It was Fallon's suggestion that they keep the news from everyone, especially Malcolm. Ramsey hastily agreed, but Larena couldn't help but worry about Malcolm; she feared he would be taken by Deirdre to be turned into a Warrior.

"Come, Fallon," she urged her new husband. "Let us bring Quinn home."

"Aye," the other Warriors shouted.

Fallon's eyes narrowed and glanced into the distance where Deirdre's mountain lay. "Hang on, Quinn. We're coming for you."

Malcolm stood on the steps of the castle and watched the small group leave. His arm ached constantly, and no matter what magic Sonya and Cara used, nothing helped. He had realized after waking in the cave that his arm was useless.

He had promised Larena that he would wait for her at the castle before heading to the Monroe lands, but it was a lie. He would never return to his clan because they wouldn't accept him. Not now, now that he was half a man.

Malcolm nodded to Camdyn, who had stayed behind to protect the Druids. At least he knew Camdyn.

Malcolm liked the other Warriors, but he didn't belong here. He wasn't a Warrior or a Druid. He was nothing but a mortal that was of no help in the coming war.

Yet, Fallon had offered him a home at MacLeod Castle. Malcolm hadn't expected that, but it reinforced his opinion that Fallon was the right man for his cousin.

He gripped his shoulder with his good hand and tried to push past the pain. It wasn't as if he were entirely useless. He had learned to wield a sword using either arm, and he was just as good with his left as he had been with his right.

Sonya's intelligent amber gaze watched him. He guessed she knew he lied about the pain. The Druid had said nothing, probably to spare his pride, but she didn't like that he had gotten out of bed that morning.

He snorted as he turned to enter the castle. The scars that now showed on his face, neck, arms, and chest would have been enough to wound any man's pride. Add the loss of an arm, and it could destroy a man.

"There are things I can give you to help with the ache," Sonya said. "More magic could help your shoulder as well."

Malcolm glanced at the Druid but continued walking. As usual, her red hair was pulled back into a single braid that fell down her back. "I need to cope with it."

"You are still healing, Malcolm. It has only been a few days since you were brought to us."

He halted and turned to her, his anger bubbling to the surface. "You know as well as I that I've lost the use of my arm. Admit it. Not even your magic could heal it."

"I won't admit any such thing. We won't know the extent of your injuries until the bone has fully mended. With my magic that could be only days. The best thing you can do is keep the arm still. Larena has been through enough. Do not hurt yourself while feeling sorry for yourself, because it will only wound her."

Malcolm blew out a breath and nodded. Her words were the truth, although he wanted to inflict pain on himself for not being strong enough to fight off the Warriors who attacked him. "I don't need your herbs, Druid. I will handle the pain."

Sonya watched him walk slowly up the stairs to his new chamber. She ached for the Highlander, but there was nothing more she could do for him. Her magic was strong, but she couldn't heal everything. What was done to his arm was more extensive than she had let the others know. It was more than just a break.

Deirdre's Warriors had crushed the bones in his hands and arm. It was why he was in constant pain, as his bones continued to mend. As much as she hated to admit it, the odds of him having the full use of his arm again were slim, even with as much magic as she had used.

She knew there was a future for him at MacLeod Castle, but to what depth she couldn't see. It was one of the few times she wished her sister, Anice, was near so she could see into the future.

But maybe it was better this way.

Sonya blew out a breath and returned to her chamber to finish making the brew that would keep Cara and Larena from becoming pregnant. Everyone doubted the possibility of a Druid getting with child by a Warrior, but Sonya knew differently. Now was not the time for any of them to be pregnant.

Quinn opened his eyes not to the darkness of his prison, but to a room filled with light from many candles. He knew instantly where he was—Deirdre's chamber.

He sat up slowly, disgusted to find he was naked beneath the single linen sheet. When he spotted clothes folded on a chair, he jumped from the bed and hastily dressed in the trousers, tunic, and boots.

After taking quick stock of his body, he realized he was completely healed. He had no idea how long he had been in Deirdre's bed, or just what she had done to him while there, but he wanted out. Immediately.

"You're finally awake."

He jumped at the sound of the hated voice. Quinn turned and found Deirdre in the doorway. He could barely stand to look at her as she leaned against the door frame in what was intended to be a seductive pose.

"What did you do to me?" he demanded.

Her brows lifted. "Do? Why, I healed you. After I punished the Warriors, of course, for beating you as they did."

"Isn't that what you wanted?"

She pushed away from the door and walked to the bed. She leaned down and touched the pillow where his head had been. "I want you as mine, Quinn. You've always known that. I thought I could break you. When I captured you, your god almost had complete control over you."

"Almost."

She lifted a thin shoulder. "I will do what I need to do to ensure you are mine in the end. I have great plans for us, Quinn."

"And if I don't want to be a part of them?"

"Oh, you will."

He fisted his hands and struggled to manage his rage. It would do no good for him to lose control now. "I would rather die first."

Suddenly, Deirdre's hair lashed out to wrap around his neck and squeezed. Quinn wanted to claw at the strands, but he held himself still, his gaze never leaving hers.

God's blood, how he hated looking at her, talking to her. Her shell of a body might be beautiful, but her soul was so drenched in malevolence that it made him gag.

"I offer you power beyond your wildest dreams."

"Keep it," he said through clenched teeth. "I'm not interested."

Her hair tightened around his throat. "I thought showing you how things could be by my side might change your mind, but I can see that I was wrong. Maybe some time in the Pit is what you need."

Quinn grinned. There was nothing she could do to him that would frighten him now. Not even sending him to the Pit, which he knew men rarely came out of alive. He was already in hell, already dead as far as he was concerned.

"Do your worst, you evil bitch."

Read on for an excerpt from
Donna Grant's next book

WICKED
HIGHLANDER

Coming soon from St. Martin's Paperbacks

"You've got a rather nasty bump on the back of your head, and I think your ribs are bruised."

Marcail stilled at the sound of the deep, rich voice that sliced through her like the mist that came down from the mountains. A shiver raked her body that had nothing to do with the cool temperatures that surrounded her.

For that short moment, she forgot the throbbing of her head and how it hurt to breathe. All she could think about was who belonged to such a sensual, commanding voice.

And did she dare find out?

With each pounding inside her head, she recalled everything that had happened over the past week, beginning with her running through the forest and being cornered by Dunmore and the wyrran. Then she had been brought to Deirdre and thrown into the Pit.

She remembered being surrounded by Warriors before something big and black leapt on top of her. She sucked in a sharp breath and instantly regretted it as the ache exploded in her chest.

"Easy."

The same seductive, smooth voice surrounded her

once more, his tone left her feeling safe and protected. It was a ruse, she knew, but in her current condition there was nothing she could do about it.

Marcail licked her lips, then bit back a moan as that simple movement caused pain to burst in her head once more. She lay there a moment, thinking she heard what sounded like a chant. The more she tried to listen to it, the faster it faded until there was nothing.

Any moment she expected her head to explode from the pain. When nothing happened, she cracked open an eye to see she was surrounded in darkness. She hated the dark because of what it represented—evil. With a sigh, she closed her eyes and concentrated on alleviating the aches of her body.

She placed her hand on her forehead and felt a large, warm hand cover hers. "I have nothing to help with your pain."

Was there concern in his voice? She swallowed to wet her dry mouth. "I will be all right."

"You are a healer then?"

She went to shake her head, but his hand held her still. Instead, she said, "Nay. I was taught how to speed the healing of my body."

Marcail wasn't sure why she'd told the stranger that. She shouldn't trust him, even if he had saved her. Or had he? Was it just another trick by Deirdre?

"You need to mend yourself then," he said, his husky voice dropping even lower. "By saving you, I've put you in terrible danger. I will protect you, but with your injuries, it will make it more difficult."

She never liked being a burden to anyone, but there

was something in his voice, a thread of despair and heartache that mirrored her own and caused emotions to stir within her. She had to have his name. "Who are you?"

"My name doesn't matter. Rest and heal yourself, Druid."

The pain of her body began to drag her under, but she fought to stay awake, to learn more about the mysterious man beside her. "Marcail. My name is, Marcail."

"You have my word I will protect you. Now, sleep."

She could have sworn as she drifted off to sleep that he whispered her name.

Quinn lifted his hand from Marcail's forehead once he was sure she was asleep. He picked up her small hand and placed it on her stomach. Unable to help himself, he ran his fingers over the back of her hand feeling her soft, supple skin. It wasn't until his claws touched her that he worried about her discerning what he was.

It was Warriors, after all, who had thrown her into the Pit. She trusted him now, but how long would that last once she realized she was surrounded by more Warriors—most of whom wanted her for her body?

He told himself to leave her and let her sleep, but he couldn't make himself rise. He didn't fight the urge to stay near her. It seemed harmless enough. But when the desire to touch her rose within him, he fisted his hands on his thighs until he shook with the crushing need to lay his hands on her again. Was this how Lucan had felt when he'd had Cara in his arms?

Quinn knew in that instant that he had made a fatal

mistake. There was something about the female that moved a deep, dark primordial reaction inside him. That emotion could very well be the death of him.

With a curse Quinn leaped to his feet and stalked to the cave entrance. Marcail was too tempting, too sweet to be left alone with the likes of him. He would only bring her down as he had everything else in his life.

"She woke?" Arran asked.

Quinn almost didn't answer. "Briefly. She's in a tremendous amount of pain. However, she told me she knew how to help herself heal."

"Not surprising. Every Druid holds a special kind of magic. It's lucky for the female that she can mend herself."

Quinn grunted, not wishing to speak of Marcail anymore since his body hungered for her so. "Any sign of trouble?"

Arran crossed his arms over his chest and jerked his chin to the left. "They smell her. God's blood, Quinn, we all smell her. She's like a feast to a starving man, in more ways than one. We're going to have our hands full."

"I'll be watching her myself." Quinn knew his voice came out more of a growl than anything, and Arran's narrowed white gaze let Quinn know the Warrior had heard the challenge in it.

"Do you think I would fight you for her?" Arran asked, his voice hard with disbelief. "I gave you my word I would stand by your side. Do you doubt me?"

"What I question is the need within all of us—myself included."

Arran blew out a breath and raked a hand down his face. "None of us deserves to be here, the Druid especially because she doesn't stand a chance against us in a fight. Did she say anything else?"

"She told me her name. It's Marcail."

"Marcail," Arran repeated. "An unusual name. She didn't happen to say why Deirdre didn't kill her, did she?"

Quinn shook his head. "Not yet."

"Let's hope she wakes soon so we can learn more about her." Arran turned and looked at Marcail over his shoulder.

Quinn watched Arran, waiting for the moment when he would have to battle one of the few men he gave his trust to.

"She reminds me of my sister," Arran said after a lengthy pause.

"You had a sister?"

Arran nodded and looked away from Marcail, his brow furrowed. "Two actually. One older and one younger. Marcail reminds me of my younger sister. She was small and always into some kind of trouble. I used to call her my little sprite."

"What happened to her?" It was out of Quinn's mouth before he thought better of it.

"She died," Arran murmured absently.

Quinn didn't press for more. There wasn't a Warrior out there who hadn't suffered terribly when Deirdre found him. Quinn had found this out the hard way.

With Arran lost in the memories of his past, Quinn walked to the twins. Both brothers were tall and thickly muscled. They stood similarly with their feet apart and their arms crossed over their chests as they stared at the other Warriors, waiting for someone to make a move against Quinn.

Duncan and Ian looked so much alike that they wore their hair differently to help people know who was who. Both had light brown hair that was streaked with gold, but Ian wore his shorn close to his head while Duncan preferred to let his grow down his back.

Ian turned his head to glance at him. "The Druid woke."

It wasn't a question. Quinn nodded. "She's healing herself now. I plan on questioning her more once she wakes again."

"Does she know where she is?" Duncan asked.

Quinn shrugged. "If you two find any food, let me know. Marcail is going to be hungry."

They only got fed once a day, and then only some bread. But it was enough for them. Quinn planned on giving her most, if not all, of his food if she needed it.

"I'll see to it," Ian said and walked away.

Duncan scratched his chin and watched his twin. "How long do you think it will take for Deirdre to realize the Druid isn't dead?"

"Not long enough," Quinn admitted. "Not nearly long enough."

Look for the other novels in Donna Grant's
sensational Dark Sword series

DANGEROUS HIGHLANDER
ISBN: 978-0-312-38122-6

FORBIDDEN HIGHLANDER
ISBN: 978-0-312-38123-3

WICKED HIGHLANDER
Coming in November 2010
ISBN: 978-0-312-38124-0

Available from St. Martin's Paperbacks